Eye of
Flame

EYE of FLAME

• FANTASIES •

PAMELA SARGENT

• INTRODUCTION BY •
CHELSEA QUINN YARBRO

Five Star • Waterville, Maine

This collection of stories is a work of fiction. Names, characters, places and incidents are either the product of the author's imagination, or, if real, used fictitiously.

First Edition
First Printing: December 2003

Published in 2003 in conjunction with Tekno Books
and Ed Gorman.

Set in 11 pt. Plantin.

Printed in the United States on permanent paper.

Library of Congress Cataloging-in-Publication Data

Sargent, Pamela.
    Eye of flame : fantasies / by Pamela Sargent.—1st ed.
      p. cm.
    ISBN 1-59414-064-2 (hc : alk. paper)
    1. Fantasy fiction, American.   I. Title.
  PS3569.A6887E94 2003
    813'.54—dc22   2003049465

To Connie,
who deserves a book of her own

TABLE OF CONTENTS

PAMELA SARGENT, WRITER

Writer: it can mean so many things—wordsmith, reporter, story-teller, illusionist, artist, visionary. Most professional writers are fortunate if they can combine two of those elements on a regular basis. Pamela Sargent is one of the rare ones who combines them all. She gives herself over to her story, and that enables the reader to succumb to it, too. In the best sense of the word, she seduces you into her conception and reveals it to you with concision.

She has been doing this consistently for more than thirty years, and at a level of quality that most writers are happy to achieve a quarter of the time. Her meticulous sense of place, her ability to create real, tangible, convincing environments for her stories shines out in *"The Broken Hoop"* and in *"Outside the Windows,"* both of which bring you into the story so effortlessly that the reader is immersed on the strength of the quality of the place of the story. This is very hard to do, even harder to do well. Pamela Sargent makes it look easy.

Another example of her literary dressage is found in the way in which she focuses attention without obviously pointing a crucial story element out. She uses theme-and-variations on images to mark the events that shape her stories. Consider the recurring telephone images in *"Ringer,"* and the way they culminate in the last four paragraphs of the story. Hers is a very deft touch, the sure sign of the mastery of the craft of story-telling. Do not think slightingly of craft: in writing, as in any art, the craft comes first, providing solid support for the art, so that it all hangs together and works with the unity of horse and rider in passage and piaffe.

She handles first person narration very well—and that's a lot trickier to do than it looks. *"Big Roots"* and *"Bond and Free"* show off her first-person characterizations in all their strength. She is able to see through the eyes and the lives of her characters in a way that dazzles. Plus she tells you bang-up stories in the process.

Another of Pamela Sargent's gifts is the wonderful ability to imply, to bring a sense of more beyond the story than is presently apparent on the page. This is most effectively displayed in the two shorter works in this collection, *"The Shrine"* and *"The Leash."* In very different ways, each story contrasts the perception of the characters with the larger implications of what she is telling in the immediate instances. This is another form of the on-the-page seduction at which she excels, and it makes these two fairly short tales particularly affecting, so that the possibilities of the stories linger in the mind, evocative as perfume.

"Eye of Flame," taking place in the long-vanished Mongolian culture, manages to bridge that formidable gap in time and locale, making that society accessible and genuinely comprehensible to the reader, so that the behavior of the fascinating people in the story makes contextual sense. This, believe me, is very difficult to pull off—anachronisms and current social issues have an unnerving tendency to try to creep into the tale. Pamela Sargent is able to take the time on its own terms, and to accept the characters as part of their time and culture, without apology or softening the rough parts.

To top it all off, she slings the language around acrobatically but not interferingly, letting her style serve the story instead of the other way around. She has a fine sense of internal rhythm, particularly in characterization. Her writing is vivid and generous but not intrusive—and although I don't want to contribute to any confusion between writer and work, in this vivid, generous, non-intrusive way, her work is very much like Pam herself.

Read and enjoy. But take a little advice from me: don't wolf all of the stories down at once. Savor each one. You're not likely to find better literary nourishment anywhere.

Chelsea Quinn Yarbro
June, 2003

The Broken Hoop

There are other worlds. Perhaps there is one in which my people rule the forests of the northeast, and there may even be one in which white men and red men walk together as friends.

I am too old now to make my way to the hill. When I was younger and stronger, I would walk there often and strain my ears trying to hear the sounds of warriors on the plains or the stomping of buffalo herds. But last night, as I slept, I saw Little Deer, a cloak of buffalo hide over his shoulders, his hair white; he did not speak. It was then that I knew his spirit had left his body.

Once, I believed that it was God's will that we remain in our own worlds in order to atone for the consequences of our actions. Now I know that He can show some of us His mercy.

I am a Mohawk, but I never knew my parents. Perhaps I would have died if the Lemaîtres had not taken me into their home.

I learned most of what I knew about my people from two women. One was Sister Jeanne at school, who taught me shame. From her I learned that my tribe had been murderers, pagans, eaters of human flesh. One of the tales she told was of Father Isaac Jogues, tortured to death by my people when he tried to tell them of Christ's teachings. The other woman was an old servant in the Lemaîtres' kitchen; Nawisga told me legends of a proud people who ruled the forests and called me little Manaho, after a princess who died for her lover. From her I learned something quite different.

Even as a child, I had visions. As I gazed out my window, the houses of Montreal would vanish, melting into the trees; a glowing hoop would beckon. I might have stepped through it then, but already I had learned to doubt. Such visions were delusions; to accept them meant losing reality. Maman and Père Lemaître had shown me that. Soon, I no longer saw the woodlands, and felt no loss. I was content to become what the Lemaîtres wanted me to be.

When I was eighteen, Père Lemaître died. Maman Lemaître had always been gentle; when her brother Henri arrived to manage her affairs, I saw that her gentleness was only passivity. There would no longer be a place for me; Henri had made that clear. She did not fight him.

I could stay in that house no longer. Late one night, I left, taking a few coins and small pieces of jewelry Père Lemaître had given me, and shed my last tears for the Lemaîtres and the life I had known during that journey.

I stayed in a small rooming house in Buffalo throughout the winter of 1889, trying to decide what to do. As the snow swirled outside, I heard voices in the wind, and imagined that they were calling to me. But I clung to my sanity; illusions could not help me.

In the early spring, a man named Gus Yeager came to the boarding house and took a room down the hall. He was in his forties and had a thick, gray-streaked beard. I suspected that he had things to hide; he was a yarnspinner who could talk for hours and yet say little. He took a liking to me and finally confided that he was going west to sell patent medicines. He needed a partner. I was almost out of money by then and welcomed the chance he offered me.

I became Manaho, the Indian princess, whose arcane arts had supposedly created the medicine, a harmless mixture of alcohol and herbs. I wore a costume Gus had purchased from an old Seneca, and stood on the back of our wagon while Gus sold his bottles: "Look at Princess Manaho here, and what this miracle medicine has done for her—almost forty, but she drinks a bottle every day and looks like a girl, never been sick a day in her life." There were enough foolish people who believed him for us to make a little money.

We stopped in small towns, dusty places that had narrow roads covered with horse manure and wooden buildings that creaked as the wind whistled by. I remember only browns and grays in those towns; we had left the green trees and red brick of Pennsylvania and northern Ohio behind us. Occasionally we stopped at a farm; I remember men with hatchet faces, women with stooped shoulders and hands as gnarled and twisted as the leafless limbs of trees, children with eyes as empty and gray as the sky.

Sometimes, as we rode in our wagon, Gus would take out a bottle of Princess Manaho's Miracle Medicine and begin to sing songs between swallows. He would get drunk quickly. He was happy only then; often, he was silent and morose. We slept in old rooming houses infested with insects, in barns, often under trees. Some towns would welcome us as a diversion; we would leave others hastily, knowing we were targets of suspicion.

Occasionally, as we went farther west, I would see other Indians. I had little to do with them, but would watch them from a distance, noting their shabby clothes and weatherworn faces. I had little in common with such people; I could read and speak both French and English. I could have been a lady. At times, the townsfolk would look from one of them to me, as if making a comparison of some sort, and I would feel uncomfortable, almost affronted.

We came to a town in Dakota. But instead of moving on, we stayed for several days. Gus began to change, and spent more time in saloons.

One night, he came to my room and pounded on the door. I let him in quickly, afraid he would wake everyone else in the boarding house. He closed the door, then threw himself at me, pushing me against the wall as he fumbled at my night-dress. I was repelled by the smell of sweat and whiskey, his harsh beard and warm breath. I struggled with him as quietly as I could, and at last pushed him away. Weakened by drink and the struggle, he collapsed across my bed; soon he was snoring. I sat with him all night, afraid to move.

Gus said nothing next morning as we prepared to leave. We rode for most of the day while he drank; this time, he did not sing. That afternoon, he threw me off the wagon. By the time I was able to get to my feet, Gus was riding off; dust billowed from the wheels. I ran after him, screaming; he did not stop.

I was alone on the plain. I had no money, no food and water. I could walk back to the town, but what would become of me there? My mind was slipping; as the sky darkened, I thought I saw a ring glow near me.

The wind died; the world became silent. In the distance, someone was walking along the road toward me. As the figure drew nearer, I saw that it was a woman. Her face was coppery, and her hair black; she wore a long yellow robe and a necklace of small blue feathers.

Approaching, she took my hand, but did not speak.

Somehow I sensed that I was safe with her. We walked together for a while; the moon rose and lighted our way. "What shall I do?" I said at last. "Where is the nearest town? Can you help me?"

She did not answer, but instead held my arm more tightly; her eyes pleaded with me. I said, "I have no money, no place to go." She shook her head slowly, then released me and stepped back.

The sudden light almost blinded me. The sun was high overhead, but the woman's face was shadowed. She held out her hand, beckoning to me. A ring shone around her, and then she was gone.

I turned, trembling with fear. I was standing outside another drab, clapboard town; my clothes were covered with dust. I had imagined it all as I walked through the night; somehow my mind had conjured up a comforting vision. I had dreamed as I walked; that was the only possible explanation. I refused to believe that I was mad. In that way, I denied the woman.

I walked into the town and saw a man riding toward the stable in a wagon. He was dressed in a long black robe—a priest. I ran to him; he stopped and waited for me to speak.

"Father," I cried out. "Let me speak to you."

His kind brown eyes gazed down at me. He was a short, stocky man whose face had been darkened by the sun and lined by prairie winds.

"What is it, my child?" He peered at me more closely. "Are you from the reservation here?"

"No. My name is Catherine Lemaître, I come from the east. My companion abandoned me, and I have no money."

"I cannot help you, then. I have little money to give you."

"I do not ask for charity." I had sold enough worthless medicine with Gus to know what to say to this priest. I kept my hands on his seat so that he could not move without pushing me away. "I was sent to school, I can read and write and do figures. I want work, a place to stay. I am a Catholic, Father." I reached into my pocket and removed the rosary I had kept, but rarely used. "Surely there is something I can do."

He was silent for a few moments. "Get in, child," he said at last. I climbed up next to him.

His name was Father Morel and he had been sent by his superiors to help the Indians living in the area, most of whom were Sioux. He had a mission near the reservation and often traveled to the homes of the Indians to tell them about Christ. He had been promised an assistant who had never arrived. He could offer me little, but he needed a teacher, someone who could teach children to read and write.

I had arrived at Father Morel's mission in the autumn. My duties, besides teaching, were cooking meals and keeping the small wooden house next to the chapel clean. Father Morel taught catechism, but I was responsible for the other subjects. Winter arrived, a harsh, cold winter with winds that bit at my face. As the drifts grew higher, fewer of the Sioux children came to school. The ones who did sat silently on the benches, huddling in their heavy coverings, while I built a fire in the woodburner.

The children irritated me with their passivity, their lack of interest. They sat, uncomplaining, while I wrote words or figures on my slate board or read to them from one of Father Morel's books. A little girl named White Cow Sees, baptized Joan, was the only one who showed interest. She would ask to hear stories about the saints, and the other children, mostly boys, would nod mutely in agreement.

I was never sure how much any of them understood. Few of them spoke much English, although White Cow Sees and a little boy named Whirlwind Chaser, baptized Joseph, managed to become fairly fluent in it. Whirlwind Chaser was particularly fond of hearing about Saint Sebastian. At last I discovered that he saw Saint Sebastian as a great warrior, shot with arrows by an enemy tribe; he insisted on thinking that Sebastian had returned from the other world to avenge himself.

I lost most of them in the spring to the warmer days. White Cow Sees still came, and a few of the boys, but the rest had vanished. There was little food that spring and the Indians seemed to be waiting for something.

I went into town as often as possible to get supplies, and avoided the Indians on the reservation. They were silent people, never showing emotion; they seemed both hostile and indifferent. I was irritated by their mixture of pride and despair, saw them as unkempt and dirty, and did not understand why they refused to do anything that might better their lot.

I began to view the children in the same way. There was always an unpleasant odor about them, and their quiet refusal to learn was more irritating to me than pranks and childish foolishness would have been. I became less patient with them, subjecting them to spelling drills, to long columns of addition, to lectures on their ignorance. When they looked away from me in humiliation, I refused to see.

I met Little Deer at the beginning of summer. He had come to see Father Morel, arriving while the children and I were at Mass. He looked at me with suspicion as we left the chapel.

I let the children go early that day, watching as they walked toward their homes. White Cow Sees trailed behind the boys, trying to get their attention.

"You." I turned and saw the Indian who had come to see Father Morel. He was a tall man, somewhat paler than the Sioux I had seen. He wore a necklace of deer bones around his neck; his hair was in long, dark braids. His nose, instead of being large and prominent, was small and straight. "You are the teacher."

"Yes, I am Catherine Lemaître." I said it coldly.

"Some call me John Wells, some call me Little Deer. My mother's cousin has come here, a boy named Whirlwind Chaser."

"He stays away now. I have not seen him since winter."

"What can you teach him?"

"More than you can."

"You teach him Wasichu foolishness," he said. "I have heard of you and have seen you in the town talking to white men. You think you will make them forget who you are, but you are wrong."

"You have no right to speak to me that way." I began to walk away, but he followed me.

"My father was a Wasichu, a trader," Little Deer went on. "My mother is a Minneconjou. I lived with the Wasichu, I learned their speech and I can write my name and read some words. My mother returned here to her people when I was small. You wear the clothes of a Wasichu woman and stay with the Black Robe, but he tells me you are not his woman."

"Priests have no women. And you should tell Whirlwind Chaser to return to school. White men rule here now. Learning their ways is all that can help you."

"I have seen their ways. The Wasichus are mad. They

hate the earth. A man cannot live that way."

I said, "They are stronger than you."

"You are only a foolish woman and know nothing. You teach our children to forget their fathers. You think you are a Wasichu, but to them you are only a silly woman they have deceived."

"Why do you come here and speak to Father Morel?"

"He is foolish, but a good man. I tell him of troubles, of those who wish to see him. It is too bad he is not a braver man. He would beat your madness out of you."

I strode away from Little Deer, refusing to look back, sure that I would see only scorn on his face. But when I glanced out my window, I saw that he was smiling as he rode away.

The children stayed away from school in the autumn. There were more soldiers in town and around the reservation and I discovered that few Indians had been seen at trading posts. I refused to worry. A young corporal I had met in town had visited me a few times, telling me of his home in Minnesota. Soon, I prayed, he would speak to me, and I could leave with him and forget the reservation.

Then Little Deer returned. I was sweeping dust from the porch, and directed him to the small room where Father Morel was reading. He shook his head. "It is you I wish to see."

"About what? Are you people planning another uprising? You will die for it—there are many soldiers here."

"The Christ has returned to us."

I clutched my broom. "You are mad."

"Two of our men have seen him. They traveled west to where the Fish Eaters—the Paiutes—live. The Christ appeared to them there. He is named Wovoka and he is not a white man as I have thought. He was killed by the Wasichus on the cross long ago, but now he has returned to save us."

"That is blasphemy."

"I hear it is true. He will give us back our land, he will raise all our dead and return our land to us. The Wasichus will be swept away."

"No!" I shouted.

Little Deer was looking past me, as if seeing something else beyond. "I have heard," he went on, "that Wovoka bears the scars of crucifixion. He has told us we must dance so that we are not forgotten when the resurrection takes place and the Wasichus disappear."

"If you believe that, Little Deer, you will believe any-thing."

"Listen to me!" Frightened, I stepped back. "A man named Eagle Wing Stretches told me he saw his dead father when he danced. I was dancing with him and in my mind I saw the sacred tree flower, I saw the hoop joined once again. I understood again nature's circle in which we are the earth's children, and are nourished by her until as old men we become like children again and return to the earth. Yet I knew that all I saw was in my thoughts, that my mind spoke to me, but I did not truly see. I danced until my feet were light, but I could not see. Eagle Wing Stretches was at my side and he gave a great cry and then fell to the ground as if dead. Later, he told me he had seen his father in the other world, and that his father had said they would soon be together."

"But you saw nothing yourself."

"But I have. I saw the other world when I was a boy."

I leaned against my broom, looking away from his wild eyes.

"I saw it long ago, in the Moon of Falling Leaves. My

friends were talking of the Wasichus and how we would drive them off when we were men. I grew sad and climbed up a mountain near our camp to be alone. In my heart, I believed that we would never drive off the Wasichus, for they were many and I knew their madness well—I learned it from my father and his friends. It was that mountain there I climbed."

He pointed and I saw a small mountain on the horizon. "I was alone," Little Deer continued. "Then I heard the sound of buffalo hooves and I looked down the mountain, but I saw no buffalo there. Above me, a great circle glowed, brighter than the yellow metal called gold."

"No," I said softly.

He looked at me and read my face. "You have seen it, too."

"No," I said after a few moments.

"You have. I see that you have. You can step through the circle, and yet you deny it. I looked through the circle, and saw the buffalo, and warriors riding at their side. I wanted to step through and join them, but fear held me back. Then the vision vanished." He leaned forward and clutched my shoulders. "I will tell you what I think. There is another world near ours, where there are no Wasichus and my people are free. On that mountain, there is a pathway that leads to it. I will dance there, and I will find it again. I told my story to a medicine man named High Shirt and he says that we must dance on the mountain—he believes that I saw Wovoka's vision."

"You will find nothing." But I remembered the circle, and the robed woman, and the woods that had replaced Montreal. I wanted to believe Little Deer.

"Come with me, Catherine. I have been sick since I first saw you—my mind cannot leave you even when I dance.

Your heart is bitter and you bear the seeds of the Wasichu madness and I know that I should choose another, but it is you I want."

I shrank from him, seeing myself in dirty hides inside a tepee as we pretended that our delusions were real. I would not tie my life to that of an ignorant half-breed. But before I could speak, he had left the porch, muttering, "I will wait," and was on his horse.

On a cold night in December, I stared at Little Deer's mountain from my window.

I was alone. Father Morel was with the Indians, trying again to tell them that their visions were false. The ghost dancing had spread and the soldiers would act soon.

Horses whinnied outside. Buttoning my dress, I hurried downstairs, wondering who could be visiting at this late hour. The door swung open; three dark shapes stood on the porch. I opened my mouth to scream and then saw that one of the men was Little Deer.

"Catherine, will you come with me now?" I managed to shake my head. "Then I must take you. I have little time." Before I could move, he grabbed me; one of his companions bound my arms quickly and threw a buffalo robe over my shoulders. As I struggled, Little Deer dragged me outside.

He got on his horse behind me and we rode through the night. Snowflakes melted on my face. "You will be sorry for this," I said. "Someone will come after me."

"It will soon be snowing and there will be no tracks. And no one will follow an Indian woman who decided to run off and join her people."

"You are not my people." I pulled at my bonds. "Do you think this will make me care for you? I will only hate you more."

"You will see the other world, and travel to it. There is little time left—I feel it."

We rode on until we came to a small group of houses which were little more than tree branches slung together. We stopped and Little Deer murmured a few words to his companions before getting off his horse.

"High Shirt is here," he said. "A little girl is sick. We will wait for him." He helped me off the horse and I swung at him with my bound arms, striking him in the chest. He pulled out his knife and I thought he would kill me; instead, he cut the ropes, freeing my hands.

"You do not understand," he said. "I wish only to have you with me when we pass into the next world. I thought if I came for you, you would understand. Sometimes one must show a woman these things or she will think you are only filled with words." He sighed. "There is my horse. I will not force you to stay if your heart holds only hate for me."

I was about to leave. But before I could act, a cry came from the house nearest to us. Little Deer went to the entrance and I followed him. An old man came out and said, "The child is dead."

I looked inside the hovel. A fire was burning on the dirt floor and I saw a man and woman huddled over a small body. The light flickered over the child's face. It was White Cow Sees.

The best one was gone, the cleverest. She might have found her way out of this place. I wept bitterly. I do not know how long I stood there, weeping, before Little Deer led me away.

A few days after the death of White Cow Sees, we learned that the great chief Sitting Bull had been shot by soldiers. Little Deer had placed me in the keeping of one of his companions, Rattling Hawk. He lived with his wife, Red Eagle Woman, in a hovel not far from Little Deer's mountain. I spent most of my days helping their three children search for firewood; I was still mourning White Cow Sees and felt unable to act. Often Rattling Hawk and Red Eagle Woman would dance with others and I would watch them whirl through the snow.

After the death of Sitting Bull, I was afraid that there would be an uprising. Instead, the Indians only danced more, as if Wovoka's promise would be fulfilled. Little Deer withdrew to a sweat lodge with Rattling Hawk, and I did not see him for three days.

During this time, I began to see colored lights shine from the mountain, each light a spear thrown at heaven; the air around me would feel electric. But when daylight came, the lights would disappear. I had heard of magnetism while with the Lemaîtres. Little Deer had only mistaken natural forces for a sign; now he sat with men in an enclosure, pouring water over hot stones. I promised myself that I would tell him I wanted to go back to the mission.

But when Little Deer and High Shirt emerged from the lodge, they walked past me without a word and headed for the mountain. Little Deer was in a trance, his face gaunt from the days without food and his eyes already filled with visions. I went back to Rattling Hawk's home to wait. I had to leave soon; I had seen soldiers from a distance the day before, and did not want to die with these people.

Little Deer came to me that afternoon. Before I could speak, he motioned for silence. His eyes stared past me and I shivered in my blanket, waiting.

"High Shirt said that the spirits would be with us today. We climbed up and waited by the place where I saw the other world. High Shirt sang a song of the sacred tree and then the tree was before us and we both saw it."

"You thought you saw it," I said. "One would see anything after days without food in a sweat lodge."

He held up his hand, palm toward me. "We saw it inside the yellow circle. The circle grew larger and we saw four maidens near it dressed in fine dresses with eagle feathers on their brows, and with them four horses, one black, one chestnut, one white, and one gray, and on the horses four warriors painted with yellow streaks like lightning. Their tepees were around them in a circle and we saw their people, fat with good living and smiling as the maidens danced. Their chief came forward and I saw a yellow circle painted on his forehead. He lifted his arms, and then he spoke: 'Bring your people here, for I see you are lean and have sad faces. Bring them here, for I see your people traveling a black road of misery. Bring them here, and they will dance with us, but it must be soon, for our medicine men say the circle will soon be gone.' He spoke with our speech. Then the circle vanished, and High Shirt leaped up and we saw that the snow where the circle had been was melted. He ran to tell our people. I came to you."

"So you will go and dance," I said, "and wait for the world which will never come. I have seen—" He took my arm, but I would say no more. He released me.

"It was a true vision," he said quietly. "It was not Wovoka's vision, but it was a true one. The Black Robe told me that God is merciful, but I thought He was merciful only to Wasichus. Now I think that He has given us a road to a good world and has smiled upon us at last."

"I am leaving, Little Deer. I will not freeze on that mountain with you or wait for the soldiers to kill me."

"No, Catherine—you will come. You will see this world

with me." He led me to Rattling Hawk's home.

He climbed up that evening. Rattling Hawk and his family came, and High Shirt brought fifteen people. The rest had chosen to stay behind. "Your own people do not believe you," I said scornfully to Little Deer as we climbed. "See how few there are. The others will dance down there and wait for Wovoka to sweep away the white men. They are too lazy to climb up here."

He glanced at me; there was pain in his eyes. I regretted my harsh words. It came to me that out of all the men I had known, only Little Deer had looked into my mind and seen me as I was. At that moment, I knew that I could have been happy with him in a different world.

We climbed until High Shirt told us to stop. Two of the women built a fire and I sat near it as the others danced around us.

"Dance with us, Catherine," said Little Deer. I shook my head and he danced near me, feet pounding the ground, arms churning at his sides. I wondered how long they would dance, waiting for the vision. Little Deer seemed transformed; he was a chief, leading his people. My foot tapped as he danced. He had seen me as I was, but I had not truly seen him; I had looked at him with the eyes of a white woman, and my mind had clothed him in white words—"half-breed," "illiterate," "insane," "*sauvage.*"

I fed some wood to the fire, then looked up at the sky. The forces of magnetism were at work again. A rainbow of lights flickered, while the stars shone on steadily in their places.

Suddenly the stars shifted.

I cried out. The stars moved again. New constellations appeared, a cluster of stars above me, a long loop on the horizon. Little Deer danced to me and I heard the voice of High Shirt chanting nearby.

I huddled closer to the fire. Little Deer pounded the ground, his arms cutting the air like scythes. He spun around and became an eagle, soaring over me, ready to seize me with his talons. The stars began to flash, disappearing and then reappearing. One of the women gave a cry. The dancers seemed to flicker.

I leaped up, terrified. Little Deer swirled around me, spinning faster and faster. Then he disappeared.

I spun around. He was on the other side of the fire, still dancing; then he was at my side again. I tried to run toward him; he was behind me. A group of dancers circled me, winking on and off.

"Catherine!" Little Deer's voice surrounded me, thundering through the night. His voice blended with the chants of High Shirt until my ears throbbed with pain.

I fled from the circle of dancers and fell across a snow-covered rock. "Catherine!" the voice cried again. The dark shapes dancing around the fire grew dimmer. A wind swept past me, and the dancers vanished.

I stood up quickly. And then I saw the vision.

A golden circle glowed in front of me; I saw green grass and a circle of tepees. Children danced around a fire. Then I saw High Shirt and the others, dancing slowly with another group of Indians, weaving a pattern around a small tree. The circle grew larger; Little Deer stood inside it, holding his arms out to me.

I had only to step through the circle to be with him. My feet carried me forward; I held out my hand and whispered his name.

Then I hesitated. My mind chattered to me—I was sharing a delusion. The dancers would dance until they dropped, and then would freeze on the mountain, too exhausted to climb down. Their desperation had made them mad. If I stepped inside the circle, I would be lost to the irrationality that had always been dormant inside me. I had to save myself.

The circle wavered and dimmed. I saw the other world as if through water, and the circle vanished. I cried out in triumph; my reason had won. But as I looked around at the melted snow, I saw that I was alone.

I waited on the mountain until it grew too cold for me there, then climbed down to Rattling Hawk's empty home before going back up the mountain next day. I do not know for how many days I did this. At last I realized that the yellow circle I had seen would not reappear. In my sorrow, I felt that part of me had vanished with the circle, and imagined that my soul had joined Little Deer. I never saw the glowing hoop again.

I rode back to the mission a few days after Christmas through a blizzard, uncaring about whether I lived or died. There, Father Morel told me that the soldiers had acted at last, killing a band of dancing Indians near Wounded Knee, and I knew that the dancing and any hope these people had were over.

I was back in the white man's world, a prisoner of the world to come.

THE SOUL'S SHADOW

The man had followed Jacqueline onto the pier. He stepped toward her, smiled, then walked back toward the steps leading down to the beach.

He had nodded at her when she passed him before; his grayish-green eyes seemed familiar. He might be a former student. Her memory for faces was poor, and often she forgot what even her best students looked like once they graduated. All she noticed about most of them now was their youth; they were currents in an ever-renewed stream while she aged on the shore, eroded by their movement through her life.

She leaned against the railing. He was below her on the sand, gazing out at the ocean; he glanced up as the wind ruffled his blond hair. She looked away. He couldn't have been a student; even with her poor memory, Jacqueline was sure she would have remembered him. He had the tanned, handsome face of a television actor and the body of a man who frequented gyms; he was exactly the kind of man she would expect to see here on a California beach. He would not have been in her classes, which drew intense or slightly neurotic humanities majors; aggressive and grade-conscious pre-law students; or studious, asexual, aspiring scientists trying to fulfill a philosophy requirement. She would have noticed anyone so atypical.

She turned her head slightly and caught a glimpse of his light brown windbreaker. As she felt his eyes on her, she looked away again. Was he trying to pick her up? She was flattering herself by assuming that. She supposed that he was either wealthy or out of work; vacationers were not likely to come here in February. He might be one of those Californian psychopaths who her friends back East assumed haunted these shores.

From the pier, it seemed that a structure had been built on every available piece of land; houses, condominiums, and other buildings covered the hills overlooking the wide bay. The Strand was a wide sidewalk and bicycle path running north and south; beneath the low wall separating the Strand from the beach, the sand was white and clean. Everything seemed cleaner here; the beach was tended, the houses kept up, the cars unmarked by rust or mud. Jacqueline could not smell the sea; the odors of fish and salt water were absent. The past did not exist, only a continuous, ever-changing present.

She gazed south toward another, larger pier that held shops and restaurants; beyond, a green peninsula marked by sheer, precipitous cliffs jutted into the sea. She propped an elbow against the rail, then noticed that the blond man was gone. He had been there only a moment before; she turned toward the row of houses overlooking the beach. Two skaters, legs pumping, rolled along the Strand; three joggers were trotting south. The man had vanished.

Jacqueline opened the refrigerator door, took out a jug of wine, then leaned against the counter as her cousin and her old friend gossiped in the living room.

"You've got to come," her cousin Patti had told her over the phone a month before. It had seemed a good idea then. Jacqueline was on sabbatical, while Patti and her husband were moving out of their condominium to a house nearby. The condo would be vacant for a couple of months until the new tenants moved in; she could stay there and have the place to herself. Jacqueline had been unable to refuse; the monograph she was working on was finished and needed only retyping. Patti had mentioned getting together with their old friends Dena and Louise only after Jacqueline already had her plane ticket.

She folded her arms, thinking of other times, twenty years before, when she had gone into her mother's kitchen to fetch Cokes and potato chips while Patti, Louise, and Dena had gossiped about parties and boys. She had gradually become part of their group, hoping that some of their lofty social status in high school would rub off on her. By associating with them, she did not have to endure the slights and cruel comments many of the more studious students suffered.

She had escaped them with a scholarship to an eastern women's college. She had found new friends among young women she would have avoided in high school, people with whom she could share her intellectual interests. She had occasionally reflected on the time she had wasted in her struggle to be liked and accepted by Patti's circle, but she did not have the courage to group herself with the outcasts then, had preferred her place, however tenuous, with the clique of cheerleaders, jocks, and partygoers.

Jacqueline had nearly forgotten this aspect of the youthfulness she sometimes longed for—the fear of rejection, of being different, awkward, unliked. Her doctorate, the fellowship, the published papers and books would mean little to the other women, who led the kind of life others envied.

"There you are!" Dena was standing in the entrance to the kitchen; somehow Jacqueline had missed hearing her enter.

"Dena," she said, trying to sound pleased. Dena's body,

like Patti's and Louise's, seemed shaped by aerobics and starvation.

"Funny, isn't it? We kept saying we had to get together sometime, but you had to come three thousand miles just to get us all into the same room." Dena shook back her long black hair. "Well, you finally got here." Patti and Louise had said exactly the same thing. "It'll be just like old times."

They caught up with one another as they sat on the floor around a glass-topped coffee table. Louise had moved from Palos Verdes to a house a few miles away and was living on a generous divorce settlement, while Dena, who had recently bought a place in Manhattan Beach, sold real estate.

"I was out here for a year before I bought my old place," Dena murmured in her husky voice as she poured more wine. "That was a mistake. I should have bought something—anything—the minute I stepped off the plane. Things are slower now."

"Joe really lucked out on that piece of land he bought," Patti said. "He wants me to stay home when we have our kid, and I guess we can afford it."

Dena lifted a brow. "A kid, huh?"

"We're trying. Deadline decade, you know."

Louise shook her blonde head. "Stop with one. One's enough, believe me."

Dena turned toward Jacqueline. "Didn't you say you were living with a guy?"

"Another professor," Jacqueline replied. "He's in the English department. We've been together for almost ten years."

Dena sighed. "Long time. Is he cute?"

Jacqueline thought of Jerome's long face, graying beard,

and thinning hair. "He's tall. He's in pretty good shape. I don't know if I'd call him cute."

"Well, now that you're here," Louise said, "when are you going to move?" Jacqueline was silent. "Don't tell me you want to stay back East now. You could teach out here, couldn't you?"

"It's not that easy. I'm lucky to have the position I've got. The world isn't exactly short of Ph.D.'s in philosophy."

Louise tapped one manicured finger against her cheek; she had a faint, golden tan, just enough to make her glow without turning her skin leathery. "Patti said you were writing a book."

"A monograph on Plato's *Philebus*. I figured I'd pick a dialogue people hadn't written that much about. That's hard to find when scholars have had over two thousand years to mess around with Plato."

Louise stared at her blankly. "I saw Clint Eastwood in the airport last month," Patti said, "just from a distance. He looked emaciated."

"If they look thin on the screen," Dena said, "they look absolutely anorexic in person." She nibbled at a shrimp. "Didn't David Lee Roth make a video around here?"

Jacqueline stood up. "I think we need some air." The others didn't seem to hear her. The topics of real estate and celebrity-spotting could probably keep them occupied for hours, and Louise had been married to a celebrity of sorts herself.

She crossed the room, opened the sliding glass door, and stepped out onto the terrace. The condo was on the second floor; the Strand and the beach beyond it were less than a block away. The wind had grown warmer. The sun was a bright red disk just above the gray water; she had watched it set last evening, surprised at how suddenly it dropped below the horizon. To the south, Catalina was a misty gray form, barely a suggestion of an island. Cyclers and runners moved along the Strand; other people were entering a restaurant across the street.

She reached into her shirt pocket for her cigarettes and lit one. She would call Jerome later; he had told her not to waste the money, but she needed to hear his voice. Her eyes narrowed. The blond man she had seen by the pier was sitting on the low wall between the Strand and the beach; he stood up and began to walk toward her.

"—very eastern habit," Louise said behind Jacqueline.

"What?"

"Smoking. The only time anyone smoked in my house was when somebody from back East was visiting." Louise moved toward the railing as the other two women came outside, then lifted a hand to the collar of her blue silk shirt. "Will you look at that." She lowered her gaze to the blond man.

Dena moved closer to Louise. "Do you know him?"

Louise shook her head. "But I saw him just this morning, near my driveway. He was definitely flirting."

"That's funny," Dena said, sounding annoyed. "I saw him last night at Orville and Wilbur's, at the bar. He smiled at me, but when I looked back, he was gone."

"Sure it was the same guy?"

"I don't forget men who look like that."

"He gets around, then." Patti's thick, pale hair swayed as she leaned over the railing. "He was outside my house when I left for work. I thought he was casing the place."

"Hello," the man said then. The sound of a passing car and the music coming from the nearby restaurant seemed to fade as he spoke. The sun disappeared; he moved closer to the light over the sidewalk below. "So you're all together again."

Louise's hands fluttered. "Do we know you?"

"I know you," he replied. "Couldn't forget you, Louise, or Dena there, or Patti, and especially not Jackie."

Jacqueline swallowed. "Who are you?" she managed to say.

"An old classmate." He thrust his hands into the pockets of his windbreaker. "Maybe you don't remember me—I wasn't exactly part of your crowd. I'm Tad Braun."

Patti started. "You're Tad Braun?"

He nodded. Jacqueline now recalled the last time she had seen those grayish green eyes, but they had looked out at her from the flaccid, pimply face of a fat, awkward boy. Tad Braun had transformed himself. The awkwardness was gone, the oily hair golden, the fat turned into muscle; perhaps a plastic surgeon had chiseled his face and smoothed his skin.

"You sure have changed," Dena said.

Tad shrugged. "So have all of you. You were attractive then, but you look even better now." That might be true of the others, Jacqueline thought, but it couldn't be true of her. "Maybe I'll see you again." He moved away into the shadows before any of them could speak.

Patti let out her breath. "Who would have thought Tad Braun would turn into such a hunk? I wonder what he's doing now."

"I barely remember him," Louise said. "Wasn't he that awful boy who we—"

Jacqueline did not want to remember. "We were pretty cruel to him, weren't we? But we were cruel to a lot of kids when they didn't meet our standards."

Dena's dark eyes widened. "Oh, come on. That was a long time ago. Nobody remembers things like that."

"The victimizers probably don't," Jacqueline said. "The victims do."

The night air was colder. The four walked back into the empty room and settled around the coffee table. The shrimp and raw vegetables were nearly gone; Jacqueline stubbed out her cigarette as Patti lit a joint.

"Maybe we should have asked him up," Louise said. "Of course, I have to be careful about the guys I see."

"Herpes," Patti muttered.

"No, visitation rights. I wouldn't put it past my goddamn ex to use any excuse to cut them back. I see Chris little enough as it is."

"He has custody?" Jacqueline asked, surprised.

Louise's mouth twisted. "I guess you professors don't read *People* regularly. I needed the settlement, and if I'd fought for Chris, I might have gotten much less."

Jacqueline said nothing. "Look, I couldn't have raised him without a good settlement. You need at least thirty thousand a year here just to stay off the streets. And just try to go up against one of the NFL's former golden boys in court." Louise poured more wine. "Bob's been born again, you know. I suppose he'll marry that Baptist bimbo he's been going to Bible study with." The blonde woman glanced at Dena. "Well, there's nothing to stop you from seeing old Tad."

"There's Sadegh," Dena replied, "but I don't know how long that'll last. I'm too old for him—he's forty-two and I'm thirty-six. Trouble is, he likes eighteen-year-olds."

"And I'm an old married lady trying to get pregnant." Patti took another toke on her joint. "Guess I should give this up. I don't even know if 1 really want a kid, but Joe does. Anyway, what else can I do?"

"Jackie could ask Tad over for a drink," Louise said.

"I'm living with somebody."

"Yeah, but he's three thousand miles away."

Patti propped her elbows on the table. "You told me it was no strings with you and Jerome."

No strings, Jacqueline thought. She had fashioned the strings and turned them into cords. Except for a brief trip to Chicago for a classics conference, she had not even been on a plane without Jerome until now. She could not even tell if she still loved him or was only afraid of being alone.

Lately he made her feel old. Neither of them even went through the motions of trying to find positions at a better school. They had their tenure, published enough to keep up the reputation of scholarship, and revised lectures each of them had given several times before. Each year, they were confronted by a sea of ever-younger faces. At night, suspended in the moment between consciousness and sleep, Jacqueline often imagined that she was suddenly an old woman, that the years had flown by and had left her ill and weak with no one to tend her, no one to care what became of her.

"I can't imagine why Tad Braun would want to see any of us." Jacqueline looked around at the pretty, ageless faces of the other three women, certain that they would not understand what she was about to say. "Tad was a gentle, sensitive boy, but we didn't care about that, couldn't see it. Now, at least, his beauty reflects the truth about what he was inside."

Patti finished her joint; the others were silent.

"Well," Patti said after a moment, "I've got an early day tomorrow. Listen, why don't you all come to the house on Saturday? Joe's going to be out. Come over around noon. We'll sit around and swill wine and go out to dinner."

Dena nodded. "I think I can take the day off."

"Fine with me," Louise said.

"Sure," Jacqueline murmured. "It'll be fun."

★ ★ ★ ★ ★

It was admitted near the beginning of the Philebus *that pleasure and intelligence are both parts of the good life, and yet we cannot decide which is closer to the good (or which determines the character of the good life) without concerning ourselves with what "the good" is.*

Jacqueline looked up from her typewriter. This was hardly a concern of the people out here, who had their own ideas about the good life. They would have taken Callicles' position in this dialogue and argued for pleasure. She ruffled through the pages of the manuscript she was retyping, unable to concentrate; the intellectual pleasures Plato valued so highly could not overcome her restlessness.

She glanced at her watch. She had not called Jerome last night, but he might be in his office now. Sarita Ames was teaching at UCLA; she could get together with her old classmate and bitch about how many philosophy departments still held Aristotle's view of women. Giles Gunderson was at Irvine; there were a number of colleagues she might contact out here. They might draw her out of the spell Patti and her friends had cast, remind her that she was no longer a high school girl who envied the pretty and popular.

She stood up and crossed to the bed. Telephone directories lay next to the telephone on the floor. She was leafing through the B's before she realized that she was looking for Tad's number. No Thaddeus Braun was listed in the local directory, and the Los Angeles book seemed a formidable obstacle.

She went to the bedroom window and peered out. Tad was standing near the beach; she felt as though she had summoned him somehow. She hurried into the living room, but hesitated in front of the sliding glass door before she opened it.

Tad strolled up the street, then halted below the terrace and raised a hand in greeting. "Hello, Jackie."

"Tad." She tried to think of something to say. "Are you vacationing, or do you live out here?"

"I've been out here for a while." He had not really answered her question. Was he unemployed, looking for a position? Tad had been one of the better math students when she knew him; perhaps he did freelance consulting work for computer firms. "You're visiting, aren't you?"

She nodded.

"Mind if I come up for some coffee? You can tell me what you've been doing."

"I'll come down," Jacqueline said hastily. She backed away, closed the glass door, and hurried to the bedroom for her jacket. Better, she thought, to talk to him outside; she might have known him once, but he was a stranger now.

As she came outside, he took her arm and led her toward the Strand. She almost pulled away, surprised at how ill at ease she felt.

"How are all of you doing?" Tad asked. "You know—you and the other members of the Bod Squad." She glanced at him sharply. "Come on, Jackie—a lot of guys in school called you that. Not the ones you went out with, just the ones who didn't have a chance with you."

"Oh, we knew. We didn't much care for the term." She paused. "You might have read something about Louise's ex-husband; he used to play for the Rams. He gave her a good settlement. Dena's selling houses to rich people and going out with an Iranian millionaire from Beverly Hills."

"What about you?"

"I'm just a philosophy professor on sabbatical. Patti invited me out when she and her husband were moving into their house, said their condo would be free until their new tenants moved in. Her husband's a car dealer, kept pointing out his showrooms all the way in from LAX."

Two women cycled by as they came to the Strand. Tad gripped her arm more tightly. "Let's walk down to the water."

She was about to refuse. Except for a couple of surfers in wet suits near the pier, the beach was nearly deserted. She was suddenly afraid of being alone with him, but he could hardly harm her there, in sight of the houses lining the Strand.

He led her through the opening in the wall onto the sand. A group of gulls alighted near them, watching with beady eyes as they passed. She shivered; Tad, in a tweed jacket and jeans, did not seem to notice the chill. "It's colder than I expected," she said. "I guess all that propaganda made me think you have an endless summer out here."

"I was surprised to see you," Tad said. "I wanted to speak to you on the pier, but then I thought you might not want to see me. I was thinking of the last time—"

"I was hoping you'd forgotten that," she said quickly.

"Oh, I can't blame you. I must have seemed pretty hopeless."

She slipped her arm from his and walked toward the ocean. It was all coming back to her now, more vividly than she had ever recalled it before.

He had been the fat, pimpled boy who sat next to her in geometry. She had paid little attention to him, but he had surprised her by calling her up one day to talk about their homework.

Tad did not ask her out; she doubted he had ever dated

anyone. But she pitied him a little and could talk to him about her ambitions, the books she read, the interests she usually cloaked. She did not ask him to her house, but occasionally met him in places where her friends were not likely to see them—at the playground for small children near her street, or at a delicatessen in the city adjoining their suburb. They met only to talk; she did not think of their meetings as dates. She might have guessed that Tad would assign more importance to them.

He called her early one Friday evening. He had walked two miles from his house to her neighborhood and was calling from a pay phone; he wanted to come over. Carelessly, she agreed.

Patti, Louise and Dena arrived only moments after she hung up. Her face burned as she listened to the babble of her friends and tried to think of how to get rid of them. Patti was saying something about a party; Jacqueline could guess what her cousin would think when she saw Tad.

Her friends were unusually perceptive that evening and noticed her nervousness almost immediately; she had to speak. "I can't go," she blurted out. "Someone's coming over."

"Who?" Patti asked.

"It's—well, it's Tad Braun. It's just—he's supposed to help me with some homework."

Dena rolled her eyes; Louise looked disgusted. "Tad Braun?" Patti shrieked. "You're going to see Tad Braun on a Friday night?"

"It's almost like having a date with him," Dena said.

"I need some help in geometry," Jacqueline mumbled. She knew it was a poor reason to give as soon as she spoke. The other girls were aware of her grades; they had copied her homework often enough.

"Maybe Jackie likes him," Louise said maliciously. "Wait until I tell—"

"I don't!" Jacqueline cried, terrified of what the other girls might do. She was in the middle of denying Louise's suspicions when Tad came to the door.

She knew that she should have sent him away quickly, tried to tell him she would call him later, but that hadn't been enough for her friends. They pulled him through the door, ushered him to the sofa, and made the bewildered boy sit down as they grouped themselves around him.

Their words, their callous remarks and cruel comments about his weight, his complexion, his clumsiness, awful clothes, and wretched personality had been designed to show him his place and rob him of any shred of self-esteem. His face grew mottled with humiliation; Jacqueline saw the message in his pained eyes as he looked at her. Tell them I'm your friend, his eyes said; tell them that you hate what they're saying, that I mean something to you.

But she said nothing; she even laughed with her friends. He shot her one last glance before he fled the room; she had been surprised to see no anger, only despair.

She had made her choice and betrayed him. Tad had disappeared from school after that amid rumors he was ill; she had not even called his parents to find out how he was, and found out only later that his parents had sent him to another school elsewhere.

The sand shifted under her feet. She turned as Tad came up to her side. "What are you thinking about?" he asked.

"How heartless I was before."

He adjusted the collar of his jacket. "I thought I was in love with you back in high school. I think I had a crush on all of you in a way, but you were the only one who would

44

talk to me. I kept hoping, I thought I'd never get over—"
He paused. "Well, that's past. I doubt the others even remember."

She looked up at his handsome, even-featured face. At
close range, his features were almost too perfect, as if he
were hardly human at all. "You've changed a lot, Tad.
You've probably had plenty of opportunities to forget us."

He shook his head. "I couldn't forget you. You were the
first girl I loved. You don't forget that."

She sat down on a sandy slope; he seated himself next to
her. "I was a fraud then," she said. "It was all a pose. I was
so afraid of—"

"I can understand that."

"I'm still a fraud. I do my work, and I suppose I do it
well enough, but it isn't really my life in the way it should
be. I'm supposedly a Plato scholar. Plato valued the life of
the mind above all, but I don't know if I do or not." She
laughed softly. "How naive that sounds. I used to think that
once you assented to an argument's validity, you'd have to
change your views, even your life if necessary. One of my
professors found that notion quite amusing. He said I had it
the wrong way around, that philosophers find arguments to
justify only what they already believe."

Tad was gazing at her steadily; she was surprised to see
warmth and sympathy in his eyes. "I'm supposed to be
writing a monograph on Plato's *Philebus*," she continued.

"I studied some philo in college," Tad said. "Mostly
courses in symbolic logic, but I did read some Plato."

"It's the dialogue where Plato deals with the relation of
pleasure to the good and tries to show the comparative
worthlessness of physical pleasures. He shows the contradictions involved in asserting that pleasure alone is the
good, but he can't conclusively disprove that purely hedo-

nistic belief. All he can really do is to show that the life of the mind, the intellect, is a truer pleasure than those most people seek." She sighed. "Maybe I shouldn't have come out here. It's just made the contradictions in my own life more evident. If I really believed in the choices I made, I wouldn't still envy my friends."

"I'm afraid my intellectual pleasures were the only ones I had," Tad said. "Math interested me the most. It seemed to take me to that realm of forms Plato wrote about, where objective truth could be found. I could forget the world then, see it as an illusion, as only the dimmest reflection of the real realm of truth and beauty, as only shadows on the wall of a cave in which people are trapped. Mathematics was far more real to me than the physical world."

That, she thought, was a Platonic enough notion. Tad went on speaking of how much each thing in the world also existed as a mathematical possibility; the world would change and eventually die, but the possibilities mathematical sets expressed would always exist, were in fact eternal. But he also seemed to think that the barrier between the physical world and this mathematical one could be breached, that a way of breaching it could be expressed mathematically, that the manipulation of certain symbols by itself could transform physical facts. As he spoke, she lost the thread of his argument, unable to tell if he was talking about applied mathematics or some sort of magical mumbo-jumbo. Words seemed inadequate for what he was trying to say.

"I explored this for a long time," he went on. "I was trying to see past the illusions of time and space. Each moment of time became another bead on an endless chain, while the world itself seemed almost like a series of cross-sections, a cutaway set in which, if you could see it all, you could move to any place in it almost instantly."

He fell silent; she heard only the rhythmical pounding of the waves against the shore. She felt that if she turned, she would see only bare hills, discover that the world she knew had vanished.

"We used to talk this way," he said at last. "I've missed you, Jackie. I kept imagining that I'd meet you again. I think I'm still in love with you."

He pulled her to her feet and drew her toward him. As he kissed her, she stepped back, startled at how aroused she felt.

"This is ridiculous." Another woman seemed to be speaking the words, not Jacqueline herself. "We haven't seen each other for twenty years. I don't know anything about you. You can't be in love with me."

"I know what I feel. I wouldn't be here with you now if I didn't think you wanted me, too."

"There's someone else. I'm living with a man."

"Jackie." He kissed her again. Her arms were around him, clutching at his back. He drew away and encircled her waist with his arm. "I love you," he said as they walked back up the beach.

Jacqueline opened her eyes and stared at the bedroom ceiling. Tad was gone; she could not remember when he had left. For the past three days, it had been like that; Tad had exhausted her with his lovemaking and had been absent when she awoke. She would shower, dress, and go to the terrace; he was inevitably below in the street, waiting.

Her memories were hazy and blurred. She dimly recalled that Tad had driven her in the Fiat that Patti had loaned her to a restaurant overlooking the beach. There had been a drive up the coast to Marina del Rey and drinks at a bar, but she had only the faintest recollection of the sailboats and yachts in the harbor there.

Other memories were more vivid—the touch of Tad's hands, the feel of his muscled body, his whispered endearments as he made love to her. Thinking of him made her want him even more; he had awakened desires she had believed dormant or dead.

She sat up abruptly. Three days, and she knew about as little of Tad's life as she had known when she first saw him. They had talked about her life and her problems, or had sat together in a comfortable silence, whenever they were not making love. He had to live nearby, since she had never seen his car, but he had not shown her his home. He had enough money to buy her overpriced drinks and an expensive dinner, but she did not know how he got it. She had been content to tell him about herself while asking no questions about his life; he had been the perfect lover, responding to her needs without imposing his own.

Now she was appalled at herself, thinking of the risks she had taken. Tad might have herpes or some other disease. She had not even thought of contraception; her diaphragm was back East in her apartment, where its presence might serve to reassure Jerome.

It was Saturday; Jerome would be home, perhaps hoping she would call. She reached for the telephone, dialed the number, and waited until it had rung fifteen times before hanging up.

She climbed out of bed, reached for the watch on the folding table where her typewriter stood, then saw that it was nearly noon. Patti would be expecting her. Her cousin had not called during the past days; she wondered why.

Jacqueline hurried into the adjoining bathroom, pressing the light switch as she entered. The face staring at her from the bathroom mirror looked haggard; the harsh light revealed all her flaws. Tiny lines she had never noticed before marked the skin around her eyes; at her temples a few strands of silver stood out against her auburn hair. She had gained almost fifteen pounds since high school, but her face had stayed youthful; the light made her seem ten years older.

Tad had insisted that she was still beautiful to him. He might be waiting for her now, below the terrace; she wanted to be with him, to hear his reassuring words. She forced the thought of him from her mind.

Patti's house was a wooden structure with large, glassy windows overlooking the sloping road. Stone walls separated the house from its neighbors; a stocky, dark-skinned man was toiling in Patti's tiny flower garden. Jacqueline parked, then climbed the steps leading to the side door.

Patti led her to the patio out back; Dena and Louise were sitting by the pool. Dena stood up, smoothed down her shorts, then handed a glass of wine to Jacqueline. "Tried to call you," Dena said. "Hope you've seen some of the sights. When you live out here, you turn into a tour guide for visitors."

"I would have called," Louise said, "but—" She smiled and lowered her eyelids. "I thought Bob had vaccinated me against serious relationships, but there's someone—"

Dena sat down again. "Do tell."

"Oh no. This is something special. I don't want to ruin it. You'll find out soon enough."

The weather had grown warm. Jacqueline set down her glass, then shrugged out of her jacket. In the daylight, Louise's face seemed puffier; her chin sagged a little, and her breasts drooped slightly under her red halter. Dena brushed her black hair from her face; Jacqueline thought she saw some gray, then noticed a small, bulging vein on one of

Dena's tanned legs. Even Patti looked a bit older; her cheeks sagged just a little. Jacqueline felt a guilty pleasure, quickly suppressed, at seeing that the others were not quite so ageless after all.

They talked about high school days, real estate, and men. Dena and her millionaire had parted company, but she did not seem all that unhappy about it. Louise mocked her ex-husband, while Patti enumerated Joe's various faults. Louise remained sober enough to drive them to a restaurant in her Mercedes; there they giggled and recited old high school cheers over margaritas. Yet somehow, to Jacqueline, their joviality seemed forced. They all lapsed into awkward silences before rushing to fill them with words; Dena seemed distracted, while Louise kept staring into space.

Jacqueline had expected the two to linger at Patti's house after dinner, but both women seemed in a hurry to get home. "We should get together this week," Patti said as Dena got into her Jaguar. "I'll call you—maybe we can meet at your place, or Louise's." Dena nodded, then followed Louise's Mercedes down the street.

"I'm really beat," Jacqueline said. "Good thing I don't have far to drive. Anyway, Joe should be home soon."

"I have to talk to you." Patti hurried up the steps; Jacqueline followed her into the house. Patti turned on a light and crossed the living room to the wide window, keeping her back to Jacqueline.

"What is it, Patti?" Jacqueline sat down on one end of the modular couch. "Is something wrong between you and Joe? You were being pretty hard on him this afternoon."

"I'm having an affair."

This was a surprise. "Is it just a passing thing, or is it serious?"

"At first it was just curiosity. I've never been unfaithful to Joe before. You know how it is. The spark goes out, you fall into a routine, you want something different. But I think I'm really in love this time." Patti continued to stare out the window. "I can tell you. I don't think I could say it to Dena or Louise. I'm sleeping with Tad Braun."

Jacqueline struggled for control, grateful that Patti could not see her face. The pain of Tad's betrayal was sharp. "How long?" she managed to ask.

"You must know—just since that night we saw him. He came here the very next day, right after I was home from work. He says he's been in love with me for years, that he had a crush on me in high school. I called in sick the next day and saw him again. Joe's always home late—it was easy to see Tad."

Jacqueline was silent. Patti turned and paced toward the fireplace; Jacqueline composed her face. "It's crazy, I know," Patti said. "I don't even know where he lives, or what he's doing, I just know I have to be with him. It isn't just the sex—he understands me; he listens to me."

Jacqueline closed her eyes for a moment. She should have guessed she wasn't the only woman in Tad's life, that his sincere-sounding words were only a line designed to hook the vulnerable, but he might have found someone besides her cousin. How had he even managed it? He had been with her for much of the past three days, would have had to rush away while she was asleep. That was possible; Patti's house was only half a mile from the condominium. She had lost track of time with him, but was his energy limitless? How could he have had any strength left for Patti?

"You're shocked," Patti said.

Jacqueline lit a cigarette. "I'm a little startled," she said, trying to mask her hurt. "You have a pretty good life with

Joe. Do you want to throw it away?"

"I don't care about that now. Tad's what I want; I think he's the kind of man I wanted all along. I can't even think of anything else when I'm with him."

"But you've admitted you don't know anything about him."

"I know what I have to know, and he says he needs me."

She would be doing her cousin a favor if she told Patti that Tad had seen her as well. Patti would be angry, but the news might be enough to make her give him up.

Jacqueline was about to speak, then hesitated. Patti might only get angry at her or refuse to believe the story. If she got jealous enough, Jacqueline could hardly stay on in her condo with a car borrowed from one of Joe's showrooms; she would have to go home, and might not see Tad again. That possibility tore at her. Even now, she still longed for Tad; he must have sensed her weakness, her need.

"You feel that way now," Jacqueline said, "but it won't last. You might find out later that Tad isn't what you wanted, either. Stop seeing him before it's too late. Joe doesn't have to know."

"I'm in love with Tad."

"You just think you are." Jacqueline took a breath, wondering if she was trying to help Patti or only trying to win Tad for herself. She stubbed out her cigarette. "Patti, you're tired, and we've both had too much to drink. It'll look different tomorrow, believe me."

Patti sank down onto the stone hearth. "You don't understand; you don't know how I feel." She looked up suddenly. "You won't say anything."

"Of course not." Jacqueline stood up. "Look, maybe you can take an afternoon off this week and show me the sights. I don't think I'm ready to take on the freeways alone."

"I'll see." Patti's voice was flat.

Jacqueline tossed on her bed restlessly, unable to sleep. The sound of passing cars outside was competing with the noise of a party somewhere in the building. The weekend crowds had thronged to the beach and later to the bars along the Strand in search of the pleasures so low on Plato's hierarchy.

Tad was outside; she could feel it. She was afraid to confront him. She was imagining things; he might be roaming with the people outside, looking for another victim.

She heard a knock at the door; maybe it was Patti, wanting to talk. She pulled on her robe and left the bedroom; the living room's track lights came on as she slapped a switch. Her bare feet padded across the thick beige carpeting. "Who's there?"

"Tad."

"Go away." She had to force the words out.

"Jackie, I have to see you. Please open the door."

Her hand reached for the knob; she recoiled. "I don't want to see you—can't you understand?"

"Let me in." His voice had risen. The knob twisted in her hand; the door swung open. She let go of the knob and stepped back as he entered.

"Jackie." He was wearing a casual suit tonight, with an open-collared blue shirt; perhaps he had been in a bar trying to pick someone up. As she looked up at his face, her anger began to dissipate. He gazed at her intently, almost apologetically; before she could speak, he took her hands in his.

"I want you to know this," he said. "Maybe you think this is just a momentary thing, a few nights and no more. It isn't. I'm serious, Jackie. I have to be with you."

She pulled her hands away. "You're quite an operator, aren't you? I talked to Patti before, and she told me about you two. You can't fool me anymore."

"I won't deny it. I have some feeling for her, but I think part of that's because she's your cousin. She can't be what you are to me—no one else can be."

She clenched her fists. "Then leave her alone, for God's sake. Don't break up her marriage and ruin her life. She thinks you're in love with her. She doesn't know about me; I couldn't tell her."

"How do you know I won't improve her marriage? It happens sometimes. I'm attracted to her, and she seems to need me now, but she'll tire of me. Later on she'll be grateful for the memories and the bit of romance."

"So you're a psychologist now," Jacqueline said acidly. "You're just trying to help her out."

"I'm attracted to her. Look, just staying with one woman—it's something I've never been able to do. But I could do it with you; you can be that one woman for me. I've been waiting for you all my life. I can't change overnight, but I will if you let me have the chance."

His words seemed so plausible, his expression so sincere. Already she was weakening; she wanted to believe him. He reached for her, loosening her robe. "I love you," he said. "You brought me here; you'll understand. I won't let you leave me." She sagged against him as he drew her down to the carpet.

Jacqueline shivered. Her body ached; the bedroom seemed colder. The pillow next to her still bore the scent of Tad's cologne. She listened to the silence before realizing he was gone.

How long had they been together this time? She couldn't

recall leaving the condominium. They had made love, she had slept, and then he had reappeared at the door with groceries and wine. He had assured her of his love, but had not spoken of any plans they might make. She did not even know if he expected her to live out here or was willing to follow her east.

She stretched, then felt a sharp pain in her shoulders. Her hands were stiff, she flexed her fingers. Her shoulder pains stabbed at her again as she reached over the edge of the bed for the telephone. She set it on the mattress, lifted the receiver, and dialed.

"May I help you?" a voice chirped.

"What day of the week is this?"

"Why, it's Thursday, February—"

She hung up. She had been with Tad for nearly five days, besotting herself with him. Her hand still lay on the telephone; she gazed at it in surprise. The joints of her fingers had swelled a little; a few tiny brown spots marked the back of her hand.

She threw off the covers, ignoring her pain, and made her way to the bathroom. The sight of her face in the mirror nearly made her cry out. The lines around her eyes were deeper now, the skin of her cheeks looser. Her neck was crepy and lined, while her hair was streaked with gray. She gripped the sink, closed her eyes, then opened them again; the middle-aged face was still staring out at her. It isn't possible, she thought; no one could age so much in five days.

She stumbled out of the bathroom and reached for her watch. It was nearly five o'clock; Jerome would be home. She sat down on the bed and dialed the number. The telephone rang twenty times before she gave up. She took a breath, then dialed another number.

"Directory assistance. For which city?"

"Do you have a listing for a Thaddeus Braun?" Tad, she vaguely recalled, bore his father's name. The operator gave her the number; she dialed it quickly.

"Hello," a woman's voice said.

"Mrs. Braun?"

"This is she."

"Uh, my name is Jackie Sloane. I'm calling long-distance from California. I'm staying in Hermosa Beach, and I'm an old friend of your son Tad. I wanted to look him up, but he doesn't seem to be listed—I thought maybe you could give me his number and address."

There was no reply.

"I heard he was living somewhere near L.A. Do you think—"

"When did you know my son?" The woman's voice sounded strained. "In college?"

"No, in high school. He was in a couple of my classes."

"And you were his friend? I know who Tad's friends were. He had few enough of them, certainly none who were girls." She sounded angry. "Forgive me. There was one. He wouldn't say anything about her. He'd tie up the phone talking to her, and I think he met her a couple of times. And then—"

The woman was silent for so long that Jacqueline thought their connection had been broken. "Hello?"

"Tad had a breakdown," Mrs. Braun continued. "We were too ashamed to admit it at the time, but it hardly matters now. We sent him away for help and then to a boys' school after that. If you were his friend, you might have called us then, asked about how he was."

"I meant to, but—"

"Oh, I understand. So easy for all of you to ignore him, to make his life even more miserable. I'm afraid I can't help you. We don't know what happened to Tad. He was living near here, and then he accepted a job offer out there a couple of years ago. He told us he'd let us know when he got settled. He never showed up at the job. We finally hired someone to track him down. Apparently, Tad rented a car at the airport when he arrived and then vanished. The car was found parked near a beach." The woman's voice broke. "His things were in the car, and there was no sign of violence. The police think he's dead, that he walked into the ocean to die."

Jacqueline nearly dropped the receiver. He's not dead, she wanted to say, but how could she tell his mother that? The woman would think it was some kind of cruel joke. Tad must have had reasons for disappearing; she did not want to think of what they might be.

"I'm sorry," she said at last.

"Sorry. It's too late for you to be sorry." Jacqueline heard a click as Mrs. Braun hung up.

Someone was knocking at the door. She pulled on her robe and hurried into the living room, then halted. "Who's there?" she called out.

"Tad."

She wanted to open the door; that urge frightened her as much as Tad himself did. "I talked to your mother," she shouted. "I don't know why you decided to disappear, and I don't want to know. Maybe you're working for the CIA or the Mafia. I suppose you had plastic surgery, and maybe you use another name, too. I don't know what you're up to, but you're not going to drag me into it."

"Jackie, let me in. I love you; I have to talk to you."

"Go away." She sank to the floor and pressed her head against the carpet, longing for him in spite of what she suspected.

★ ★ ★ ★ ★

She took to driving on the roads along the coast, going north past Santa Monica, then south until she came to the cliffs of Palos Verdes. She was afraid to stay in the condominium; she continued to drive along the same route, retracing it until she was too tired to drive anymore. Whenever she returned to the condominium, she made certain that the door was securely locked, then drank wine until she was able to fall asleep.

Tad had said that he cared about her, she thought as she drove. She still wanted him in spite of what she now knew; her reason was powerless against him. Perhaps he had been planning to tell her why he had to disappear once she had committed herself to him. That was what she wanted to believe, but she couldn't know his purpose; he might be trying to use her in some way. Tad had heartlessly deceived his own parents; all his professions of love were probably a lie.

She could go to the police, but wondered what she could tell them, what Tad might do if he found out. If he were engaged in something illegal and had accomplices, she would then be in danger. The longer she dwelled on her fears, the more they seemed to grow. She knew she should warn Patti and leave the area, yet she could not bring herself to make that decision. Another fear began to take shape in her mind—the fear that Tad would not let her leave.

The telephone was ringing. Jacqueline stirred on the bed. She had forgotten to take off her shirt and jeans, and had stumbled inside around dawn to drink more wine before collapsing.

Her mind cleared. She had to pull herself together, decide what to do. She reached for the telephone; maybe Jerome, stingy as he was about long-distance calls, was finally calling. He might be able to advise her. "Hello?"

"Jackie, it's Joe."

She propped herself up on her elbows. "What is it?"

"Is Patti there with you?"

"No."

"This is important. I called her friend Louise, and she swore up and down she wasn't there, and then Dena came by about a couple of minutes ago, so I know she's not with her. I've called all our friends. Look, I just want to know she's O.K."

"She isn't here, honest. What's wrong?"

Joe sighed. "I know I should have seen it earlier, but I've been working late all this week, and she was always asleep when I came home. I found out yesterday by accident that she'd taken a leave from work, and that was when I went home and took a good look at her. Jackie, she's sick—she looks like an old woman who's wasting away. I couldn't believe it, couldn't see how—"

Her stomach knotted. "And it took you days to notice it?"

"Give me a break! I've been putting in a lot of time—and why didn't you bother to come around? You might have—" Joe cleared his throat. "I told her I was calling our doctor and then taking her to the hospital. She went into this rage, started yelling at me that she'd be all right, that—" He paused. "Then she calmed down, begged me to wait until this morning before I did anything, told me how afraid of hospitals she was, convinced me that she was starting to feel a little better. I shouldn't have listened. When I woke up, she was gone; she took her car. I've been calling people ever since."

Jacqueline sat up. "Did she say anything about—" She swallowed. Patti might not have mentioned Tad; it would do her cousin no good to reveal that secret to Joe. "Did she say anything about where she might go, even a hint?"

"Do you think I'd be calling you if she had?" He choked and was silent for a bit. "I'll have to call the police, and they won't even start to look for her right away. I don't know if I can handle this. I mean, Jesus, I've got a business to run; I didn't need this right now. Look, if she shows up there, give me a call and then see if you can talk some sense into her. Maybe she'll listen to you."

"I'll call if she does."

"Thanks."

She hung up. The darkening sky outside the window told her that evening was approaching. She got up and entered the bathroom, expecting to look even more ravaged than she had before. Strangely, her hair didn't seem quite as gray, while the skin of her face and neck was firmer. She thought of what Joe had said about Patti; she should have told her cousin what she had learned from Mrs. Braun. Irrational suspicions were forming in her mind; she shuddered.

The doorbell rang. Her heart fluttered as she hurried toward the door. "Who is it?"

"Dena."

Jacqueline pulled the door open. Dena was wearing a dark linen suit and a wide-brimmed hat with a veil. "I thought I'd better come by," she said. "I stopped at Patti's for a moment. Her husband's frantic about her. She—"

"I know. He called. She isn't here."

"I couldn't understand what Joe was saying. I wanted to talk to her. I was over at Louise's. We had a falling-out, I'm afraid." Dena's ankles wobbled a little as her high heels dug into the thick carpet; she crossed the room and perched gingerly on the glass table. Her movements seemed awkward and stiff. "You look like hell, Jackie. What have you been up to?"

"Sleeping, drinking, driving around. What day is it?"

"Sunday."

Jacqueline shook her head and sat down on the floor. "Don't tell me you put on a suit and a Princess Di hat to go to church."

Dena said nothing for a moment; her face, behind the veil, was indistinct. Jacqueline lowered her eyes. She had never noticed before how Dena's veins stood out on the backs of her hands, how gnarled her fingers were.

"Louise called me today," Dena said at last. "She just had to tell me about her new love. I was always the first one she told when we were kids, and she seemed to enjoy it the most if it was a guy I had the hots for. She's been seeing Tad Braun. He had her in the sack about a day or so after he showed up here. She went on and on about how she's really in love, how much he adores her. There's only one problem. Tad's been seeing me, too. He says he's in love with me."

Jacqueline's neck prickled. "But he couldn't—"

"He's in love with me; he told me so. I drove over to Louise's to get this settled, but she wouldn't let me in. I stopped at Patti's on the way back."

"It's impossible," Jacqueline said. "Listen, Tad hasn't just been seeing you and Louise; he's been seeing Patti, too. She told me so herself. She might even be with Tad now."

"She must have been lying!" Dena's hands clawed at the air; she shivered, then folded her arms. "He was with me only this morning; he's been with me nearly every day. Maybe he made it with Louise, but not Patti. He wouldn't have had the strength. He couldn't have found the time."

"Why would Patti lie?" Jacqueline took a painful breath. Tad must have nursed a grudge for years, and now he was having his revenge; she thought of the effort he must have put into preparing to hurt them. "Dena, listen to me. He's playing some sort of sadistic game. Go back to your millionaire and forget him."

Dena reached up and removed her hat. Jacqueline started, too shocked to speak. Dena's hair was nearly completely white; her face had grown so wrinkled, she was barely recognizable. "Do you think Sadegh would have anything to do with me now? I haven't worked for nearly a week; I don't want anyone to see me like this." She put on the hat and adjusted the veil. "But Tad doesn't even seem to see it; he says it's an illusion. And when I'm with him, I don't feel achy and old—I feel the way I was. He's like a drug—I don't care about anything else when I'm with him. He says he wants to take me somewhere else, that he'll never leave me, that—"

Jacqueline clutched at Dena's hand. "You don't know everything," she said forcefully. "Tad's been seeing me, too." A harsh laugh escaped her. "Don't ask me how he could do it; he'd hardly have time to sleep. He told me the same thing he told you—that he loves me."

"I don't believe you."

"Joe told me about Patti; he said she looked old and sick. Look at yourself; look at me. This didn't start until after we—" Her throat locked for a moment. "He must have infected us somehow. I looked worse a few days ago. That's when I told Tad I wouldn't see him anymore. Maybe it wears off if you don't—"

Dena pulled her hand away.

"You've got to listen," Jacqueline continued. "I talked to Tad's mother. She doesn't even know he's alive. He disappeared a while back, and she thinks he's dead." Her hands shook; she clasped them together. "I read a nutty article once about AIDS being some sort of conspiracy, a plot to infect the world or an experiment in germ warfare that went wrong. I thought it was ridiculous, but now I'm not so sure. Maybe Tad's involved in something like that, and now he's found the perfect subjects."

"Never."

"Is it any crazier than what you told me?" Jacqueline stretched out an arm. She no longer ached; the spots on the backs of her hands were gone. "It might not be permanent. We've got to warn Louise and find Patti, then look for help."

Dena stood up slowly. "You're pathetic. Why should I listen to you? Tad loves me, he wouldn't do anything to hurt me, and I believe him. You just want to have him yourself. You're just like you were, ready to take our castoffs, the guys that would settle for you if they couldn't have one of us. You'd make up any story to get him away from me. He's everything I ever wanted. I won't give him up." She stepped around Jacqueline and walked toward the door. "I have to get home; he'll be waiting."

"Dena!"

The other woman walked into the hall, then slammed the door.

She had Louise's address and a map; her house was only ten miles away. Jacqueline drove up and down hills, squinting through the evening light at the houses she passed until she found Louise's street.

Her Tudor house stood at the end of a cul-de-sac. An ambulance was parked in the driveway, under a tree; a few people had gathered in the street. On the small front lawn, three men in white were kneeling over a stretcher.

Jacqueline braked, then got out of the car as a young man walked toward her. "You a friend of Louise's?" he asked. She nodded. "She isn't home." He gestured toward the stretcher. "A neighbor saw someone come out of the house and collapse on the lawn, so he went to check and then called the ambulance. Turns out this old woman was carrying a purse of Louise's, with all her cards and ID. Senior citizen burglar, I guess." The man shrugged. "Louise'll sure be surprised."

Jacqueline walked toward the lawn. Two of the orderlies lifted the stretcher and carried it toward the ambulance. She caught a glimpse of the woman's white hair, then recognized the blue silk shirt; Louise had worn that shirt the night they had all spoken to Tad from the terrace. The third orderly stopped in front of her. "Do you know the woman who lives here?" he asked.

"Yes."

"I put her purse back inside. The police'll be here soon, but it doesn't look like there'll ever be a trial. The thief's practically flat already." He disappeared inside the ambulance; she stepped aside as it backed out of the driveway and sped down the street.

The young man came to her side. "If you want to wait for Louise—" he started to say.

She spun around and ran toward her car.

"I thought you'd want to know," Joe said over the telephone. "We found Patti. Her car was outside a motel. She looked a lot worse; we took her to the hospital. She kept talking about some guy; said he'd come for her, that I couldn't take her away from him." His voice broke.

"I have to see her," Jacqueline said.

"It's no use. She had a stroke in the hospital. They've got her in intensive care. The doctors don't think she's going to make it; they can't even tell how this happened." She heard a sob.

"Is there anything I can do?" she whispered.

"I've got a couple of friends here in the hospital with me. You could call Dena and Louise. They might want to know."

She squeezed her eyes shut.

"I called Patti's mother," he went on. "She said she'd tell your mother. She's going to fly out as soon as she can." A sigh rasped in her ear.

"Maybe I should leave," she said quickly. That sounded heartless. "I mean, if there's nothing I can do. My mother might want me to come home. Patti's almost like another daughter to her instead of just a niece."

"You can leave the keys there, I have a set. Same with the car keys. There's no reason for you to stay unless Dena or Louise want you to. We may be taking Patti back East if she—" Joe groaned. "Oh God, she's really dying. I'm already—"

"Joe," she said helplessly.

"I've got to go."

"If you need me for anything before I leave—"

"Yeah, I know."

The receiver clicked. She could not stay; she knew what was waiting for her if she did. She walked toward the terrace and opened the sliding door.

The street below was quiet; she could hear the distant roar of the sea. Tad was waiting, his hands inside the pockets of his jacket; his hair shone in the morning light. He lifted his head as she leaned against the railing.

"Jackie."

She closed her eyes so that she would not have to look at him. "I don't know what you are," she said. "I don't know how you did what you did, but it's not going to happen to me."

"Jackie—"

65

She turned away and went back inside.

She dialed Jerome's office. The telephone rang twice before he picked it up. "Hello."

"Jerry, it's Jackie. I tried to call before."

"Well, you know how it is. That seminar, and all the department politics—"

"I'm coming home tomorrow," she said. "My flight should be in around five o'clock your time. I'll take a cab if you can't pick me up."

"Sounds as if California wasn't what you expected."

She swallowed, wondering how she could tell him what had happened. "Patti's sick," she said. "Joe's worried about her, and there's nothing I can do for her, and he thought—" She would have to try to explain it all when she was home. "The airline told me I couldn't use my return ticket, the super-saver, so I'll have to pay full fare, but—"

"Then maybe you should stay."

"I can't. I'll explain it when I'm there. Don't you miss me?" She heard the desperate whine in her voice as she spoke. "I need you now; you don't know how much."

"I didn't want to tell you this yet," he responded. "I thought I'd have more time to think it over, to work it out alone before you got back. I think—I need some space, Jackie. I'm thinking of moving out, at least for a while, until I can decide—"

She gripped the receiver. "There's someone else, isn't there?" He did not reply. "You wouldn't be leaving if you didn't have someone else lined up."

"It isn't just that." He was admitting that her guess had been right. "We've been in a rut; you know that. It's as if we've just been going through the motions. I kept feeling that my life was over. I thought maybe you felt the same way, that it was why you needed to get away for a while."

"I see," she said bitterly. "Who is she? That grad student you've been advising, or that Milton specialist the department hired so you'd all have a babe to ogle between classes?" She thought of Tad and the accusations Jerome could hurl at her. "You don't know . . . Patti's really sick; she may—"

"Jackie, this isn't the time. I've got a class in a few minutes. We can talk it all over when you get back. I don't want to be unfair to you, but it's not as though we made a final commitment or anything. It isn't fair to you to let you hang on just because I couldn't bring myself to make the break."

"I know," she muttered. "No strings. I'll take a cab. I trust you'll have the grace to get her out of the apartment before I get back." She slammed down the receiver.

Her life would never be more than it was, than it had been; that thought stabbed into her brain with the sharpness of a weapon. She could struggle to transcend the impermanence of this world only to lose that battle in the end. She seemed to sense the world dissolving around her, leaving only a mind impaled on despair.

The shuttle bus was to pick her up in front of the building. Jacqueline glanced at her watch as she waited on the sidewalk. The bright sunlight hurt her eyes; she squinted as she glanced toward the Strand.

She had escaped Tad; he had lost his power over her. It might have been easier to leave had there been someone to return to, but she had lived alone before; she wondered if, after Tad, she could ever be satisfied with another man. It didn't matter. She still had her work; she could lose herself in it, become the scholar she had pretended to be. She had learned for herself how fleeting physical pleasures were without having to consult Plato's writings; the fate of her cousin and friends had demonstrated that all too vividly.

She had called her mother, had promised to drive down to see her; she had left a message on Joe's machine. Her eyelids felt gritty; she had not slept well. Her old nightmare had returned the night before, the one in which she was alone, abandoned, her body aged and riddled with illness.

A jogger was running along the Strand, racing in the futile battle to preserve his youth. She thought of Tad and how alive she had felt with him. A shadow suddenly appeared near her feet; she had not heard anyone approach. She looked up.

"Jackie." Tad touched her arm gently. "You can't leave me now."

She wanted to run. The street was silent; no one was near. If she called for help, nobody would hear her.

"You've had your revenge," she said. "You've more than evened the score with the others, but you're not going to get me."

"Is that what you think? I'm past that. What I told you is true—I want you with me forever."

She turned toward him. For a moment his features were blurred; she seemed to see the boy she had known. He smiled, showing his even white teeth. "I have Louise," he said. "Patti and Dena will be with me soon. You're the only one left, the one who means the most to me. I can't let you go."

"What are you?" she whispered.

"You know. I was in that realm of eternal truth, of forms, of mathematical possibilities. I passed through the barrier, apprehended that world fully at last. Other souls are trapped there for a time and forget that world when they're reborn into this one again, but I was able to become what I am now. I was able to step through the barrier again and keep the knowledge of the truth I saw there. Time and space no longer exist for me. I can step from here to another time and place as easily as you would step from this curb. I've run you on fast forward, to age you past death. I've demonstrated the reality that lies out here, the change, decay, and death that await all physical things."

"No," she said.

"You drew me here, Jackie. You glimpsed that other world, however dimly, but this one still held you. Part of your soul called to me, and I reached out."

"No."

"What do you have now? This is all an illusion, nothing but shadows inside a cave. You can come with me now, or you can live out this illusion, but I'll still be waiting for you when it's past. Give it up. You'll never have to return to it again. I'll always be with you."

She was still, unable to move. He picked up her bags, carried them into the lobby, then closed the door as he came outside.

He held out his hand as he moved closer to her. "Come with me," he said. Love and gentleness were in his eyes, but his voice was hard, promising an eternity bound by his will. "This body's already weaker—you have to cast it off. Come."

His hand was cold. A madman, she thought; I'm going to die. His grip was crushing her fingers; she thought of his mind crushing her soul. "You may be lying," she said. "How can I know?"

He shook his head and smiled as he led her toward the ocean.

RINGER

Cheryl saw the telephone ring. The chirping sounds exploded behind her eyes as a series of flashes. She pulled a pillow over her face, yearning for the dark silence to return. After months of nagging, she had finally persuaded Nick to get rid of their old black telephone with the rotary dial and the bell that hit her with the force of a lightning bolt, but this chirper wasn't much better.

The phone kept chirping. Cheryl prayed for it to stop, unable to bring herself to pick up the receiver. Nick was probably calling from his office, checking up on her, seeing if she was out of bed yet. She could tell him that she had gone out to a job interview. Pressing the pillow more tightly around her ears, she composed a possible story for her husband. Adele from Ronald Associates had called to tell her that the personnel manager at Trahel Engineering was looking for a new file clerk, had seen Cheryl's résumé, and wanted to interview her at eleven. That would be detailed enough to satisfy Nick, who would be delighted that she had miraculously managed to answer the phone and too busy to check on her story.

The phone stopped chirping. Cheryl peered out from under the pillow. The glowing numerals of the clock-radio told her that it was almost eleven now. She had to get up. If she could pull herself together and go out on a few errands, she would not be here to answer the phone.

Years ago, when Cheryl was a small child, the sound of a

telephone ringing had filled her with dread. She did not know why; it had always been that way. She had once thought that she must have picked up the receiver and heard something so frightening or upsetting that she had blocked it from her mind, recalling only that the telephone had carried the horror to her. But what could she have heard? Why had her parents known nothing about such a call? Surely she would have run to them, however emotionally distant they were, for comfort.

So, she had concluded years later, something else had to be at the root of her fear. Maybe it was the intrusiveness of the instrument, the fact that she was forced to pick it up without knowing who was calling or what she would hear. The chaotic outside world, the world her parents had tried to escape inside their neat orderly house in a dull small town, was always threatening to intrude through the phone. Cheryl could not know whether the call was from her best friend Marcy or from that creep Julie Colton, who always rushed to tell her what everybody was allegedly saying about Cheryl behind her back. She might be dreaming that Joe Wentworth, the best-looking boy at school, was finally going to ask her out, then pick up the phone only to discover that Mrs. Nance, her math teacher, wanted to see one of her parents for a conference on why Cheryl was doing so badly in that subject. She could answer to find that her life was on the verge of some precipice. The torment of wondering whether the voice at the other end was going to launch her into ecstasy or plunge her into depression was usually so great that she could not bring herself to answer the phone at all. The ringing would stop, and her life would remain as it was, placid and undisturbed, at least for a while.

She had supposed that the other kids, even Marcy, sometimes thought she was weird for being so abrupt with them whenever one of their calls did get through to her. Unlike them, she didn't mind when her mother or father picked up the phone first, and she usually hung up as quickly as possible instead of staying on for hours and hours to gossip. She could even feel relieved when her mother told a friend that Cheryl was doing her homework and could not come to the phone. She could not explain to anyone, even Marcy, how the ringing made her tense with terror.

By the time Cheryl graduated from high school, she could barely bring herself to say anything over the phone even when she was able to answer it. Sometimes words lodged in her throat, forcing her to hang up as she gasped for breath. Sometimes the disembodied voice at the other end of the line seemed alien and unfathomable, and she would find herself hanging up to escape the sound. "We must have been disconnected," she would tell the caller later. "Lots of trouble on this line lately."

When she went away to college, at a university only one hundred miles from her home town, she did not follow the example of other students and plague her parents with collect calls. She never called them at all. Her mother sent her a short letter twice a month; Cheryl mailed a postcard back every six weeks or so. The lives of her mother and father remained uneventful according to her mother's letters, and she sometimes wondered if they were secretly relieved not to have her living at home for most of the year. Even one shy and docile daughter had occasionally seemed more than the quiet withdrawn couple could handle. Her mother often looked vaguely distressed whenever any of Cheryl's friends dropped by on their infrequent visits, and her father seemed happiest when he was alone in his den with his books and records.

Getting through college without having to deal with telephones proved to be simpler than expected. Her roommates usually rushed to answer any calls first, and soon Cheryl had talked them into covering for her. The other girls took messages, called out for pizza, accepted dates, or turned down guys Cheryl wanted to avoid with excuses agreed upon earlier. As time went on, word got around the dormitories that any compulsive phone freak wanting to have a telephone entirely to herself ought to room with Cheryl Manfred. By the middle of her sophomore year, Cheryl was much in demand as a roommate.

During her senior year, she moved off-campus to an apartment with her friend Beth Terrence. Beth, as had her previous roommates, gloried in the opportunity to monopolize the phone. Because of that, Cheryl was surprised when, only two weeks before they were to graduate, Beth answered the loudly ringing phone, but insisted that Cheryl speak to this particular caller herself.

"Can't you tell them I'm not here?" she whispered, terrified as always.

"It's important," Beth replied, and then Cheryl noticed how pale her friend looked and how Beth's eyes refused to meet hers. "You'd better take this call."

Somehow she managed to hold the receiver to her ear and listen as Mrs. Redfern, her mother's closest friend, told her that both of her parents had died in a car accident. Mrs. Redfern's choked voice kept breaking as she spoke of rain-slicked roads and of the car going through a guard rail and into a river swollen by late spring flooding. Cheryl knew then that all her terror of telephones, her fear of what might happen to her world if she responded to the ringing, had anticipated this incident, as if the future had been calling to the past through the telephone lines. Even through her grief, she felt a bitter satisfaction. Her fear, as it turned out, had been completely justified. She had been right to fear the phone.

Nick was pacing in the living room, talking to his mother over the cordless phone. Cheryl knew that her husband was talking to his mother because he was speaking in Greek and also sounded more tense than usual. He spoke to only two people in Greek, his mother and Mr. Vassilikos, the butcher who rented one of the commercial buildings Nick owned. In the three years she and Nick had been married, Cheryl had been unable to learn a single word of Greek, but she could tell to which of the two he was speaking by the tone of his voice. With Mr. Vassilikos, Nick sounded patient and resigned; with his mother, his voice was strained. Both Mr. Vassilikos and Nick's mother usually called only when they had complaints, one reason to dread their calls.

Nick's voice was rising; soon he would be shouting at his mother. They could not discuss even the most innocuous subjects without engaging in histrionics and high drama. Cheryl, out in the kitchen, tried not to listen. She hated it when he was talking on the phone to his mother, and speaking in a language she could not understand only made things worse.

Mrs. Christopoulos could be complaining about almost anything. She still thought of her mother-in-law as "Mrs. Christopoulos," since the woman was much too formidable to be addressed by her first name and Cheryl could not bring herself to call her "Mother." She could endure Mrs. Christopoulos's annual visits, even if the two or three weeks sometimes seemed like an eternity. Usually her mother-in-law would keep herself occupied by watching soap operas while commenting on the moral degeneracy of the characters, and she liked cooking Greek dishes for her son that Cheryl had failed to master. When Mrs. Christopoulos was here, Cheryl did not mind hearing her conversing in Greek with her son; it saved Cheryl the trouble of having to talk to her. Whatever complaints the older woman might have, she usually kept them to herself in Cheryl's presence.

But the telephone, combined with a language foreign to Cheryl, gave Mrs. Christopoulos freedom to vent her feelings and say anything she liked to her son, and Cheryl could never know if her husband was sticking up for her or siding with his mother. She could sense her mother-in-law reaching through the phone lines from a thousand miles away, still clinging to the son who could never give her enough attention.

Cheryl, tearing at lettuce leaves, wondered what Mrs. Christopoulos was bitching about now. Nick should call more often, even though he called her at least once a week. He should talk some sense into his sister, who was almost thirty and still hadn't settled down. He could visit her once in a while, or even move back home instead of leaving her to rattle around alone in their old house, and it was about time he visited his father's grave, which he had not been to since the funeral. He could give up being Nicholas Christopher, as if Christopoulos wasn't a good enough name for him, and change his name back to what it had been. He could tell Cheryl that it would be nice to have her get on the phone once in a while and say a few kind words to her old and neglected mother-in-law.

Mrs. Christopoulos could be complaining about any and all of those things, but Cheryl suspected that the lack of telephone conversations with her daughter-in-law was one of the complaints being batted around now. Nick had explained to his mother that Cheryl was shy, which had not done much good. Shyness was a concept that apparently did not exist in Mrs. Christopoulos's mental universe, where people were classified as either warm-hearted or cold-blooded and neurosis was considered self-indulgence. Cheryl tore up the last of the lettuce and began to peel a carrot, hating the sound of the Greek words she did not know, the words being drawn from her husband out along the telephone lines by his mother's voice.

Nick fell silent. She had put the salad into the spinner when he wandered into the kitchen. "Mom tried to call today, twice," he said.

"Must have been when I was out getting groceries."

"She tried at ten o'clock her time, and again at around two."

"Oh. Well, I had to go over to the mall to see if that screwdriver you ordered came in." She had decided to save her excuse about having an appointment with the personnel manager at Trahel Engineering for another time.

"You could have phoned the store about that."

"I was going there anyway. Benetton was having a sale. I don't know why she was calling anyway, when she knew you'd be at the office."

"Maybe she wanted to talk to you. Ever think of that? You are her daughter-in-law. It wouldn't hurt if you'd try to be a little friendlier to her."

"I do try. All she ever talks about is the soaps, cooking tips, what a fine little boy you were, and all those crazy people who lived in her village in Greece."

"They weren't crazy. It was just a different way of life. Look, I know she's a little difficult. She can drive me nuts sometimes, but she's not a bad person." Nick leaned against the counter and folded his arms. "You're not an-swering the phone again. I'll bet that's what it is. I never get an answer when I call home, either."

She stared at the salad, unable to reply.

"I got rid of the old phone. I thought that'd help. I know that old ringer brought back some bad memories."

He knew about the call that had told her of the death of her parents. That call, she had let him believe during the years he had known her, was the source of her inability to handle telephones; he did not know that she had suffered from her fear of phones since childhood. He had been patient, making excuses to his mother and their friends and taking care of all their phone calls himself. Her anxiety still persisted, making her queasy whenever the telephone rang, even when he was there to answer it. Sometimes, unable to control herself, she would find herself begging him to let it go on ringing and not to answer it at all.

"An answering machine," she said. "We can get an answering machine. It's about time we had one. Everybody else in the world does."

"You know I can't stand those damned things. It's bad enough having to have one at the office—I don't want one in my home."

Cheryl had never been enthusiastic about getting an answering machine herself, not wanting to dwell on anything having to do with telephones. Now she was wondering why she had not seriously considered such a device before. The machine could answer the phone for her. She could surely calm herself enough to listen to messages left hours before. The machine could screen calls, meaning that she might actually be able to overcome her phobia enough to pick up the receiver once in a while. An answering machine might even cure her.

"I used to feel the same way," she said, "but you know how it is. Once everybody else has something, you almost have to get it yourself in self-defense. I mean, people sort of expect you to have them, so they can leave messages if you're not around and not feel they have to keep calling back."

"I still don't see—"

"Look, if I get a job, we may need an answering machine. There wouldn't be anyone here during the day to take calls then." Not, Cheryl admitted to herself, that there was much chance of her getting any kind of a job soon, although it eased things with Nick to pretend that she was looking for one. Too many jobs—almost all of them, in fact—seemed to require encounters with telephones sooner or later.

"You're not taking calls now," Nick said. "You've got to get over this, Cheryl."

"You're right." She turned toward him, trying to smile and look determined. "That's why we should get a machine. I'll be able to know who called, and if I can screen calls, so I know what to expect, maybe I can get into the habit of answering."

"I suppose it's worth a try."

"It is. I'm sure. I know it'll help," she said, wanting to believe that.

Cheryl had gone back home after graduating from college. The attorney handling the estate of her parents had told her that she was the sole heir, which was hardly a surprise. Each of her parents had been an only child, too.

The details of the estate were as tidy as her mother's house had been. The mortgage was paid off, the house now belonged to Cheryl, and there was enough money from cautious investments and an insurance policy to give her a modest annual income. It had been surprisingly easy to move back home, and to tell herself that she might as well stay there until she decided what to do.

The house was still as quiet, as peaceful, as it had been when she was a child. Days would pass in which she got up late in the morning, ate her usual breakfast of cereal and fruit, took her early afternoon walk, and spent most of the rest of the day reading one of the books in her father's den or a volume borrowed from the town library. Occasionally people who had known her parents or one of the few old school friends who still lived there would invite her to dinner. When she was feeling especially adventurous, she would drive to Wellford, the nearest city and only a hour away, to shop in its new mall and see a movie.

Only the telephone disturbed her tranquility. She had grown so used to other people answering it for her that she could not pick it up herself or even bear listening to it after two or three rings. There was no reason for anyone here in town to call her. She always made the rounds during her walks, passing the houses and shops where she was likely to run into anyone wanting to see her later; the people in town knew her routine. She wrote letters to her college friends, although their responses were becoming less frequent. Soon she had turned off the telephone; the damned thing could ring all it wanted to as long as she couldn't hear it. There was, she realized, no reason why she had to have a phone at all as long as she lived here, yet she could not bring herself to have it disconnected.

Somehow, she needed the phone there, much as she feared it. She would gaze at the telephone and think: If it weren't for you, everything would be fine. I wouldn't have anything to worry about then; I'd be content. It's your fault that I'm afraid. Such thoughts soothed her, reminding her that only an intrusive technology over which she had no control was responsible for most of her fears.

Eventually, Cheryl sometimes told herself, she would come to grips with her fear, maybe by forcing herself to make the occasional call to the local doctor or dentist for an appointment instead of dropping by to schedule one in person. She could work up to the occasional personal call and eventually to picking up the phone when it rang. But whenever she had such thoughts, her mouth grew dry and her body stiffened with fear. She would be hearing nothing but a voice, one created from electronic signals. There would be no visual cues to tell her what the unseen person might be thinking. She would be nothing except an insignificant, halting, hesitant voice herself, an invisible being that the one at the other end of the line could easily crush with only a few words. One call could destroy the peace she had managed to find.

The lines snaked down telephone poles, along streets, and through windows, then slipped into telephones. The world was encased in a web of shining wires and fiber optic cables over which voices babbled, shrieked, moaned, muttered, and screamed. No matter how many hallways she ran through and how many doors she closed behind her, she could not escape the tentacles through which all the world could demand her attention. Once she picked up the receiver, her thoughts would be drawn out of her, her soul trapped inside the wires.

Cheryl woke, afraid to move. The dream was a warning. The telephone was just waiting to ensnare her in its net along with everyone else.

The telephone on the night stand chirped, making her tense. She gritted her teeth, knowing that the answering machine would take the message after four more rings. She counted them, then let out her breath when the phone fell silent.

At last she forced herself out of bed and went downstairs. Nick had bought an answering machine with a cordless receiver; the device sat on an end table in the corner of the living room, its light blinking at her. Two calls had come in already that morning; she had heard the phone ring earlier, before falling asleep again.

Cheryl lifted her hand, steeling herself to retrieve the messages. Her finger moved toward the "message" button, then froze. She could not know what was on the tape, what she would hear. The machine had not eased her fear, but had only compounded it. Nick had installed the machine three weeks ago, and she had not retrieved a single message. Even if she listened to the messages, she would never be able to return the calls.

Nick could listen to the messages later, not that this would solve anything. In fact, it would only make matters worse. He now had something else to hold against her; not only did she refuse to take phone calls, she left all the messages for him to handle.

The phone suddenly rang. Cheryl stiffened, knowing that if she did not pick it up, she would still hear the caller when the machine began to take the message. There was no escape. She longed to grab the machine and dash it against the wall.

Somehow she seized the receiver and pressed it to her ear. "Hello?" she squeaked.

"Hello," an unfamiliar male voice responded, "am I speaking to Mrs. Christopher?"

"Wrong number!" Cheryl screamed, then hung up and fled from the room.

★ ★ ★ ★ ★

Although Cheryl had welcomed a calm, serene life far removed from the turmoil of most of the world, she began to grow restless after nearly two years of living alone in her parents' house. She had taken on a part-time job at the local library two days a week, work that required her only to shelve volumes and arrange displays near the desk, but felt the need for more activity to fill her time. She did not see the people she knew here as often, and their conversations with her were more brief; their invitations to dinner came less frequently. Sometimes she could even feel that they were avoiding her.

While in Wellford one day, she picked up a flyer from the local branch of the state university listing evening non-credit courses for adults seeking self-improvement. During her next trip, she went to the small campus on the outskirts of Wellford to sign up for a course, knowing it would be impossible to register over the phone. Over the next two years, she took courses in calligraphy, conversational Spanish, Chinese cooking, and drawing. There was no need to call up any of the students in her courses, since they could easily get together after class for the occasional bull session, and she never grew close enough to anyone to worry that someone might try to call her. By now, she supposed, her phone would almost never ring even if she turned the ringer back on. She was safe.

She met Nick Christopher after signing up for a course in macramé and going to the wrong classroom, where Nick was teaching a course on rental property management. He was a lawyer by profession and a stocky, energetic man with curly black hair and a wide grin. "Why don't you check out my first lecture?" he told her. "Maybe you'll want to switch to my course," and she had been powerless to leave his class after that.

She never did master the intricacies of managing property, but Nick was soon taking her out for late dinners after class. He had a law office in downtown Wellford and owned two commercial buildings and two apartment complexes. He had reached that point in his life when he was looking for a nice woman to settle down with, someone who wasn't as driven and hard-edged and career-minded as a lot of the women he knew, someone who was more gentle and old-fashioned.

When Nick asked her to marry him, Cheryl quickly said yes. The warm, kindly feelings she had for him had to be love, and he accepted her as she was. He had hoped to find a quiet soul, a contrast to his outgoing and vociferous temperament, someone for whom he could play the outmoded role of protector. He did not mind the quirks he thought of as her charming eccentricities.

"What do you do all day? Why can't you ever finish anything instead of just dabbling in one thing after another? Why can't you find a job so you'd at least have something to do? Why can't you even answer the goddamned phone and retrieve messages?"

Those were the kinds of questions Cheryl got from Nick lately. She no longer looked forward to having him come home in the evenings, when he was likely to destroy whatever serenity she had won during the day. What did he expect her to do with her days, anyway? She did the housework and shopping, and would still have been doing all the cooking if he had not recently decided that he preferred cooking spicier dishes she didn't much like. She took a course at the state college every semester, her favorite ones lately having been anthropology, Italian Renaissance art, and the nineteenth-century novel, and could not see why she had to limit herself to one thing in order to get another useless degree. There was no economic reason for her to get a job, one that would undoubtedly force her into confronting a phone.

Nick was on the telephone now. He had been on for almost half an hour, ever since the end of dinner, and now he had retreated to his study next to the living room with the cordless. She could hear him talking behind the closed door. Hearing his voice indistinctly through a closed door only made the call seem much more ominous. He had never gone to his study, closing her off, to take calls before. He was speaking in English, so he could not be talking to either his mother or Mr. Vassilikos.

Cheryl put her book down, got up from the sofa, and crept toward the door. ". . . don't know," she heard Nick say. "It's driving me . . ." She leaned closer. ". . . try to get there by one."

She could not listen any more. She would never be free of the calls, the messages, the efforts of all these callers to wrench her from her refuge. Because she could not pick up a phone and speak to someone at the other end, her husband now considered her disturbed and possibly in need of help. He no longer saw her horror of telephones as a charming eccentricity; he had, the day before, raised the possibility of counseling.

Maybe he was talking to a counselor now, the kind of person who would consider her healthy and normal if she went around routinely spilling her guts over the phone to all and sundry. Maybe Nick was complaining to a friend. He could hatch a plot against her with impunity over the phone. He knew she would be incapable of tiptoeing up to the bedroom and listening in on the extension.

The door opened; Nick came back into the living room

and hung up the phone. He sat down in his chair in front of the television, picked up the remote, channel-surfed for a while, then turned off the set.

"We have to talk," he said. Cheryl stared at her book, refusing to lift her eyes. "We've had that answering machine for four months now, and it hasn't helped at all. It's probably made things worse. You're just using it as a barrier, something else to put between you and everything outside. I could put in one of those things that gives you the number of who's calling, and it wouldn't do any good, because your problem isn't just the phone—it's something more."

"You're wrong," she said. "You don't understand."

"I've been trying to," he said. "You can't say I haven't been patient. I thought you'd get over it, but it's becoming pathological."

How could she explain her fear to him? How could she convey her horror of phones? Having to speak to someone she could not see, having to fear that at any moment a call might come from someone she could not see or touch, with a message she could not anticipate—the thought was unbearable. Throughout her life, on those rare occasions when she had picked up a phone, she had imagined invisible callers listening to her stammered, uncertain words with mockery and contempt and indifference while feigning friendliness.

It was the interconnectedness of it all that got to her, the vision of a world hooked up and wired and always in contact, with fibers and cables and satellites carrying messages that no one could escape. It wasn't enough to put telephones in everyone's home; now people could carry pagers and drive around with cellular phones. They would all be sucked into the constant babble, the noise that would allow for no peace. There would be no solitude, no time for quiet moments; they would all be nothing but automatons reacting to the latest stream of messages. Nervousness, some might call her fear, or a speech problem, or a lack of interpersonal communication skills, but at last she knew it for what it was—her defense of her innermost self.

"You can't keep going through life," he went on, "without coming to terms with telephones. I mean, you can't escape them."

"Yes, I know," she murmured. "I know that only too well."

"I don't care how you do it. Go to a psychiatrist, or a group—if there is such a thing as a group for people like you—or just sit there and practice picking the damned thing up when nobody's calling, but you've got to get over this. I have to cover for you all the time. Even making a dinner reservation or calling back a friend is beyond you."

"I can't," she said.

"You can. You'd better."

"All *right*," she said, because that was easier than arguing with him.

He picked up the remote and went back to channel-surfing. Cheryl stared at her book. He had not even told her who had called, something he had always done before, as if trying to reassure her that her fears were unfounded.

The telephone rang. Nick got up, muttered a greeting, then retreated to his office and closed the door.

There was no one Cheryl could turn to, no close friend or confidant who might offer her some sympathy. Acquiring and cultivating close friends seemed to require making telephone calls at some point. The people she met in her classes, or the couples who occasionally went out with her and Nick to dinner, remained only distant acquaintances.

She had lost track of her college classmates, and would have to drive to her home town to consult her few friends there.

Nick was up to something. He had stopped nagging at her about counseling, and she had stopped lying to him about the psychologist she was allegedly seeing in Fensterburg, a small city one hour's drive from Wellford. He wasn't likely to discover her deception, since there was little chance of his running into her alleged psychologist. She had always taken a long drive on the days she supposedly had appointments, in case Nick checked on her mileage. The driving soothed her; she was enclosed in a protective carapace, away from chores and disturbances and telephones. Sometimes she would drive as far as her home town. She still owned her parents' house, but Nick had rented it out to a couple with two young children; Cheryl could not even park near the house to gaze at it nostalgically without hearing the sound of ringing telephones through the open windows.

Nick seemed to be getting more phone calls than ever. He often spent most of the evening in his study, behind his closed door, taking one call after another. In the evening, before he came home, the light on the message machine was often blinking nine or ten times. He was doing it deliberately, just to annoy her. Sometimes she was sure she saw him smile whenever the phone rang, seemingly glorying in her distress before he went to answer it.

He was in his study now, speaking in a voice so low that she could barely hear him from her chair. He had been talking to his mother before; she had overheard an occasional shouted Greek phrase. She had also heard her own name spoken several times. Nick had not sounded as though he was sticking up for her. He had probably been telling his mother that there was no excuse for his wife's rudeness, that he had pressured her to make the occasional phone call to Mrs. Christopoulos until he was blue in the face, that he no longer knew what to do.

She got up and moved toward the door. ". . . sorry I ever got married," she heard before Nick's voice again fell. Cheryl crept back to her chair. So her suspicions were correct. With the telephone as his tool, he could call up anyone he liked and say whatever he wished, and her phobia made her powerless to stop him, to have any control over his actions.

The door to the study opened; Nick came toward her and sat down on the sofa. "I may not be home for dinner tomorrow," he said. "There's a chance I'll have to talk to a colleague about a case, and I can't call you up later to let you know for sure, so just don't worry if I'm not here."

"Fine." She did not believe him. He was probably getting together with a friend to drink and commiserate. "By the way, didn't you mention a while back that the lease on my old house is almost up?"

He leaned back. "Yeah, I did. Almost forgot—the Ruddocks are moving out in three weeks. I was going to bring that up. I've been thinking—" He sat up again. "Maybe we ought to sell. I know you feel attached to it, but trying to rent it and keep an eye on it from here is kind of a pain."

"I know."

"It's your house, though. We ought to decide what to do with it together."

An inspiration came to her. "We shouldn't rent it out again," she said quickly. "We could live there ourselves. The town's quiet and safe, there's plenty of room for the two of us, and you could still get to your office here." This was, she realized, the answer to a lot of problems. Nick's business, and its potential disruptions, would be farther away. There was less chance his various tenants would pester him with phone calls about relatively insignificant problems if they had to call long distance, and his clients would have to leave messages at his office. Perhaps Nick would come to appreciate the virtues of a life without so many distractions.

"Absolutely not," he muttered, shattering her reverie.

"Why not?"

"For one thing, because I don't feel like commuting for two hours a day, and it'd probably take even longer in winter. Also because it'd be harder to tend to all my business from there."

Cheryl looked down. "Well, you could cut back on some of your business."

"No, I don't think I could." His hand was suddenly around her wrist, gripping her tightly. "Oh, there's one way I might manage it. I could get another computer for the house, and hook it up to a modem. I could put in a fax machine, and another phone line to handle any business calls that come there. I might be able to do more of my work at home, and drive into my office less often. How would you like that, Cheryl?" She lifted her head; he was smiling now, but his eyes glittered with anger. "Pretty soon everything'll be on the phone lines. You won't just be worrying about phones—it'll be more and more: home computers, modems, faxes, TV, and God knows what else. What are you going to do then?"

She pulled her hand from his. "Stop it!"

"Don't you understand? I'm trying to help you, shock some sense into you."

She jumped to her feet. "Is it so wrong to want to be free of that damned thing?"

He gazed up at her. "You've got to do something about this, Cheryl. It's for your own good." He sighed. "I'll give you a month. That's about as patient as I can be at this point. If you can't answer a simple phone call by then, or ring me up for a couple of minutes at the office—" She waited for him to complete the threat. "You've got to put this phone bullshit behind you."

"We'll see," she said softly, then walked toward the stairway. Her parents had never raised their voices, she thought as she climbed toward the bedroom. She suddenly hated Nick for insisting that she change, for making a scene, for trying to frighten her with his talk of faxes and modems and all the other devices reaching out for her through the wires.

No, she told herself. I won't let them.

Cheryl parked her car a block from Nick's office and walked to the boutique across the way. Nick came out at six; a beautiful blonde young woman was waiting for him in a blue BMW. The blonde beauty looked familiar; Cheryl dimly recalled meeting her a year ago at a local bar association dinner. She had to be the colleague Nick was meeting for dinner. How convenient for him, she thought, to have to discuss business with such a babe.

A week later, when Nick told her once again that he had to meet another lawyer for dinner, Cheryl drove to his office once more. She was not surprised to see the same blonde pick him up again. There had been even more mysterious phone calls lately, calls that came in the evening and that Nick took in his study. The two were plotting against her, and the telephone was their ally.

She had tried to give Nick a refuge. She had thought that was what he wanted. How great it would have been if he could have come home to her and retreated from the out-side, at least for a while.

She had known what was happening, long before she was fully conscious of the source of her fear. Telephones had only been the harbingers. The networks people had built to communicate with one another would soon flood them with so much babble that they would be unable to tell which thoughts and feelings were their own. They would become no more than receivers passing on the messages of the net-works. Their most private thoughts would be overwhelmed by all the noise; they would call out to others through their phones and modems and microphones and never truly be heard. Solitude would be impossible.

The information lines were a growing nervous system, drawing her into itself, but she did not want to be part of it. She desperately needed to be apart, to be herself. She could not fight the system alone. But at least she could protect herself.

Nick was spending more evenings away from home, al-legedly at business dinners. It was easy for Cheryl to pack some of her belongings each night and hide the suitcases and boxes in the basement before he came home.

She was ready to leave in a week. It was surprisingly easy to walk out the door with the last of her packed belongings and turn the key in the lock, having avoided an unpleasant confrontation. In a way, she was grateful that Nick had found someone else; that made it even easier to leave.

Her spirits lifted as she approached her home town. The family in her parents' house had moved out; except for some crayon scrawlings on a couple of walls and worn spots on the living room carpet, the rooms were in good shape. She could sleep on the futon she had brought with her until she got a bed, and would drive to the electric company's local offices in the morning to get the power turned on. The Ruddocks had installed telephone jacks in both of the bedrooms and the kitchen, but had apparently taken their phones with them. The only telephone left in the house was her parents' old black one in the basement recreation room, and its receiver was off the hook.

Cheryl approached it hesitantly, then leaned down, picked up the receiver gingerly, and managed to put it back in its cradle. The telephone company would have disconnected this line by now. She could always drive over to the local offices to see about having it reconnected.

Assuming, of course, that she could come up with any good reasons to have the phone hooked up.

Nick came to the house two days later, just after the two men from the local furniture store had delivered her new bed. She managed to lock the front door just before he reached the porch.

He pounded on the door. "Cheryl! Cheryl! Open the goddamned door! I have to talk to you!"

"Go away!"

"You can't just walk out like this!"

"Oh yes I can."

"Cheryl!" He pounded on the door again, then stepped back. She could see him through the peephole. "Are you still there?"

"I'm here."

"Then I'll just have to shout at you through the door. I found somebody. He can help you. I've got it set up, he works with people like you all the time. He's actually kind of interested in your particular disorder. It took me a while to set it up, but he'll take your case on right away."

Cheryl said, "I'm not a case."

"Damn it, will you listen to me? You can beat this thing!"

"What do you care if I do or not? You've got that gorgeous blonde to run around with, that colleague who's been joining you for dinner."

He gaped at her. "Rita? You know about Rita?"

"You're goddamned right I know about Rita," she replied, wallowing in righteous fury. "I was outside your office. I know who you were meeting. Bet she was calling you up all those times, too."

"Then you should have spied on me some more and followed me to the restaurant, because her husband always met us there. You idiot! Rita had this massive phobia herself once, about airplane flights! She told me about this psychologist, the one who wants to see you. She helped me set it up."

She would not let him trick her into leaving her refuge, now that she was safe. "You wanted a quiet home," she said. "At least you said you did. You liked having someone around who wasn't competing, who looked after you, who just wanted some peace. I kept my side of the bargain. You're the one who's changed."

"Maybe you made me change." He thrust his face closer to the peephole. "If I'm ever crazy enough to get married again, I'll find somebody who's aggressive and loud and a workaholic and who's always on the phone." He wiped an arm across his brow. "You're not afraid of phones. You're afraid of life. You'll have to cut yourself off from everything to be happy."

"Go away."

"Cheryl—"

"Go away."

He turned around and left.

Nick did not give up right away. For two months, he drove up every weekend to shout at her through the door. Because she knew he would come on weekends, when there were fewer demands on his time, she was prepared for him. Sometimes she came to the door to listen, although she never opened it. Sometimes she stayed upstairs and pretended she was not home.

At the beginning of autumn, he arrived with an older man, who turned out to be another lawyer. Cheryl let them inside. Nick was ready for a formal separation, with the divorce to be final in a year. She would have her house, the money her parents had left her, the furniture and books they had taken from this house shipped back to her, and a cash settlement from Nick because he wanted to be fair. There was no point in contesting the terms. Nick was being more than generous, and for her to fight a long legal battle would inevitably require telephone calls.

Nick looked miserable when he left with his attorney. Cheryl did not know why. They had solved everything in a civilized, reasonable way, and he would get over her in time.

Her life was hers once more, Cheryl thought as she went upstairs to her bedroom. She had left the phone in the living room disconnected. She would no longer be plagued by the demands of others, by the need to make herself understood to them, by calls from the outside world. How odd it was that she couldn't feel happier about that. She had what she wanted; why did she still feel vaguely uneasy and afraid?

She went to bed early and fell into a dream.

She was standing in an empty room with walls of

glass. Through the walls, she saw people pressing against the glass, calling out to her soundlessly. She knew what they were saying; they wanted her to come out. Nick was there, and his mother, and several of her college class-mates. They wanted her to join them, to throw herself into the messy, painful, disorderly, unpredictable and upsetting business they called life. She shrank back, afraid they might shatter the walls and drag her outside.

Cheryl woke up the next morning feeling drained, as though she had not slept at all, and glanced at the clock on her nightstand; it was nearly noon. Then she heard the sound, one she had never expected to hear again.

Two telephones were ringing in unison. One chirped at her; the other had the loud, jarring ring she remembered from her childhood. She could almost believe that the phones were right there in her room.

She quickly got out of bed. The telephones stopped ringing, then started up again.

Cheryl ran downstairs, then clambered down the steps to the basement. The black telephone in the recreation room still sat on a table in the corner. She had never had it reconnected; it could not be ringing. Yet the ringing went on, the chirping near her right ear, the more grating bell near her left.

The ringing stopped, then began again.

Chirp. Ring. Chirp. Ring. Chirp. Ring. Chirp. Ring.

Silence.

Chirp. Chirp. Chirp.

Silence.

Ring. Ring. Ring. Ring.

Cheryl found herself kneeling on the floor, hands over her ears.

Ring. Ring. Ring.

Chirp. Chirp. Chirp. Chirp.

The phones would never stop ringing, she realized, because they were inside her now, and they would never stop.

Ring, Ring, Ring.

Chirp, Chirp, Chirrrrrp . . .

BOND AND FREE

I can't remember anything that happened to me before I came here, and neither can the others, or if they can they're not saying. Tamu says he can, but he's lying, as he lies about everything else. He is squatting on the balustrade now, peering at the green meadow that surrounds us on all sides. He sits on his heels and balances on his toes. His brown skin seems to gleam in the sunlight. He is mocking me, waiting to see how long I can stand it before I get up and rush across the balcony to him, afraid that he might slip and fall to the ground a hundred feet below. But I no longer care. I realize at last that Tamu with his almost perfect reflexes will not fall and will not do anything that will actually endanger him in any way. His balancing act is a lie, his precariousness on the edge of the balustrade a falsity. He turns his head toward me, and I smile.

"Stop moving your face," Tomas says. Tomas is busy applying my make-up, and he gets upset if I ruin his handiwork. It takes him at least an hour to do it every day, and that doesn't include the time he spends on my hair. Then he expects me to spend the rest of the day doing nothing that would endanger his creation. That usually means doing nothing at all except reading or talking with the other patients. Last week I defied him and went down to swim in the pool. When I came out of the water with my hair plastered flat against my head and my make-up ruined, poor Tomas almost cried; he had spent three hours on me that day. He sulked for two days afterward, and I was able to

97

roam around outside letting the wind whip my hair, able to eat without worrying about my lip paint. Then Tomas stopped sulking and my holiday was over.

Tamu is standing on his head now, hands in front of him, knees on his elbows. "There," says Tomas. "I think you're done." He holds his hand mirror in front of me. I am black and gold today, black lines over eyelids and brows, gold dust heavy on my lids and sprinkled on my cheekbones. My hair too is thick with gold dust, my lips painted gold, my eyes made black by lenses. Tomas has dressed me in a black velvet dress, and golden earrings hang like chains to my shoulders. Even my skin is golden today; my tan has begun to fade. "Please don't," he says, "move unnecessarily."

"I can't," I say, "move at all." The heavy velvet dress, stiff with stays that push my breasts up and pinch my waist in, is a cage. I can feel sweat under my arms and between my breasts. "I don't know why you couldn't find something more comfortable; I can hardly breathe." I am taking short, shallow breaths, unable to inhale deeply, and I am afraid that if I stand at all, I may faint.

"You were comfortable yesterday; you don't have to be today." Yesterday was a green leotard, green eyes, green spray on my hair. Tomas didn't like that effect and he didn't like the leotard. My thighs were too thin; my stomach was a bit too round. He had told me not to eat any supper because I was getting fat, and so I ate twice as much as I usually do. He is retaliating. It will be a miracle if I can eat at all now, with the stays pinching at my waist.

"Perfect," Tomas murmurs, "perfect. I love you, Alia; that's why I make you beautiful. And I love you even more today; you're more beautiful than I've ever made you." I glance at him and notice the bulge in his crotch, under his shabby pants.

"Why are you such a slob, then?" I ask. Tomas is heavy around the waist and his dirty brown hair hangs down to his chest. He is wearing what he always wears, brown pants and a torn white vest. The vest is unbuttoned and spotted with stains. "Why don't you use some of your expertise on your own ugly self?" I look at his paunch and make a face. He seems upset now, not because of what I've said, but because he is afraid I'll disturb my make-up by showing any expression at all.

"I'm making *you* beautiful," Tomas protests. "Why should I waste the time on myself when it's obvious that nothing will come of it anyway." He pats his stomach. "I suppose I could diet. I love you, Alia. You're perfection today, a vision. . . ."

"A vision!" says Tamu, who has given up on his balancing act for now. "A vision I would prefer to see naked and on the bed inside."

"You had enough last night," I say. Tamu leers at me. I stick out my tongue at him.

"Stop that," says Tomas, "you're going to ruin your make-up."

"I'm dying," says Tamu. He sits on the arm of my chair. "Dr. Ehlah said I was dying. My insides are rotting away. I'm going to suffer terribly."

"Why don't you jump off the balcony, then?" I reply. Tamu is unable to keep from lying.

"Because then I couldn't see you any more, Alia," he says. "Because then I couldn't spend all that time plowing your furrow. I don't mind suffering when I think of all the happy hours that await me in your presence, hours that will take my mind off my suffering if only for a little while." Tamu stands and begins to turn on his toes, stretching his arms toward the sun.

Pamela Sargent

"Let's go downstairs," Tomas says. "Let's go and sit in the ballroom so that everyone else can see you."

"I can't move. I can't even get through our room in this thing, let alone down the stairs." I feel perspiration on my face. Tomas begins to dab at it with a handkerchief.

"I don't want to die," Tamu suddenly shouts. "I want to live long enough to see my parents again, they were such fine people. They lived in a beautiful house in a large city. We had purple carpets on the floor, velvet carpets, and I would stand on them for hours, rubbing my feet on them, and sometimes I would even roll across them naked. They used to bring me little girls to play with."

"I thought they had a fine ranch with horses," I say, "and that they used to bring you little boys."

Tamu is pouting now. I am not supposed to notice his lies and have hurt his feelings by mentioning an old story. He sulks for a few seconds, then brightens. "They had the ranch too," he goes on, "and a cottage near a woodland glade. I used to watch my mother there while she was taking on the gardener."

I have to admire Tamu, in a way. At least he can invent a past. He and Tomas are much more intelligent than I am, and they can always find something to say about anything. I can do nothing but respond to their talk, rarely having anything of my own to offer. I expect this with Tomas; he is older and has been here for ten years or more. But Tamu is only fourteen. I should be cleverer than he. I have been here three years and am almost seventeen. Tamu has been here three months. I introduced him to Tomas, I let him move his bed into our room, and he doesn't show me proper deference. He is only the intermediary between Tomas and me, the tool through which Tomas expresses his love for me physically, and yet he insists on acting as if he is autono-

100

mous. But he is only a tool which pounds away in my open orifice while I cry out my love for Tomas, and afterward presents his ass to Tomas while Tomas cries out to me. It is I who lie in the big bed with Tomas during the night while he gazes down at my ruined make-up and speaks to me about how short-lived his art is, how soon beauty dies. Tamu has to lie in the small bed. Let him prance around with his pretty ass! He is only a tool.

"Why are we here," Tomas says, "and why can't we remember? I must have asked myself that a million times."

"I don't know why you do," I say. "The doctors told us. We're prone to certain illnesses and have to be kept in a restricted environment."

"I don't think that's true. I didn't believe it when I first came here, and I don't believe it now."

"What difference does it make?"

"Aren't you curious, Alia?"

"Sure," I say. "But I'm not going to sit around thinking about it. One day, I'll just get up and walk out of here, and I'll keep going until I see what's outside. You can come along if you want."

"But you can't just walk out of here," he says, looking worried.

"Why not? No one will stop me. I can just keep going, as far as I want to. I walked out once and stayed away for the whole day; I didn't come back until after supper; you remember, you were really upset. But the doctors didn't care."

Tomas is agitated. "You can't," he says. "You're susceptible to certain diseases; that's why you're here."

"But I thought you didn't believe that."

"Well, I don't entirely, but I haven't disproved it either. If I'm going to find out anything, I'll find it out here."

"Suit yourself," I say. "You should come along, though; it might be a real adventure. This place is so boring I'd think you'd welcome the chance."

"I don't think it's boring. There's a library, plenty of people to talk to, and you, Alia. Why should I be bored?"

I begin to shrug my shoulders, then feel the pinch of my stays. Tamu is turning cartwheels now. "I'm dying," he shouts to us. "My bones will rot away until I can only flow across the floor." He begins to dance across the balcony, whirling faster and faster, his arms straight out from his shoulders, until I am almost dizzy watching him. I reach for Tomas's hand. He holds it, then kisses my golden-nailed fingers.

"You are beautiful," he says.

The fire of sunrise blazed beyond the balcony. Awakening, Alia sat up in her large brass-railed bed and gazed across the room.

Tomas had betrayed her again, creeping out of bed in the middle of the night to Tamu. She could see their bodies huddled together under Tamu's sheets, moles burrowing under the bedclothes.

Tamu was only an intermediary. Alia had never made love to him unless Tomas was present and able to witness the act. Yet Tomas had gone to Tamu while assuming that she still slept; she had heard their moans and remembered that it was Tamu's name he called out and not hers.

Well, thought Alia, it hardly matters now. She was leaving this morning. If the others were content to sit around here, that was their business. She had wanted Tomas to accompany her, but he, along with everyone else, preferred to huddle in the hospital even though he, and almost everyone else, did not really believe what the doctors had told them. No one had forbidden them to leave; none of them really wanted to go.

She put on her walking boots, straightened her slacks, and checked her small knapsack. It was filled with food packets stolen from the kitchen and a canteen of water. She had a knife and could sleep on the ground using the knapsack as a pillow.

Alia hoisted the knapsack onto her back, then turned toward Tamu's bed. The two were still sleeping. She opened the door and walked out into the red-carpeted hallway.

No one else was up yet. She walked down the hallway to the elevator and pushed the down button. Tomas was afraid of the elevator and never let her use it; Tamu laughed at Tomas for his fear but wouldn't ride it either. The doors opened and she stepped aboard.

The elevator hummed down to the first floor lobby and stopped with a jolt. Alia paced through the lobby. Her booted footsteps echoed on the smooth white surface of the floor. Other Alias marched on either side of the large room, reflected from the mirrors that lined the halls. All of the Alias moved toward the arched doorway, then disappeared, leaving only one to pass through the doorway and outside the hospital.

The morning air was cool and the grass around the building still dewy. As she walked, Alia saw the tips of her boots darken with moisture. She pivoted and looked back.

The hospital seemed to tower above her. It was an ugly building, tall and square with baroque balustrades surrounding balconies on every floor of the thirty-story structure. The heavy wooden doors, propped open, which led into the lobby seemed out of place, an afterthought. She turned away from the hospital. Grasslands surrounded the building on all sides; the only tree she had ever seen was the weeping willow near the back entrance.

Alia set out across the green field in front of her. She hoped Tomas wouldn't worry, remembered seeing him under Tamu's sheets, then began to wish that he would worry a little. He would have to dress someone else today, if anyone would sit still that long. She laughed to herself.

The knapsack had grown heavier. Alia stopped, removed it, and sat down. She was still surrounded by green meadows, and she could still see the hospital. It was small and close to the horizon, a grey block against the blue sky.

She couldn't have made much progress if she could still see the hospital. Annoyed, she stood up and began to drag her knapsack behind her. The cursed thing seemed to be made of lead.

Alia trudged on, dragging the knapsack. Occasionally she turned and, seeing the grey block, would keep going. The weather had grown warmer, and her clothes were sticking to her. She pushed on, dragging the knapsack up a small hill and down the other side, through a field of dandelions and up another small hill. She moved on until she was exhausted and had to stop once more.

She fell next to the knapsack and stretched out on the ground, catching her breath. At last she sat up and climbed to her feet.

The hospital had vanished.

She sat down again, facing her long afternoon shadow. At last she was free of the place. If Tomas had been with her, he would be trying to guess what was beyond the meadow, if indeed there was anything beyond the meadow. Alia was content to wait. She shivered, suddenly apprehensive.

Alia had found some trees by nightfall and decided to sleep under them, feeling somehow, that she would be safer there. By morning, she regretted the decision. The ground under the trees had been harder than the soft meadowland.

She began to walk around the trees, feeling numb in the cool morning air. Her jacket was damp with dew. "This is ridiculous," she said aloud, "walking all this way to see five trees." Her voice sounded hollow. She shuddered and decided not to talk to herself again.

She hoisted the knapsack onto her back and set off. Occasionally she looked back. The trees moved closer to the horizon and finally disappeared. A song Tamu had taught her ran through her mind, repeating itself monotonously.

At noon she sat down to rest. The silence of the grasslands had grown oppressive. She pulled out her canteen and drank noisily, smacking her lips between swallows. She opened a packet and gnawed at the rubbery chicken inside, then let out a loud belch.

Ahead of her was a very high hill, higher at least than any she had seen so far. She noticed a small structure on the side of the hill, squinted at it nearsightedly, but couldn't see what it was.

She hurried toward the hill, curious now. She moved quickly, ignoring the warmth of the sunlight and the increasing heaviness of the knapsack she was dragging.

Reaching the hill, she began to climb toward the structure. It was a well. She had seen a painting of a well in the library; in fact, this looked like the same one: brown stones, wooden bucket parked on the edge, wild violets growing nearby.

There was one difference. She could see a wooden plank resting against the well. Someone had painted white letters on the plank. She read the message:

WATER—FILL UP

YOU'RE GOING TO NEED IT

Alia sat down and stared at the plank. Tomas, she thought, would have been terrified by now. She reached over and touched one of the white letters with her finger.

The paint was still wet.

She jumped up quickly and looked around. She saw nothing but grassy fields on all sides. Her hands were trembling. Someone had painted the sign very recently.

Whoever it was might be just over the hill.

Alia paced near the well, clenching her hands, trying to calm herself. Someone is telling me I need water, she thought, that's all; I'll fill my canteen and the empty packets and reseal them, and then I'll see what's over the hill.

She lowered the bucket into the well, then filled her canteen and empty food packets. She resumed her climb. The hill was steeper than it looked, and her legs ached from the exertion. The weather had grown extremely warm, and the air seemed dryer. The knapsack was pushing her toward the ground, and her calf muscles tightened.

At last, panting, she reached the top of the hill and looked around.

The green grass continued to the bottom of the hill, then stopped abruptly. In front of her, Alia could see only dry, flat desert land. The desert stretched to high mountains far in the distance, at least a day's walk away. There was no sign of life anywhere on the desert wastes except at one point midway to the mountains. There, she could see what looked like a small group of buildings. They seemed to shimmer before her eyes.

People. There might be people there.

A wave of panic swept over her. I should go back, she thought wildly, and shuddered at the thought of the diseases to which she might be exposing herself.

She turned quickly, tripped, and began to roll back down the hill, finally sliding to a stop.

"Stop it," she said aloud, "if you panic now, you've come all this way for nothing." Her voice was harsh, and she whispered her next words. "I'll stay near the well, and I'll sleep there, and rest, and decide tomorrow."

She walked back down to the well where, after a hasty look around, she stripped off her clothes and then lowered the bucket for water. She poured it over her body, welcoming the coolness. The water was a silver stream, refreshing and calming her. She threw herself to the ground, feeling the warm rays of the sun on her back, and sniffed at the wild violets.

She set out across the desert before dawn. It was cold at first, but after walking for a while, she peeled off her jacket and put it into the knapsack.

The sun was burning her face, and she could feel the desert heat through her boots. Alia began to whistle, marching in time to the tune. The desert blurred around her, and the thin layer of sand over rock seemed almost white. She kept marching, pausing only long enough to drink from one of the food packets.

Ahead of her, the buildings in the center of the desert shimmered. As she came closer, she noticed something odd about them. The ones at the edge of the town were not buildings at all, but only facades supported by wooden rails, as if the entire town were nothing more than a stage set. Moving nearer, she saw that in fact there was only one real building in the town, in the center of the facade.

She suddenly felt foolish, trudging across the desert to meet this display. She walked over to the building in the center, an old rickety wooden structure three stories high, feeling more alone than ever. It would at least shade her from the desert heat for a while. She peered inside the front window and saw an unlighted room with round tables, chairs, and a long bar on one side near the wall. She tried the door. It opened easily and she walked inside.

Everything in the room was coated with a layer of grey dust. Alia walked to a table near the bar and took the knapsack off her back, placing it next to a chair. Rummaging in the sack, she pulled out her jacket and dusted off the table. Then she sat down, resting her head on the tabletop.

She had come on a fool's errand. She should have turned back at the well, but she had come too far to turn back now. She sighed and closed her eyes.

"My God, honey, don't look so sad. What you need is a cold beer."

Alia sat up quickly. A tall busty red-headed woman was standing near her, arms resting on the dusty bar. She smiled at Alia.

"Who are you?" shouted Alia, almost rising to her feet.

"Don't look so worried, honey. My name's Eta. I own this establishment." The woman walked toward her, carrying a bottle. She wore a long purple dress which trailed behind her, picking up dust and leaving a streak on the floor. She put the bottle in front of Alia and sat down across from her, placing her elbows on the table. "Go ahead, it's on me. Business is so lousy lately, I can't lose much more giving it away." Eta smiled and fluttered her thick black eyelashes.

Alia picked up the beer. It was cold and wet with beads of condensation. She sipped at it tentatively, then began to gulp it down.

"You know," said Eta, "everyone used to come here. Why, you couldn't hardly find a place to rest your ass. But you know how people are; they go to a place, and before you know it they're moving on to a new place because it's got a band or hot horsy dervs or some other fool thing. I don't have all that, but I run an honest bar, and I don't care if people get boisterous or the girls want to make some spare money on the side or somebody wants to throw some chairs around, but I guess Eta's place just isn't good enough any more."

Alia stared at the woman. She could not understand what Eta was talking about and was afraid to ask. "This whole damn town used to come here," Eta went on. "I remember when Gar Tuli got so mad he threw a whole table through that window over there, and his woman—she was big, honey—sent him through the window when she found out about him and Neela. What a night!"

Alia looked down at her beer bottle. The woman must be mad. This could never have been a town, not unless everyone had moved and taken the buildings with them. "Maybe they'll all come back someday," she said, trying to smile sympathetically, "when they get tired of the other place." She finished her beer. Eta's eyes seemed to flicker a bit as she watched Alia. The woman was silent for a few seconds; then she slapped her thigh and laughed loudly.

"You're all right, honey. You know the right thing to say. I feel better already." Eta got to her feet. "You want another beer?"

Alia shrugged. Eta sailed over to the bar, making another trail in the dust with her train. She bent over behind the bar, then stood up. Alia could see silver beads on the bottle Eta was holding and wondered how the woman kept the beer cold.

"Where you headed for?" asked Eta.

"I thought I'd take a look at the mountains," Alia muttered. Eta came back with the beer and sat down again.

"There's nothing over there, honey," the woman said.

"How long does it take to get there?"

"A few hours. But I'd advise you to head back where you came from. Or you can stay here and maybe we can figure out how to get some customers. We oughta think of something between the two of us."

Alia stood up. "You're insane," she said quietly. Eta didn't respond. "You are really demented. There aren't any people here; there aren't even any buildings except this one. I've got better things to do than spend time with a madwoman." She picked up the knapsack, watching Eta. The woman was silent. Alia moved toward the door.

Suddenly Eta chuckled. "You sound like Gar Tuli," she said. "You know what he used to say? He used to say, 'Eta, you got cobwebs in the attic.' I think you better go back where you came from."

"Thank you for the drink," said Alia. "If I see anybody, I'll be sure to recommend your hospitality." She left Eta sitting at the table and stepped into the hot dry air outside. As she walked away from the building and past the facades on either side of her, she began to feel a bit more energetic in spite of the heat. Tendrils of guilt brushed at her mind, and she speculated about Eta, thinking that perhaps she should have stayed with her for a day, talked to her, and offered some help. She pushed Eta out of her mind. The woman was demented, after all; she could have done nothing for her. It was a wonder she had lasted in the middle of the desert; the woman must be more resourceful than she seemed.

Alia burped, then began to whistle again as she marched toward the mountains.

Alia had reached the mountains during the night and slept on the hard desert ground with her jacket wrapped around her. By morning she was shivering from the cold, and she welcomed the sight of the blood-red sun as it began to climb above the now-orange wilderness.

She looked up at the mountain above her. It was rocky and not quite as high as she had thought, although it would take some time to get to the summit. She opened her knapsack and removed some food.

"Mind if I join you?" said a voice. Alia turned her head quickly. A skinny old man sat on the rocks above her.

"Come on down."

The old man clambered over the rocky slopes and was soon sitting next to her. He had an untrimmed grey beard which seemed to wobble on his face, and his shabby brown shirt, black slacks, and boots showed signs of wear.

"I sure am hungry," the man said, eying her dried beef.

"I can only give you one packet." She rummaged in the sack and took out one of the apricot bars, which tasted sour anyway, and tossed it to him.

"I can take you up the mountain," said the man, tearing open the food packet. "You can go up yourself, but it'll take you a lot longer; you don't know the mountain. I can take you up in three, four hours maybe."

Alia looked around at the mountain, then back at the man. "Halfway up it gets hard," he went on. "But I know a quick way."

"All right," said Alia. It would be safer going up with someone anyway, whether the old man could take her up more quickly or not. "All right, old man."

"I could use some more food first and water too." She took out another apricot bar and a packet filled with water.

"Where are you from, old man?"

He squinted at her. "None of your business."

"You wouldn't happen to be acquainted with Eta's place?"

"I'm not acquainted with anybody. I keep to myself and you should do the same." The old man finished his food and got to his feet. "Come on," he said. He began to climb over the rocks. Alia followed him, then noticed that there was a clearly defined path through the rocky slopes.

"I could have found this path myself, you old fraud," she shouted at the figure ahead of her.

"I told you," he shouted back, "it's halfway up you run into trouble." Alia sighed and kept going. Her muscles soon began to knot painfully.

"I don't suppose you could help carry this knapsack for a while," she shouted.

"Why the hell should I? It isn't mine."

"What's over the mountain?"

"You'll find out." His voice was faint. He was getting ahead of her.

She kept climbing, trying to ignore the hot sun. She could go on for another two days before heading back to the hospital, maybe longer on short rations. She should have brought more. She wiped the sweat from her face and wished for a bath. Tamu's mindless song circled her mind once more as she climbed, stopped to rest, then climbed some more. The old man had disappeared.

At last she came to the end of the path. A smaller path forked to the right between two boulders. Alia looked up and saw only sheer cliff surface above her.

The old man had apparently been waiting. He sat on the ground, smiling complacently.

"What now?" she asked.

The old man groaned and got up. "And I just got comfortable too," he grumbled. He turned and she followed him along the small path until they reached a cave in the side of the mountain.

"Here we are," said the man. Above the cave in large letters someone had painted:

ENTER CAVE.

CLIMB STAIRS TO TOP.

"You old fraud," said Alia. She grabbed the man by the shoulders and pushed him against a boulder. "I could have found this cave myself." He twisted loose and ran past her back along the path. "Come back here," she shouted after him. "Aren't you going to the top?"

"Why bother?" The old man's voice floated back to her. "There's nothing up there."

She stood beside the cave, feeling angry and foolish, then walked inside. Someone had carved a flight of stairs in the rock; the steps curved around the cave walls in a spiral. She looked up and saw a speck of light above her.

She chuckled, then began to laugh. This is too easy, she thought; they're not making it hard enough; anyone can just walk out of the hospital and keep going. It wasn't consistent with the doctors' desire to prevent the exposure of susceptible people to disease.

On the other hand, she thought as she began to climb the stone steps, I haven't really seen anybody I could get a disease from except a couple of lunatics. Suddenly she felt cold. Maybe they *were* sick; maybe they, like her, had left the hospital and become ill, losing their minds in the process. Her stomach turned. She should go back.

She kept going up the steps. She would at least see what was over the mountain first. The stairway was dark and only intermittently lighted by phosphorescent green bars attached to the walls. She kept close to the wall, not wanting to lose her balance too close to the edge of the steps, which had no rail.

Alia climbed, stopping frequently to rest. She began to

count steps and lost track of the number. She started to sing and lost track of the time. She was almost hypnotized by the time she reached the top of the stairs and could at last see the sky clearly. It looked like late afternoon.

Above her was a small metal ladder. It was attached to the wall and would take her out of the mountain. She hurried up the ladder. As she climbed out, a breeze wafted past her, and she smelled salty air.

She stood at the summit and looked around. A path had apparently been carved in this side of the mountain also; she could see its clearly defined boundaries among the rocks and boulders. At the bottom of the mountain there was a large expanse of white sand and beyond that a body of water stretching to the horizon. Even at this distance, she could hear the thunder of breakers as waves rolled toward the shore. An ocean, she thought. Tomas had shown her a picture of one in the library and had told her that it was thousands of miles wide, with salty water unfit to drink.

Alia sat down and stared at the grey sea. There was nowhere to go from this point. The mountains extended along the shore for as far as she could see. She could not get across the ocean. She would have to go back, get more supplies, try a different route. But maybe the doctors, who hadn't had to restrict anyone up to now, wouldn't let her leave again. They might be searching for her.

She considered the hospital. Perhaps there was nothing outside the hospital, and no one except a few demented individuals such as Eta or the old man. The doctors themselves might be susceptible to disease. But that wouldn't explain why some doctors disappeared for weeks at a time, or how supplies got to the hospital. No, there had to be other people somewhere.

If I've been exposed to disease, she thought, I'm already

dead. I might as well go on, or the whole trip is for nothing. I'll walk till I drop, I'll stretch the food and water, I have to know. The image of Tomas flickered across her mind, and she felt a pang of regret, then shrugged it off.

Alia started down the mountain.

Four more sunrises, four sunsets; on the fifth day she was still walking, seeing nothing but white sand and ocean on her left, white sand and mountains on her right. The arc of the red sun marked time for her now; she no longer divided her days with meals, eating only when she grew weak. She was almost out of food and water. She could not turn back; she would not even get to the desert.

A crab scuttled past her. She stared at it as it scurried beneath a wave, then heard a cry above her. She looked up. Three gulls circled overhead. She turned to the mountains and saw trees and bushes growing on the slopes. The landscape around her had changed. She had left the barren mountains and arid desert behind.

Her tired feet carried her on. Two days before, she had washed her feet in the ocean, crying out in pain as the salty water washed over the bleeding blisters. She glanced at the ocean. It was receding from her as if it had postponed its apology until now. It withdrew from her and began to creep toward the horizon, leaving behind beached crabs and fish.

Food. It would be simple to gather up some of the fish and store them in empty food packets. With luck, she might be able to start a fire with some wood from the mountain slopes. If necessary, she would eat the fish raw. The ocean kept retreating, leaving behind an almost unnatural silence. Alia began to walk toward some beached fish, squashing the wet soft sand under her feet.

"Hey!" a voice shouted. She turned and saw a figure

running across the beach toward her. It was a young man with black hair; he was well-tanned, clad only in a pair of ragged blue shorts. He waved his arms frantically as he ran.

He stopped near her, panting for breath. "Run!" he shouted. "Run for the mountains, run!"

"Why?"

"Don't ask, run!" The young man took off. She looked toward the ocean.

A wall of water was on the horizon. It was coming toward the shore, threatening to smash her and everything on the beach. She ran after the young man, her terror making it easy for her to catch up with him. She ran, pounding through the sand, ignoring the knapsack on her back, not even looking over her shoulder at the wave. She could hear it now, a low distant rumble coming ever closer to them. They reached the mountain, and she followed the man up the slope, ignoring the tree branches and bushes which clawed at her arms and legs. They stopped on a small ledge, and the young man turned to the sea. He stared at it intently. His jaw muscles tightened.

Alia saw the wave sweeping across the shore toward the mountain. "Come on!" she screamed at the man. "We've got to climb higher, come on!" He ignored her and continued to stare at the wave. It began to slow down, diminishing in size. By the time it reached the foot of the mountain it was a feeble sight, lapping gently at the trees there and then retreating, until the ocean was again where it should be.

The man relaxed, leaning against a tree behind him. "I'm tired," he said. "It's hard to stop them by yourself."

She was puzzled. She remembered reading something about tidal waves and knew that this one had not behaved normally.

"Don't worry about it," the man went on. "Someone was just fooling around." He smiled at her, showing even white teeth. "It happens sometimes."

Alia loosened the straps on her knapsack, letting it fall to the ground. "You're going to get awfully sick, wandering around like this," said the young man. "Don't you think you should go back?"

"Go back to where?" she asked warily.

"You know where. Whatever institution you wandered out of. Didn't they tell you that you might get sick?"

"Yes. I don't know if I believe it any more." She watched the young man carefully. "I've walked a long way. I don't think I want to turn back just yet."

"But I'll take you back. I'm sure it's much nicer there than here. Wouldn't you agree?"

Alia thought of Tomas and Tamu and her life at the hospital, free from any demands. The older patients had been there for fifty years or more and seemed content; in fact, one old man had grown terrified of the thought that a vaccine might be found for the patients and they would be forced to leave. The doctors had to tell him that no one would be forced out, and everyone else had been as relieved as the old man.

"I suppose it is nicer," she said to the young man. "It's easier at least."

"Don't you miss all your friends? They'll be so happy to see you again."

"How would we get there?"

"Oh, it's easy, and it would be fun too. I'll show you." The young man started to climb the mountain. Alia followed him, dragging the knapsack. As she scrambled over some rocks, she noticed a huge red globe hovering above some trees on a ledge just above her. The young man reached out a hand, she grabbed it, and he pulled her up. She saw a huge balloon, bright red and attached to a large basketlike bottom. The young man had apparently tied it to one of the trees.

"We can go back in my balloon," the young man said, walking toward it.

"How?"

"It's simple. When we want to descend, all I have to do is pull this—" he pointed to a rope attached to the balloon "—and we land; it lets some air out. To go up, I just pour some sand out of one of those bags there." He grinned at her. "Doesn't that sound like fun?"

"Sure does."

"We can have a great time on the way back," said the young man. "Come on, let's go." He turned toward the balloon. Alia raised her arm quickly and chopped him on the back of the neck. He toppled forward with a soft moan and lay silent.

She quickly climbed into the basket, cut the rope holding the balloon down with her knife, and poured sand out of one of the bags. The balloon rose, grazing some treetops on the way. She was soon above the mountains and could see the desert on her right. The balloon hovered above the mountains, and she waited for it to start drifting.

"What now?" she muttered. The vehicle was of no use to her if it stayed here. She felt a warm breeze on her face; then she began to move. The balloon drifted to the north. At least, she thought, it won't go back to the hospital.

Ahead, she noticed that the mountains had started to curve to her right, surrounding the desert. She moved further away from the sea and was soon over a thick green forest. She had left the desert behind.

Deer were leaping through the underbrush below her,

waving their small white tails at the balloon. A slender river wound through the trees, and she could see two horses, black and chestnut, on its banks. A flock of crystalline birds, with feathers that were prisms, swam in the river. Alia, clinging to the side of the basket, gazed happily at the forest. It was worth it, she told herself, it was worth it for this.

Then she glimpsed something on the edge of the forest. She squinted as the balloon floated on, and was able to discern large crystalline structures just beyond the wooded land. The crystals were green, gold, silver, blue and pink; some were spirals; others were slender towers. They glittered in the sunlight. As she came closer, she saw large golden insects buzzing softly in the sky over the crystal buildings. A city, she thought, and something jarred her mind.

Home, her mind whispered. *She was a child again. She stood in a garden while her mother made the roses grow.* She was over the city now and could see people moving through the streets on silver bands. A few people were floating over the city, apparently unsupported by anything. *Her father was giving a concert with his mind, and people gathered near the house to listen. Alia heard only silence and the rustle of leaves.* Silvery vines formed patterns on the sides of some of the crystals, wrapping themselves around the buildings, then unwinding and forming new patterns. There were parks scattered throughout the city with trees and ponds, and she could see children playing in them. *The other children wouldn't play with her. She could not float up to the treetops or make the thunder roar.* One of the golden insects passed near her, and she saw people inside it. They gazed at her through the transparent golden walls of the craft and waved.

Home. Bits and pieces cluttered her mind, traces of the

memories she had lost. *I have a brother, with red-gold hair like mine, and he sometimes dances with me in the garden. My home is sapphire-blue. Once he made a cloud for me, and it rained on the flowers.* She tugged at the rope attached to the balloon and began her descent. *Father is composing. He listens to the universe, the stars and winds, and adds his own notes. They tell me it is beautiful. I can't hear it. He listens to other times. I can't hear them. He travels. I cannot follow.* The balloon fell slowly toward a sapphire spiral, then landed with a bump in a small garden behind it.

A tall blonde woman was in the garden gathering pink flowers. Near her stood a man with silver hair. They wore white robes and stared at her as she clambered over the side of the basket. The balloon bobbed uncertainly next to her.

The woman let go of the flowers and they fell in a pink mass at her feet. "Mother," Alia said softly. "Father."

Alia. The name was unspoken as it entered her mind. "Let me stay," she said, "don't send me away again, let me stay." She began to run to them, arms outstretched. The woman turned away. The man still watched her, but did not hold out his arms.

She was surrounded by a blue cloud, frozen, unable to move. *I'm sorry, Alia,* something in her mind whispered, *I'm sorry, please believe that.* Then, very slowly, she fell forward, almost floating, until the blue cloud turned black.

Alia could hear a loud humming sound. She opened her eyes. She was rushing through an underground tunnel aboard a conveyance with transparent sides. The garden had disappeared. Around her, Alia could see only rock and an occasional flashing light. Someone had put her in a chair, and she struggled vainly at the straps which bound her to it.

Eta, the woman of the desert, sat in front of her, but she wore only a green robe and had removed her make-up. Next to Eta sat the young man from the beach and the old man who had guided her up the mountain. The young man was slouching in his chair, staring at the floor. The old man, also in a green robe, had trimmed his beard.

"What are you going to do with me?" asked Alia.

"You have to realize," said the young man, still looking at the floor, "that we are civilized. None of us has entered your mind; no one has since the time you were first taken to the hospital. It was necessary then, as you must know, but we haven't entered it since. If we had, you would be back at the hospital now and would never want to leave again. If I had, you could never have surprised me and stolen my balloon."

"We didn't think you'd get this far," said Eta. "You were timid when we placed you at that hospital. It seemed perfect for you. I didn't think you would become so adventurous."

"Take me home," she said. "Haven't I earned it? I know my mind is weak, but there must be a place for me. Ask my parents, they'll keep me; they have to."

The old man shook his head. "Would you want your parents to bear that?" he said softly. "They made the same decision everyone in their place has made."

"We tried to spare you all this," said the young man. "We tried to discourage you on your journey. We could have terrified you, driven you back with our minds, but that would have been wrong, using our minds like that against a helpless creature."

"Please take me home," she said. Her words seemed feeble. *On her last night at home, she sat sleepless in her room, trying desperately to raise her table with her mind, sobbing with frustration.*

"What would you have us do?" said the old man. "Structure our society around misfits and atavisms? Would you want to live with us, knowing that there was really nothing your poor mind could contribute? You can't shake the mountains or move the sea or bring meteors close to earth in showers of fire. You can't sail the clouds across the sky or make the spring come early out of the ground. You will never be free of the tyranny of time and space." The old man stood up and placed a hand on her shoulder. "I tell you this, even though you will forget. We do the best we can; we place you in environments that will make you happy. We prevent your suffering by removing memories of the past. Would it make you any happier if I told you that there are fewer of you now, that soon there will probably not be any?"

"Don't tell me all that," Alia said bitterly. She glared at the old man. "You have your own reasons for sending me away, I know that."

The old man sighed. "Yes, we do," he said. "Do you have any idea of the control we must exercise over ourselves in order to be certain that a momentary impulse isn't expressed outwardly by our minds? Helpless people such as you would be a constant temptation. You would be pawns which we could dominate, and you would make us cruel and decadent."

"That tidal wave," the young man muttered. "I couldn't resist the temptation. I was glad when I saw how terrified you were. Do you understand that? I never want to feel that way again."

"You'll be in a very nice place," said Eta.

"You'll be happy there," said the old man. "It's all arranged." Alia turned from him and looked out at the rocky walls rushing by them. They seemed to blur slightly as she watched.

★ ★ ★ ★ ★

I can't remember anything that happened to me before I came here, and neither can the others, or if they can they're not saying. The doctors tend to be a bit restrictive, but that's probably understandable. They don't want us traipsing around picking up all kinds of germs that might make us really sick. They wouldn't be too happy to know that Moro and I are on our way to the village.

Moro is skiing ahead of me. He slaloms along, then stops for a bit so I can catch up. I'm not as good a skier as Moro, and I have to go slowly. Moro has sneaked out of the hospital several times, and so has everyone else, I guess. The doctors don't make it too difficult, although they usually get annoyed if they find out.

It'll be my first time in the village. Already I can see it, just over the next slope, cottage roofs covered with inches of snow. Moro knows a tavern where they'll serve you without asking questions. The bartender there used to be at the hospital; I think most of the people in the village were once, but they're old now and were given permission to move.

Moro says that there's a city down at the bottom of the mountain, if you can call it a city. It's not much larger than the village up here. A few patients have been down there, but it's impossible to get to it in winter; you could never make it back up the mountain even if you got there. But Moro will take me in the spring, he's promised, and I'm looking forward to the trip. I don't like staying in the hospital all the time, but as long as I know I can go somewhere, I can stand it.

I manage to come to a stop near Moro without falling over. He is laughing, and there are crinkles on either side of his eyes. He kisses me on the cheek, and I begin to laugh too, stopping only to inhale some of the cold mountain air. I am falling in love with Moro, with his laughter and his talk and his sapphire-blue eyes. We will go to the tavern, and if I manage to acquire some courage with my beer, I may ask him to move into my room.

I think he will accept the offer.

BIG ROOTS

After Father died, I stayed on at his camp. I had put off leaving for a lot of reasons. One was that I felt at peace there, in a way I hadn't for a long time, and another was the need to settle matters with my sister Evie. Maybe I still would have been there, struggling against a world intruding on my refuge, if my sister hadn't appeared to me in the guise of a False Face and the spirits had not spoken.

The camp was a cabin with two bedrooms, a kitchen and living room that were on the side facing the lake, and an attic with cots and sleeping bags. We called it a camp because that's what everyone in the Adirondacks called their summer places, whether they were shacks or mansions. Father had sold his house after Mother died, and lived at the camp during the last two years of his life, before my sister put him in the hospital.

My grandfather had built the camp and cleared the land around the cabin, but the pines were crowding in, and long knotted roots bulged from the ground in tangled masses along the path that led down to the lake. One of the pines, during the year since my father's death, had grown larger, its trunk swelling to nearly the size of a sequoia.

I didn't know why this tree was growing so much faster than the others, but its presence comforted me. I would sit under the pine and think of its roots spreading out under the land, burrowing deep into the ground. We had deep roots in these mountains, my family and I, and I had felt them more lately. My grandfather's people had come there early in the nineteenth century, but my grandmother's Mohawks, the Eastern Gatekeepers of the Iroquois, had been there earlier. She had grown up on a reservation in Canada, but my grandfather had met her in Montreal and brought her back here after their marriage. This land had been a Mohawk hunting ground, the forest they had traveled to from their villages to hunt beaver and deer, and where they had sometimes encountered forest spirits, long before white settlers had moved into the mountains. My grandfather had brought his wife back to her roots.

I had pulled up the canoe and was sitting on the dock, thinking about Grandma's life while watching the loon. The bird had taken up residence in our part of the lake a couple of weeks earlier, and I wondered when more loons would join it. The loon would float on the water, moving its black-feathered head from side to side like an Egyptian belly dancer, then dive. It would stay underwater for three or four minutes, and I could never predict where in the bay it would surface. I had been like a loon underwater myself for the past year, living at the camp, diving below the turbulent surface of my own life. The bit of money I had saved was running out. Pretty soon, I would have to emerge.

The wind picked up and the trees sighed. Sometimes I heard voices, as if people were chanting and singing elsewhere in the forest. Now I heard the sound of a car in the distance. It would be Evie; I was expecting my sister. Our great-aunt and a couple of cousins lived in the nearest town, but they hadn't called since the funeral, and I wanted nothing to do with them anyway; Aunt Clara had led the family faction that disapproved of my grandfather's marriage. My brothers, who lived in Seattle and Atlanta, had already said they wouldn't be visiting this summer, and I hadn't made any friends in town. So it had to be Evie, along

with her husband Steve and her three kids by her first husband, my niece and nephews who couldn't sit in place
without a VCR and a boom box for more than two minutes.
It would be Evie, because anyone else would have called
first to ask for directions, since the only way to the camp
was along a narrow dirt road through the woods. It would
be Evie, because we had business to discuss. She was here
to change my mind.

I got up and climbed toward the cabin. A winged shape
soared overhead; I looked up as an eagle landed in the up-
permost branches of the largest pine. Evie's blue Honda
was rolling down the rutted dirt driveway that led to the
cabin. She would unload a television, a VCR, and a ton of
rented cassettes, to keep her kids quiet, and Steve would sit
in the kitchen making bad jokes while Evie and I cooked
supper. The noise from the TV would be deafening, because all the movies my niece and nephews watched had
lots of special effects. I was sure the sounds would frighten
the eagle away.

But when Evie got out of the car, I saw that she was
alone. "Got the whole weekend," she said, "and I'm taking
Monday off. Steve's watching the kids, so it'll be a real va-
cation for me." She went around to the trunk and opened
it. "Brought some food in the cooler, so we won't have to
cook tonight." Evie took after our father, and he had gotten
his looks from his mother. My grandmother had looked like
Evie when she was young—a tall woman, with coppery skin,
thick black hair, and dark brown eyes. I had our mother's
blue eyes, and my black hair had gone gray early, so now I
colored it reddish-blonde. I didn't look anything like my
grandmother, but I had her soul, which was more than you
could say for Evie.

I helped her carry the cooler and her suitcase inside, re-

lieved that the kids and Steve weren't with her, but still
wary. Ten years lay between my younger sister and me, and
we had never been that close. We had gone for years
without even phoning each other while she was having kids
and getting a divorce and I was drifting, afraid to come
home. She wouldn't have come up here alone just to relax
and visit with me.

The two bedrooms stood on either side of the bathroom,
separated by a narrow corridor. I had been using the bedroom our grandmother had slept in during her summer
visits, and took Evie's suitcase to the other. A quilt covered
the bed that took up most of the small room, and a crucifix
hung above the headboard. I never slept in that room,
mainly because I didn't like the idea of sleeping under a
crucifix, especially one that made Christ look so peaceful
hanging there, as if he were only snoozing. I also knew my
grandmother had come to hate the sight of the cross, which
only reminded her of the nuns who had tried to beat a white
soul into her. I could have taken it down, but then Evie
would have been whining, "Where's Dad's crucifix?" even
though she hadn't been to Mass since her divorce. My father had wanted to die here, in the room he and my mother
had shared, but Evie had insisted on the hospital, so an ambulance had come up the long dirt road and driven him the
fifty miles to the city. Father had lasted less than a month
there, barely enough time for my brothers to realize that he
was actually dying and to get to his side to make whatever
amends they could.

"Mother must have hated this place," Evie said as she
opened the suitcase.

"I never heard her say so."

"Well, think of it, Jennie—sitting around here, away
from all her friends, taking care of us and waiting for Dad

to come up on the weekends."

Maybe she had hated it. I wouldn't know, because Mother had been the kind of person who kept her thoughts to herself. The camp had been my father's boyhood summer refuge. Even after all our summers there, Mother had moved around the rooms, occasionally peering into a corner or picking up an object from a table, as if she were a guest exploring unfamiliar surroundings. But maybe Evie was only projecting her own feelings onto our mother. That would be like my sister, imagining that everyone felt exactly the way she did.

"But I guess you wouldn't understand that," Evie continued, "being practically a hermit yourself."

I would have to put up with three days of this, Evie asking when I was leaving, how I could possibly get through another winter, when I was going to find a job and get on with my life. She would get to the business about the land, too; I was sure of that now. It didn't matter. I was ready for her this time.

We went to the kitchen. "Hungry yet?" Evie asked.

"Not really."

"Let's have a drink then. Better make mine a ginger ale, or diet soda if you have any."

"You sure? I've got some of your bourbon left."

"Steve and I are trying for a kid," she said, "so I'm laying off the booze."

"You must be kidding," I said. "You have three already. How can you afford it? What's going to happen to your job?"

"Steve wants a kid of his own. Can't blame a man for that, can you?"

"Go sit on the porch," I said. "I'll get the drinks." She wandered toward the porch. Evie had always been big, and she had gained more weight since her last visit; maybe she was already pregnant. I poured her a diet cola, along with gin over ice for myself. Once, I had liked martinis, but had come to think of them as a drink for rich white Republicans, so now I didn't bother with the vermouth. "Your grandmother drank." Mother had harped on that, on how much trouble it had caused everyone. "Her Indian blood—that's what it was." That was Mother's explanation for any behavior she didn't want to blame either on environment or her own genes.

The screened-in porch faced the lake. Evie was sitting in one of the chairs, smoking a cigarette; apparently she hadn't given that up yet. I sat down near the standing ashtray and took out my own cigarettes. Tobacco was a sacred plant for the Iroquois; I had read that in a book. For my grandmother's Mohawk ancestors, it was a means by which their prayers could reach the spirits, and rise to their Creator. That was, I supposed, a pretty good reason not to quit. My indecision would travel out along the smoky tendrils, to be dispersed as it rose toward heaven; the spirits would answer my prayers. A stream of smoke from my cigarette drifted through the screen, then broke up into uneven strands.

Evie said, "I have to talk to you."

"I figured."

"Curt called me last night. I talked to Sam a couple of days ago, about the land. They think selling it off's a good idea. People want lakeside property, and this land's worth more now."

Of course my brothers would agree with her about selling. The land Father had left us was his only legacy. We owned everything around this small bay; the closest place, about a mile south, was another cabin overlooking the narrow channel that connected the bay to the rest of the lake. The shallowness of the channel kept large motorboats out of the bay; days could pass without my seeing more than a canoe moving along the shore. It was why the loons came there and blue herons nested in the nearby trees; I thought of the eagle I had seen earlier.

"Dad didn't leave us this land," I said, "so that we could sell it."

"He must have known we'd consider it. Why didn't he put it in the will if he didn't want us to sell?"

"Because he was too sick to think about it. Because there wasn't time. I know what he would have wanted."

"You know. You always know, Jennie. You always know all this stuff about everyone in the family that nobody else knows." Or which might not even be true, her voice suggested.

I knew things because the rest of them never bothered to listen to anybody. I said, "When I knew Dad was dying, I kept waiting for him to tell me to get on with my life. But he never did, and it wasn't until a little while ago that I figured out why. He wanted me to stay here, to protect this land."

"That's crazy. He was so doped up toward the end he probably couldn't think straight. He must have figured you'd have enough sense to get back on your feet by now. This land's worth nothing to us this way. If we sell it, we can—"

"It isn't ours," I said, "not really. It's like we're the caretakers, that it's a trust. I've been feeling that way the whole time I've been here. It isn't our land, it's our people's—Grandma's people."

"Are you on that again?" Evie stubbed out her cigarette. "How can that stuff matter to you? Look, I loved Grandma, but she wasn't all that much use to anybody when she was alive. If Grandpa hadn't had to waste so much money on her, maybe there would have been something left for us."

She took out another cigarette and lit it. "You can afford to be sentimental about these things, but the rest of us have kids. I'd like to be able to do something for them."

That was the excuse that explained everything. "I have kids, so that gives me license to be an asshole. I have kids, so I'm entitled to do things I'd shy away from or have doubts about otherwise, because I have to think of them." At least that's how it sounded to me. Whatever happened to "I have kids, so maybe I should try to pass on some wisdom and principles?" But my sister didn't live in that world. Maybe no one did any more.

"And Curt's got a son almost ready for college," Evie went on. "He told me he wants Brian to get somewhere." That sounded like Curt. My brother would think he was doing the world a big favor if he gave it another lawyer or M.B.A.

"It isn't as if the state hasn't set aside plenty of undeveloped land already." Evie gestured with her cigarette. "We're not rich, you know. We can't keep this our little private bay forever."

I tried to think of what to say, but the gin was getting to me. Evie wouldn't understand if I told her that I still caught glimpses of deer coming to the bay to drink, that we had to keep the land as it was so that the deer could still come here. I couldn't tell her that having more people around would probably frighten off the turtles that sunned themselves on the logs across from our dock. Evie would be thinking of future college bills and expensive technology for her kids and the new baby with Steve, not deer and turtles.

"It won't be the same," I said. "I saw an eagle in that big tree today. He won't stick around if builders start tearing things up. We could leave something behind, Evie, a bit of untouched land people might appreciate having someday."

"Listen." She leaned toward me. "We can still keep some of the land around this camp. You'd hardly notice the difference. We could sell the rest off in large parcels, so there wouldn't be too many places built." She sounded like a white woman, with her talk of selling the land and carving it up, but that was how Evie thought of herself. It's that Indian blood that caused most of the family troubles; better forget you have any.

"I'll just bet the developers will listen to you," I said. "They'll say, 'Sure, I'll just put one summer home here and make fifty grand instead of building five and pocketing a hell of a lot more.' "

"There are limits," Evie replied, "what with having to put in septic systems and all. If you ask me, this place could use some development." She squinted as she stared toward the lake. "For instance, that big tree there is completely out of hand. Somebody should have cut it down a long time ago. If you cleared out some of those trees, you'd have a much better view."

"That tree stays." I was on my feet. "It's Grandma's tree—she planted it herself when Grandpa built this place." I don't know how I knew that. During the year I had been living at the camp, I had looked out at the tree without ever thinking about it. Why had Grandma planted a pine there, when pines already surrounded us on all sides? Yet somehow I knew she had planted it. Maybe she had told me once, and I had simply forgotten until that moment.

I went into the kitchen, took some ice out of the refrigerator, and poured myself more gin. The evening wind was picking up when I got back to the porch. The pines sang, the wind rising into a muted cheer and then falling into a sigh, but a deeper moan nearly drowned out the song. I heard a rumble that might have been distant thunder, but the sky was still salmon pink, the clouds fingers of navy blue.

"It was cruel," I said then, "what Grandpa did to Grandma."

"What do you mean?" Evie asked.

"Buying all this land and saying he did it for her."

"You call that cruel? It showed how much he adored her."

"No, it didn't," I said. "He was saying, 'Here, I bought this land, this little piece of the mountains that used to belong to your people, because I made a lot of money in lumber. And you can have a little of your land back because a white man got it for you.' "

"You're crazy, Jennie. Grandpa loved that woman. Do you think he would have stayed with her all those years if he hadn't?"

That was the way the rest of them saw it. Grandpa was the long-suffering saint and Grandma the alcoholic he hadn't been able to help. He had checked her into every expensive hospital he could find, but that had not kept her from going back to drinking when she got home. He had sold his business to stay with her, and at the end of his life, the money was gone. Grandma had outlived him even with the drinking; she tapered off toward the end, spacing out her drinks, but not enough to save either her liver or my father from her medical bills. No wonder the rest of them blamed her for their lives of tract houses, credit card bills, and tedious jobs.

Maybe I would have blamed her myself, but I had spent too much time as a child sitting with her when my brothers exiled me from their games. To Evie and my brothers, our grandmother was only an old drunk who sat in the corner and mumbled to herself; that was the Grandma they remembered. They didn't have the patience to listen to her, to see that her disjointed musings made sense once you put them together. The Grandpa I had heard about in her words wasn't the loving husband Evie saw, but the man who had forced her to live among people who despised her, who had refused to let her go.

"The wild Indians'll get you." That had been Curt's favorite taunt at our camp when he was tormenting our younger brother Sam. "When you're asleep, the wild Indians'll climb in your window and scalp you." Indians had nothing to do with them. They had never noticed how Grandma closed her eyes when she heard Curt's words, how her hand had tightened around her glass.

"I don't even know my clan," I said.

Evie exhaled a stream of smoke. "What?"

"I don't even know my clan. Grandma used to say that. She'd say it in this low voice, so nobody else would hear, but I did." She had said it as if knowing the name of her clan would have freed her from her prison.

"Probably said it when she was drunk." Evie leaned back in her chair. "It doesn't matter, Jennie. It's got nothing to do with us." She was quiet for a while. "Being alone up here all this time—no wonder you sound so funny. Look, if we sell, you'd have enough to make a new start. You can think of where to live, have time to find a job. Hell, maybe we can get enough so you don't have to work at all."

As the gin slowed me down, I wanted to shout that I was going to find work—waitressing, office work, or whatever—in the nearest town, that I could lay in enough wood for the winter and buy enough meat for myself cheaply from a hunter once deer season started. I knew what I had to do; it was time to lay it all out and show Evie she had to go along. I was about to raise my voice when the cabin suddenly shook, and the floor dropped from under my chair.

The disturbance lasted only a moment. Before I could speak, the floor was once more firmly under my feet, the evening still except for the gentle sound of the wind.

"Whoa," Evie muttered. "Did you feel that?"

"Just a quake," I said. The mountains had them once in a while, mild ones that barely made three points or so on the Richter scale, but I had never felt one quite like that. Usually, everything would get very quiet, and then there would be a sharp sound like a sonic boom, and after that a small bounce before things settled down. This time, the quake had come from deep underground, as though the earth was giving way.

"Jesus," Evie said, "I thought the whole place was going to fall down. I'll have that bourbon after all."

I got her the drink, and then another one when we sat down in the kitchen to eat the sandwiches she had brought, and by then Evie was wandering down memory lane, droning on about our adventures at the camp when we were younger. She seemed to get most nostalgic about the times the boys had ganged up on me, or about how Curt and Sam would always push me off the dock, even when I was dressed, even when the water was freezing cold. I didn't mind. At least she had forgotten about real estate for the moment.

She went to bed early, tired from her drive, and I sat on the porch with another gin, trying to think of how to persuade her and my brothers not to sell our land. Brilliant ideas about how to convince them flashed through my mind, only to be forgotten a second or so later. My face was stiff, my body numb. I was really drunk by then, and felt as if I were wrapped in cotton and looking at everything from inside a long tunnel. The big pine tree near the path seemed larger, and then I saw a face in the bark, a carved mask like the ones my ancestors had made.

That had to be an illusion, a trick of the moonlight shining through the boughs. The face changed as I stared at it, reshaping itself into that of a wolf. Seeing a face in the tree didn't frighten me, though, because I had noticed other strange things lately—marks and symbols on trees that looked as though they had been made by knives, the throbbing sounds of drums in the night until hooting owls or the snarl of a bobcat drowned them out. I had grown to accept these passing sights and sounds, which seemed to belong to the forest and mountains.

I must have fallen asleep after that, and woke up on the studio couch in the living room, my head pounding. I lifted my head, then realized I would never make it to my bedroom without collapsing or vomiting—maybe both. My head fell back, and then I was outside, under the big pine.

Two men in feathered caps and deerskin robes stood near the tree. One lifted his hand, and then I looked up to see the eagle flutter its wings in the branches overhead.

"Do you know what tree this is?" one man asked.

"My grandmother's," I replied.

"It is more than that. Your grandmother planted the cone from which it grew, but that cone fell from an ancient pine, the one under which I had my vision of peace, the vision that united the Five Nations of the Iroquois. I am the Peacemaker, child, and this tree—"

But before he could say anything more, I was back on the couch, covering my eyes with one hand against the light. "Jennie," my sister said.

"Jesus Christ." My jaw ached, and even moving my mouth hurt. "Turn off the light."

"You're drunk," she said.

"So what?"

"Is this what you do when you're alone, just drink yourself silly?"

"No. This is what I do when you guys won't leave me alone."

She pulled me up from the couch and helped me toward my bedroom. "You ought to know better, Jennie, what with—"

"I had a dream. I have to tell you—"

"You probably had a nightmare, in your condition." She let me fall to the bed, then took off my shoes.

"It wasn't a nightmare." Something else my grandmother had said was coming back to me. Dreams were important; in the old days, an Iroquois who had a vivid dream would go to every longhouse in his settlement, recounting his dream until he found someone who could explain it to him. I didn't think Evie would be able to explain my dream to me, but it clearly had something to do with our land and the tree outside, so I felt it was something I had to tell her. Maybe the dream would persuade her to give up her plans.

"I was outside," I continued, "and these two men—I'm positive they were Mohawks, or Iroquois anyway, were standing—"

"Give it a rest," Evie burst out. "I'm going back to sleep. Talk to me when you're sober." She stomped out of the room.

I don't know why I thought telling her about the dream would bring her around. The fact was, I didn't have to come up with brilliant schemes for keeping the land. All I had to do was tell Evie I wasn't going to sign any papers, and she and my brothers wouldn't be able to do a thing. I hadn't wanted to state the matter quite so bluntly, but she had pushed me to it, so there was nothing else to be done.

But I didn't know if I would have the fortitude to hold

out against my brothers and sister forever. I could disappear, but the rest of them—Curt especially—wouldn't give up until they found me, and they might use my disappearance against me. If they got desperate enough, they might even get me declared incompetent, and they would have enough grounds, what with my wanderings, erratic work history, and bouts of manic-depression. I had gotten my mental shit together before coming home, but it could still look bad, so I'd have to make sure they couldn't find me. If that meant leaving the forest that had finally calmed the storms that often raged inside me, I would still have the comfort of knowing the land was safe.

I slept for a while and woke up with a bad case of the dries. Somehow, I managed to stumble into the bathroom for a glass of water, and then the telephone in the kitchen started ringing. I found my way to it, shading my eyes against the morning light as I leaned against the wall and picked up the receiver.

"Hello," I mumbled.

"Hey, Jennie! This is Curt. Gosh, it's great hearing your voice again—been a long time."

I sank into the chair below the phone. "Yeah."

"Evie said she was going up there this weekend. Wish I could be there with you guys."

I always got nervous when my brother sounded cheerful, especially at that hour of the day. "She's trying to talk me into letting the rest of you sell," I said.

"Well, I know, but don't think we're going to get rid of the camp or anything. I was talking to Sam last night, and we were thinking that maybe you should get the deed to the camp, along with your share of whatever we get for the land. We owe you something for taking care of Dad before he went to the hospital, for coming home when he got sick." So Curt was offering me a bribe. "I know the place means a lot to you, so maybe you should have it. Of course, I hope you'll let your old brother come to visit once in a while."

I was silent.

"You'd have enough money to get another place for yourself, get a new start, but the camp would be there for the summers. You could—"

"I won't sell."

"What?"

"I'm not going to let this land be sold. I won't sign any papers. I won't go along with you."

"Jennie? Jennie?"

I rubbed at my aching temples, refusing to answer him.

"I want to talk to Evie," he said at last.

My sister was standing in the doorway. I got up, handed her the phone, and went to my bedroom. Evie was talking in a low voice, but sounds echoed in the kitchen, so occasionally I caught a few words. "Crazy" was one. The words that disturbed me most, though, were "power of attorney." So they were considering that option already.

A rumbling sound came from under the cabin. Another small quake, I thought; they were certainly coming more often lately. I heard Evie hang up, and then the banging of pots in the kitchen. I dozed off, and woke to find Evie carrying a tray into the room.

"You need breakfast," she said as she set the tray down. "There's coffee, eggs, and toast. You'd better rest today— you look like you might be coming down with something. I'll stay here until you're feeling better, and then I'll head into town to pick up more groceries."

She handed me the coffee; I sipped at it. "You should know better than to drink so much," she went on, "what with your manic-depression and all." She was already laying the groundwork, but not out of malice. Like my brothers, she was probably half-convinced that I really was demented, and that it would all be for the best in the end. Evie could persuade herself that I would be better off in treatment, with others handling my affairs. She would play nurse this morning until I felt better, and then go off to town, where she would probably call Curt from a public phone so that they could decide what to do next. They would tell themselves they were saving my life, that they were helping me.

"You look like death warmed over," Evie said as she lit a cigarette. I set down my cup. She seemed to be holding a glowing coal to her lips as coils of smoke drifted toward the ceiling. Her dark eyes glittered, and her face was as still as a mask.

Masks, I thought, and recalled something else I had read. I had been reading a lot while living at the camp, going into town to buy old books at garage sales and to take others out of the library. That was how severed I was from our traditions; I had to pick up a lot of my people's lore from books. Now I remembered reading about the False Faces.

The shamans called the False Faces would come to the longhouses to heal the ill, bearing hot coals in their hands. They would put on their masks and sprinkle ashes over the ailing person, and if by some miracle they saved him, he had to become one of them. I drew in Evie's smoke; an ash from the end of her cigarette fell on my hand.

She was a False Face, I suddenly realized, but one who served evil spirits. She would nurse me and heal me and bring me back from the dead. Then I would have to join her and my brothers and the society of those who bought and sold and tore at the land instead of living lightly on it, giving back what they took from it. I would have to live in their world.

"Get away from me!" I was on my feet, struggling against her as she tried to restrain me. Evie was three inches taller, and a good thirty pounds heavier, but I broke her grip and pushed her against the wall. She fell, and then I was running through the living room toward the porch. It was dark out there for that time of day. I lifted my head and gazed through the screen.

The big pine had grown during the night. Its trunk was much wider, almost cutting off the dock from view. Nothing could grow that fast, and yet the great tree's roots now twisted over much of the cleared land around the cabin. I looked up through the lattice of green branches at a patch of sky. The pine had grown past the trees around it; I could no longer see the top.

"Oh, my God," I said under my breath.

"You crazy bitch." I turned to see Evie stomping toward me. "I tried to be reasonable about this. You really are nuts, and—"

"Get out!" I shouted. "Get the hell out of here." I went at her, but she jumped back before I could hit her.

"You'll be sorry for this, Jennie."

"Get out!" I swung at her, then ran after her as she retreated across the kitchen. My knee caught the table, and I was suddenly on the floor. By the time I got up, Evie was gone.

I stumbled toward the door. Evie was making for her car across a maze of roots. A bulge in the ground appeared near the cabin, as if a giant mole was burrowing nearby. "Evie!" I shouted, but she was inside the Honda and barreling up to the road before I could get to her. Brown tentacles snaked after the car, scattering dirt and grass. I don't know if Evie saw the roots. Maybe by then she was too concerned with getting away from her crazy sister to notice anything.

The ground heaved under my feet; roots spread out around me as I walked back to the cabin, swelling in size until they reached nearly to my knees. The pine now blocked most of the path leading down to the lake, and the smaller trees around it nestled in the furrows between its roots.

The cabin shook, but I felt calm as I sat down at the kitchen table. It came to me that I had been waiting for something like this, and that the pine and its burgeoning roots might solve my problem. Nobody would want to buy land near a spot where trees behaved this way.

I went to my bedroom, picked up the remains of my breakfast, then made more coffee. The floor trembled, but I made no move to leave. A glance out the kitchen window revealed that the roots had surrounded my car and that more had tunneled up to the road; I would never be able to drive over them. I might be able to get to the camp over-looking the channel on foot. Maybe the people there, the closest neighbors to me, had seen the giant pine springing toward the sky. Perhaps its roots were already moving in that direction.

Father had posted a list of numbers near the telephone. I found the number of my neighbors, then dialed it quickly.

"Simmons here," a voice said in my ear.

"Mr. Simmons, I'm your neighbor, Jennifer Relson, from the other end of the bay. I think I'd better warn you that a tree around here seems to be out of control."

"What?"

"It's growing really fast. I can't even see how tall it is any more, and the roots are going all over the place. What I'm trying to say is they might come your way."

"What?"

"The tree's roots," I said. "They're growing all around this camp now, high as walls!"

"Look, lady, I was just on my way out. I don't know what you're smoking, but—"

I hung up. Maybe he would believe me when he saw the roots moving toward him, if they got that far. How far could they spread? I went outside to find out. The tree's trunk had grown as wide as the cabin; the pines around it swayed as smaller roots twisted across the ground, then burrowed into it. I climbed over roots, into the ways between them, and over more roots again until I could see the lake.

The yodeling cry of loons greeted me; five more had joined the one I had been watching. The pine didn't seem to be growing any more, but long bands of brown bark were winding among the trees on the other side of the bay. I sat down, resting my back against a root. Dark veins snaked through the forest until the hills across the lake seemed enmeshed in a network of tunnels.

Strangely, none of the maples and pines seemed harmed by the roots, which bulged up and around the trees without crushing them. The loons bobbed on the smooth, mirror-like surface of the water, the turtles basked on their logs, and deer had come down to the opposite shore to drink. The birds and animals were undisturbed by the roots branching out around them; the loons filled the air once more with their wild laughter.

I turned away from the lake and clambered back over the roots. Above, the cabin nestled among curved brown walls, an outpost of order in the midst of disorder. The phone was ringing when I went inside. I waited for a bit, then picked up the receiver.

"Listen, Jennie," my sister said. "I'm trying to understand, I really am. I'm willing to come back if you'll promise to be sensible." There was the sound of country-and-western music in the background, which meant Evie was probably calling from the Brass Rail, the only bar in town. "If you don't," she continued, "I'm going to call Curt and Sam, and discuss this, and we'll decide what to do about you."

"But you can't do anything," I said. "You won't get past the roots. They're all over the place now."

"You're out of your mind."

"Didn't you see them on your way out?"

"I thought it was only your manic-depression, but you're really out to lunch. That does it, Jennie. I'm calling Curt as soon as—"

"Go ahead and call. You'll just be wasting your money. There's nothing you can do." She didn't answer. "Evie? Evie?"

The line was dead. I wandered through the cabin, trying to sort out my thoughts. The electricity still worked, and water came out of the bathroom faucets. If I didn't look through the windows at the bark barriers entwined around the place, I could almost believe everything was still normal. Somehow, the burrowing roots weren't affecting the cabin, but that probably wouldn't be the case for long. Eventually I would run out of food, and the roots would keep me from driving into town for more. There was no reason to stay anyway. How could my sister and brothers sell this land now?

I packed some food and a canteen of water, then struggled over the roots down to the dock. The roots winding among the forested hills had settled down, but now a brown wall cut off Mr. Simmons's camp from view. He had said he was on his way out when I called; he would certainly be surprised when he tried to drive back. There was no point in going to his place anyway. I would try for town. I didn't think about what I would do if the roots had spread that far.

I dropped the backpack into the canoe, then climbed in and paddled out, looking back when I was halfway across the bay. The pine towered overhead, as tall as a skyscraper, dwarfing everything around it, its needles as long as arrows. The surface of the lake was dappled by the green shadows of giant boughs. There had been some peace for me under the tree my grandmother had planted; maybe its limbs would grow vast enough to shelter the world. I paddled out from the shadows toward the far shore.

I beached the canoe at a spot where the land sloped gently up from the water, then shouldered my backpack. The tangle of roots on the hillside above had cut me off from a path that led to the nearest road. I scrambled over one thick root, into a ditch and up another root, then sat down to consider my options.

Even if I managed to find the road, making it to town might be pointless. If the roots had spread that far, I would only find chaos, and be forced to try for refuge somewhere else. I lifted my head and gazed across the lake at the camp. The cabin was hidden, the great tree a branching green canopy shielding the forests below. Roots were looped among the reeds near the shore; I thought of them tunneling under the water. The mountains beyond the bay, made blue by the distance, were now covered by thin brown webs.

So the roots had already spread that far. In the middle of this unexplainable event, sitting on top of a root that gently pulsated under me, I was surprised to find that I could still think rationally. Reason told me that my only choice now was to find the road, follow it to town, and figure out what to do after I found out what was going on there. If I kept climbing this hill, I would eventually reach the road, however many roots barred the way.

The tree was still stretching toward the sky, as if time was accelerating. I imagined the great pine springing into space, its boughs embracing the moon as its roots clutched at the earth. A wedge of ducks, quacking loudly, dropped toward the lake; the water blossomed around them as they landed. Maybe that was keeping me sane, the fact that the birds and animals I had seen were acting normally, that the roots had not harmed or frightened them. Perhaps the animals were somehow blind to them. I narrowed my eyes and stilled my thoughts, and the roots became translucent, as if I were gazing at one image superimposed on another. But the root under me still throbbed, as though sap and nutrients were coursing through it, and I felt the ground shake as another root slithered past my feet. The great pine and its roots might save this bay from intruders. I wanted them to be real.

As I stared at the lake, an eagle flew out from under the great pine, soared over the bay, then dropped toward me and landed in a branch overhead. It watched me for a while, waiting.

"Well?" I said. The bird fluttered its wings, then lifted from its perch.

The eagle wanted me to follow. I didn't think of why a wild bird of prey would want me to follow it anywhere, but sensed that it did. The eagle led me. Whenever I was lost and uncertain of which way to go, it would return and circle above me before flying on.

I climbed over roots and down into wide ditches, then thrashed my way through underbrush. Roots were looped around berry bushes and arched over creeks. The staccato tapping of woodpeckers filled the forest, and once I glimpsed a rabbit before it hopped over a root and disappeared. I kept going, following my feathered guide through the tangled tendrils of wood until my backpack seemed as heavy as a boulder and my arms felt like useless baggage; my legs were cramping from climbing over so many roots. It was beginning to dawn on me that I should have come to the road by now, that the eagle was only leading me even farther into the forest.

I leaned against a tree, cursing myself for my stupidity. Had I been thinking clearly, I would have stayed in my canoe, headed through the channel and then hugged the shore until I reached town that way. Now I was too lost even to find my way back to the canoe. I might have given up then if the eagle hadn't flown back and landed on a branch just above me.

"I suppose you want me to go on," I said. "Not that I have much choice." The bird tilted its head. What was the point, after all, of going back to a world where I had always felt displaced, where something inside me had constantly threatened to burgeon as wildly as these roots? My previous life had been as uncontrolled as this growth, a manic lashing out followed by a burrowing into depression. Like the pine my grandmother had planted, I had been waiting to gather my strength. I don't know whether my grandmother had meant this to happen, or if she had been ignorant of the pine's power, but I would take my chances among the roots burrowing into the earth, among the trees the great pine was protecting.

"Grandma," I whispered, "you planted some kind of tree."

The deep green light of the forest grew darker. The eagle disappeared. I struggled on until I reached a small clearing.

Ahead lay the largest root I had yet seen, a rounded ridge of bark as high as a good-sized hill.

I was too tired to go on. I stretched out, propping myself against the backpack. The air was still; the birds were silent. My ancestors had believed there were spirits in these mountains, but I was more fearful of animals that might be lurking nearby. Then a darker thought came to me, the kind of grim reflection I often had just before falling asleep, a thought that becomes a sinkhole swallowing every fragment of hope.

Maybe I was as crazy as Evie believed. Maybe the sudden growth of the pine tree and its huge, spreading roots were a delusion. I wanted to save this land so badly that I could imagine the supernatural had intervened to save it. I had called up this vision, and the small part of me that was still sane was able to perceive that the surrounding land and wildlife were unaffected by my imaginings. Maybe I would wake to find everything as it had been, and be unable to find my way out of the woods. Fear locked my muscles and dried up my mouth. I might wander these mountains until I joined the roaming spirits of Indians who had never been laid to rest.

"Perhaps you will," a voice said. "Maybe this is all an illusion after all." The voice was inside me, but I opened my eyes to see a woman standing near the root. She wore a long cloak decorated with beads and a band with eagle feathers over her brow, but the darkness hid her face. "Perhaps what you see is only a vision that will vanish, and you will return to the world you remember. But you cannot find your way back to your canoe without help, and even if you made it to the town, what then?"

"My sister's there," I replied, "and she thinks I'm a few cards short of a deck as it is. She'd have all the reasons she

needs to put me away. Can't really blame her, you know—
she has other priorities."

"Do you want to go back?"

The answer shot out from me before I could hold it
back. "No."

The woman vanished. The ground lurched; I looked up
to see trees swaying wildly. I jumped up and grabbed for a
tree limb as the earth yawned under my feet. Roots were
sinking all around me, groaning as they burrowed into the
ground. I guessed what it meant. The tree had reached out
with its roots and would now send them deep into the world
to entwine them around the earth's heart. Then I lost my
grip and was suddenly rolling down the hill until something
hard rushed up to meet me.

I must have lain there throughout the night, because
when I opened my eyes, the forest was green with light
again. I was afraid to move, expecting to feel bruises and
aches, fearing that I might have broken bones. But when I
finally sat up, my body obeyed me easily, bringing me to my
feet as effortlessly as it had when I was younger.

Most of the roots had vanished, but I felt them pulsating
beneath me. The giant root still lay across the hill, and now
I noticed that the trunks of the trees around me were
marked by lines and patterns that pointed upward. My
backpack lay near me; I slipped it on. I had as much chance
of reaching safety by following the carved markings as I did
doing anything else.

I hurried up the hill, then climbed the root, clinging to
ridges in the bark, resting my feet in its cracks. The backpack tugged at my shoulders and pressed against me with
its weight. I kept going until the ground was far below me
and it was too late to turn back. I climbed, afraid to look up
or down, until I reached the top.

There were no giant roots in the valley below me, only maples and pines of normal size. They stood around a field planted with corn and squash, and in the distance, I saw the wide leaves of tobacco plants. Smoke rose from the roofs of the longhouses beyond the field; people waited in the doorways, men and women in deerskin robes adorned with beads.

I don't know where this land is. It may be the past, or a far future, but I don't know enough astronomy to look up at the night sky and find out. It could be a world that might have been. Whatever it is, something has guided me here, to the place where I will make my home and live out my life.

I stumbled down the other side of the root and went to find my clan.

THE SHRINE

Christine heard the childish, high voice giggling out an indistinct sentence; the woman's voice was lower and huskier. She waited. A door squeaked open and then she heard her mother's rapid footsteps on the stairs.

Christine stepped into the hall and peered at the slightly open door. Her mother had been in Christine's old room again; she had been there last night when Christine first heard the voices and had recognized one as her mother's. She went to the door, pushed it all the way open, and gazed.

Her mother had done no redecorating here, as she had everywhere else. Christine entered, turning to look at the wall of framed photographs and documents above the slightly battered dresser. A young Christine with wavy blond hair and a wide smile stood with a group of other little girls in Brownie uniforms. A thirteen-year-old Christine wore a white dress and held a clarinet; an older Christine, slightly broad-shouldered but still slender, grinned up from a pool where she floated with other members of the Mapeno Valley High Aquanettes; a bare-shouldered Christine in a green formal stood at the side of a tall, handsome boy in a white dinner jacket. Her high school diploma was framed, along with other certificates; another photo showed her parents beaming proudly as they stood behind Christine and her luggage at the Titus County Airport, waiting for the plane that would take their daughter to Wellesley. There, as far as the room indicated, Christine's life ended. She had lasted less than one year at Wellesley.

She gazed at the top of the dresser, where her high school yearbook had been opened to her page. A pretty girl with flowing locks smiled up at her.

Matthews, Christine
"Onward and Upward!"
National Merit Scholar; National Honor Society, 3, 4; Student Council, 2, 3; Class Vice-President, 4; Aquanettes, 3, 4; Assistant Editor, Mapeno Valley *Clarion*, 3, 4; Dramatics Club, 3, 4; Orchestra, 2, 3, 4; Le Cercle Français, 2, 3, 4; Yearbook Staff, 4.

She closed the yearbook. The room was suddenly oppressive. She was surrounded by past glories; the room, with its embroidered pillows and watercolor paintings, was a shrine to what she had once been. Her mother could drive to her brother's house, only forty-five minutes away, to view his athletic trophies and his various certificates, but Christine's had remained here. She had been a good daughter, as Charles had been a good son. He was still a good son. Christine had not been a good daughter for a long time.

"Just coffee for me," Christine said as she entered the kitchen.

Her mother looked up from the stove. "Now, Chrissie, you know how important a good breakfast is."

"I never eat breakfast."

"You should."

Christine sat down at the small kitchen table while her mother served the food. "Well," she said, and sipped her coffee.

"Well," Mrs. Matthews replied. She poked at her eggs, took a bite of toast, then gazed at her daughter with calm gray eyes. "So it really is over between you and Jim."

"He moved all his stuff out."

"I was sorry to hear it. Maybe if you and Jim had gotten married—"

"Oh, Mom, that would have been great. The lawyers would have made everything even worse. I suppose you think a divorce would have been more respectable." Christine caught herself, too late. "I'm sorry."

"I meant that if you had been married, you would have had more of a commitment, and you both might have worked harder to stay together." Mrs. Matthews lowered her eyes. "Your father and I had almost thirty pretty good years. Maybe we wouldn't have had that much without a strong commitment. We had more than a lot of people have. Actually, I'm not alone—I think a third of my friends are divorced. Or widowed—that's probably worse."

Christine ate part of an egg, then nibbled at some sausage. "You haven't redone my room. You've redone every other room in the house. Every time I come here, the whole house is different."

"I only do a little, once in a while. If you came home more often, you'd see I don't redecorate that much."

"You know I don't have time." Christine's voice was harsh.

"I know, dear. I was only making a point, not an accusation."

Christine sighed, trying to think of what else to say.

"You never hung up my degree from State."

"I guess I never got around to it."

"You didn't put it up because you expected more from me."

"Now, Chrissie, you know that isn't true. I only wanted you to be happy."

Christine said, "I heard voices last night, in my old room."

Her mother's head shot up; Christine saw fear in her eyes. Mrs. Matthews's once-blond hair was nearly all gray. Her face was thinner, too, the hollows in her cheeks deeper; her long blue housedress seemed looser. One blue-veined hand pushed the plate of sausage and eggs aside; Mrs. Matthews had barely touched her breakfast.

"It was the radio," the older woman said at last. "One of those plays on the public station."

"It didn't sound like the radio. I heard your voice, and someone else's. A child's."

"It was the radio." Mrs. Matthews's voice was unusually firm.

"Maybe it was." Christine drummed on the table top with her fingers, then stood up. "I'm going for a walk."

"I'll clean up here. Your brother jogs now, you know. Three miles a day."

"I don't jog. I only walk."

Colonial houses stood on each side of the winding road. Christine searched the neighborhood for signs of change. Three houses now had solar panels; others had cords of wood stacked in yards under tarpaulins.

A young woman hurried down a driveway, juggling a box and a large purse. "Toni!" Christine shouted.

"Chris!" The woman opened her car door, threw in the box and the purse, and strode toward Christine. "God, I haven't seen you in ages. You haven't changed."

Christine smiled at the lie, grateful that her raincoat hid her heavy thighs. Toni was stockier, her dark hair shorter and frizzed by a permanent. "Mother told me you were back."

Toni hooted. "Back! What a nice way to put it. I guess she must have told you about my divorce."

"She mentioned it."

"My parents have really been great. Mom takes care of Mark when he gets home from school. I have a job at the mall now, with Macy's." Toni glanced at her watch. "How's that guy you're living with?"

"We broke up."

"God, I'm sorry to hear it."

"Don't be. I wasn't." Christine tried to sound hard and rational. "This place looks the same."

"It'll never change. It's stuck in a time warp or something. There's a couple down the street with four kids—can you imagine anyone having four kids nowadays? I don't know how they afford it. Mrs. Feinberg's running a day care thing in her house—you can't afford these houses without two incomes. Maybe a few things have changed." Toni paused. "How is your mother, by the way?"

"She's all right."

"I don't want to sound nosy. She looks kind of pale to me. She's in your old room a lot."

Christine looked up, startled.

"I can't help noticing," Toni went on. "I see the light at night. She's in there almost every day after she comes home."

"She likes to listen to the radio there while she does her sewing." Christine hoped that she sounded convincing.

Toni looked at her watch again. "Hey, why don't you come over tonight? We can talk after Mark goes to bed."

Christine saw two girls standing by a pool, giggling; they would swim through life as they had swum through the blue, chlorinated water. "I can't. We're going to Chuck's for supper."

"Maybe tomorrow."

"Mother has tickets for the symphony. And I'm leaving the day after."

"Well. Next time, maybe."

156

"Next time."

"See you, Chris."

As she approached her mother's house, Christine looked up at the window of her old room. The window was at the side of the house, overlooking the hedged-in yard.

A shape moved past the window; a small hand pressed against the pane. A little girl was looking at her through the glass; her long blond hair curled over her shoulders. The child smiled.

Except for the child's bright, golden hair, thicker and wavier than hers had ever been, she might have been looking at herself as a little girl. The child continued to smile, then reached for the curtains and pulled them shut.

Christine hurried around the yard to the back door and pushed it open, entering the kitchen. The house was still. At last she heard her mother's footfall in the hall above, and then the creak of the stairs.

"Chrissie," her mother said as she entered the kitchen. She still wore her long blue housedress; she had always dressed early in the morning before.

"Who's that little girl?"

"What little girl?"

"The one I saw in my room, looking out the window."

"You must be mistaken." Her mother's voice was flat. "There was no one in your room."

"I saw her."

"You're imagining it."

Christine passed her mother and pounded up the stairs. The door to her old room was still open; she hurried through it.

The little girl was not there. The room felt cold; Christine pulled her coat more tightly about her. Abruptly the floor shifted under her feet. She staggered, righted herself, and heard the sound of a child's laughter.

Christine covered her ears, then let her hands drop. The room was warm again; everything was as it had been. Her mother had said that there was no little girl; that meant she had imagined it all. She would have to put it out of her mind.

After Christine had greeted her sister-in-law, said hello to her nephew, and peeked into the baby's room, Charles led her to the basement. His bar sat in one corner in front of a stainless steel sink. He poured her a bourbon, then opened the refrigerator and took out a light beer. "My refuge," he said. He came around the bar and sat down next to her.

"Shouldn't we go upstairs?"

"It's all right. Jenny's got to nurse Trina again, and then she'll have to put Curt to bed, and then she and Mom'll watch the 'MacNeil-Lehrer Report' before supper. We can go up then." He paused. "I heard about Jim."

"He moved all his stuff out finally."

"I thought you two would be together forever. I kept expecting you to call and say you'd gotten married."

Christine sipped her bourbon, then gazed at the glass. "After he left, I came home one day and started fixing drinks. Jim always had a vodka and tonic and I always had a bourbon. Well, I fixed myself a drink and then I suddenly realized I'd fixed his, too. That was when I finally cried about it." She shook her head. "You seem to be doing all right."

"I guess so." Charles's ash blond hair was already thinning around his temples; his moustache was thicker, as if to compensate. "One thing about being a dentist—the customers can't talk back to you while you're working."

"You'll be all right. You always were. You were always the good child. I screwed up."

"Chris. Mom worries about you sometimes."

"No, she doesn't. She's never forgiven me, not since my breakdown. It was as if I was saying she was a lousy mother because I didn't turn out right. And I'm not married, and I don't have kids, and I don't have a lovely home and a fine husband. She hates me for it, but she won't say so." Christine gulped at her bourbon. "If she says she worries about me, it's only because she thinks she's supposed to say it."

"Oh, Chris, come on."

"She never came to see me when I was in that expensive bin. She never asked me why I broke down. After that, I was damaged goods as far as she was concerned. As long as I was perfect, she loved me. When I wasn't, she just turned herself off."

"What do you want her to do, say she's sorry?"

"That wouldn't change anything."

"Then forget it. It's your problem, Chris. You can't keep feeling sorry for yourself."

She glared at him. "It's easy for you to talk, Chuck. You didn't fail."

"You think so? Every time Dad visits, he asks me why I don't keep up my sports more, maybe coach Little League. I know he would have liked to see me pitch in the major leagues—hell, I wanted it, too. Nobody grows up thinking, 'Boy, I'm really into teeth.' But I'm not going to get depressed over it."

"Chuck, Mother's been spending a lot of time in my old room. It worries me. She—" Christine was about to mention the little girl, but changed her mind. "That room gives me the willies. I wish she'd put all my old crap away."

"You could take it with you when you drive back to the city."

"I don't have room. And I wouldn't care to be reminded of how wonderful I once was."

"Chris, you've got to stop it. You have the rest of your life—don't poison it. Grow up. Everyone fails in some way. You have to learn to live with that."

She heard the voices again.

Christine threw off her sheet and coverlet and tiptoed toward the door, opening it slowly. Creeping into the darkened hallway, she moved cautiously toward her old room.

A child's voice giggled. "Do you like it?"

"I think it's beautiful. But you always do everything well."

"I'm glad. I love you, Mommy."

"I love you, too."

Christine trembled as she recognized her mother's voice.

"Read to me, Mommy." Bedsprings squeaked.

"Which book?"

"*The House at Pooh Corner.*"

"You're such a good little girl. You won't disappoint me, will you, Chrissie?"

"Never."

Chrissie. Christine backed toward the guest room. How long had the child been living in this house, and what had enabled her to appear? She knew the answer to the second question—her own failure, and her mother's disappointment. She shook her head. It was a dream; it had to be.

She got back into bed and lay there, awake, for a long time.

Christine had slept uneasily and her eyes felt gritty in the morning. She got out of bed, pulled on her robe, and darted into the hall before she had time to change her mind. As she entered her old room, she closed the door behind her.

The bed had been made, or had never been slept in at all. The artifacts of her childhood and youth still hung on the walls in their usual places, and *The House at Pooh Corner* was back on the bookshelf between *Winnie-the-Pooh* and *Stuart Little*. The yearbook was open once again, this time to a picture of Christine and a boy named Lars Heldstrom under the caption, "Most Likely To Succeed."

She gripped the dresser; her hands became claws. "Come out," she muttered. "Damn you, come out." The room was still. She was having another breakdown; the breakup with Jim and the visit home had unhinged her. But her mother had been in the room, and she had seen the child in the window.

"Who are you? If you don't come out, I'll take Mother away. You'll never see her again."

"No, you won't." The voice seemed to hover above her; she clutched at the dresser, afraid to move. "She's mine now. Go away."

Christine spun around. The little girl was standing in front of the closet door, dressed in a pair of blue overalls and a white turtleneck. Her small hands held a clarinet; her blue eyes were icy.

"Who are you?"

"I'm Chrissie. Don't you know that?" The girl's voice was low and harsh. "This isn't your room any more. Mommy comes to visit me every day."

"She's not your mommy."

"She is. I could feel her calling me, and I wanted to be with her so much. I found out I could come in here and stay for a while. I'll never let her go away."

"You will. I'll force you to."

161

"You won't. She loves me. She doesn't love you any more."

Christine strode toward the child. The little girl retreated to a corner, her back against the closet door. As Christine reached for the girl, the wall suddenly dropped away; she was standing at the edge of the floor, gazing down into a thick gray fog. She teetered on the edge, afraid she would fall and keep falling, and clawed at the gray mists, then staggered back and fell across the bed.

She sat up. The room was as it had been; the little girl was gone.

Christine pressed her hands to her face. She had never had delusions; even during the worst days of her illness, she had never seen things that weren't there. Depression had been her affliction, and despair, and guilt.

She rushed from the room and was halfway down the stairs before she had time to think. Her mother would only evade a confrontation, and there was no one else to help her.

Christine climbed the front steps, reached into her purse, and removed the key she had taken from the kitchen wall that morning; she had parked her car in front of a house farther down the street. Her mother would not be expecting her; Christine had said that she was going to the mall to see Toni.

Opening the storm door, she propped it against her back while inserting the key, turning it slowly so that the lock would not snap, then pushed the door open. After closing both doors, she took off her coat and put it on the entryway's wooden bench with her purse, then slipped off her shoes.

The living room was a beige desert, its modular furniture

unstained, its only oases of color two potted plants and a Picasso print over the fireplace. Her stockinged toes curled against the thick, pale rug. She could hear nothing; she knew where her mother was.

She moved stealthily through the dining room and toward the back of the house, stopping when she reached the staircase. Her face was flushed; she pressed icy fingers to her cheeks. She had often sneaked up the stairs when she came home late from dates, always able to avoid the steps that creaked. She set her foot down on the first, skipping the second, holding on to the banister.

When she reached the next floor, she could hear the voices; the door to her room was ajar. She moved toward the crack of light, the wood under her feet was hard and cold. The child said, "I'm going to be the best, Mommy. I'm going to be the best at everything."

Christine thrust the door open violently; it bounced against the door stop. The little girl, still dressed in overalls, looked up; she was kneeling on the floor, her arms around Mrs. Matthews's legs. The older woman sat in a rocker; she gazed past Christine, her gray eyes empty.

"Mother," Christine said. The woman's face seemed even paler now, her hair more silvery. "Mother."

The child stood up slowly. "Leave her alone," the little girl said. "You can't have her. She's mine. She'll always be mine."

"Mother, listen to me." Mrs. Matthews stirred slightly at Christine's words. "You have to come away from here."

"She gave you everything," the child said. "She did everything for you, and you failed. But I won't."

"Mother, come out of this room."

"It's too late," the little girl said. "It's too late. You can't change anything now. You can't say you're sorry—it won't help." She grabbed the older woman's hand. "She's mine."

Christine looked around the room, the monument to her past. She strode to the wall, pulled off a framed photograph, and smashed it on the floor. "This isn't me now. You should have thrown all this out years ago." She pulled down another photo, then hurled the National Merit certificate against the wall.

"Chrissie." Her mother was standing now. Christine took a step toward her, then noticed that Mrs. Matthews was gazing down at the child. "May I go with you now?"

The little girl smiled. "Yes. We'll never come back, never."

"No," Christine cried.

"I need her now," the child said. "You don't." She tugged at Mrs. Matthews's hand, leading her toward the corner next to the closet door.

Christine darted after them, stepped off the floor, and was surrounded by fog. "Come back!" The gray formlessness swallowed her words; the thick masses pinned her arms to her side. She could feel nothing under her feet. "Mother, don't go." The mists parted for a moment, revealing a distant room, a tiny canopied bed, the small figures of a little girl and a woman in a blue housecoat. "I need you, too." The fog closed around her again, imprisoning her.

Hands gripped her shoulders; she was being pulled back. She flailed about, stumbled, and found herself leaning against the closet door, clinging to someone's arm.

"Chrissie. Chrissie, are you all right?"

Christine raised her head. A woman was with her. She wore a long housedress; her face was Mrs. Matthews's. But her blond hair was only lightly sprinkled with silver and her gray eyes were warm.

"I'm fine," she said, letting go of the woman's arms.

"I hope so. You look a little pale. I thought I'd find you here." The woman waved a hand at the wall. "Maybe I can help you decide what to take with you—I'll just store these old things in the attic otherwise." She poked at the broken glass on the floor with one toe, then tilted her head to one side. "Are you sure you're all right?"

Christine managed to nod her head.

"Good. I'd better get dressed so we can get started. I wish you could stay longer—I do so enjoy having you home."

Before she left the room, Christine leaned for a moment against her new mother, the one who, through some slip in possibility, would understand and forgive, the one she had always wanted.

THE LEASH

Carla was half-awake when she heard the mournful moan, the sound of a man in torment. The mattress shifted under her as the moan became a shriek. Clutching at the blanket, she struggled to sit up.

Ted was having a nightmare. She reached toward him; he let out another cry, sat up suddenly, then bolted from their bed. He landed on his feet and leaped toward the door, covering the floor in two bounds. "Who's there?" he muttered. "Whazit—who's there?"

Carla squinted, barely able to see him in the dim blue light of their digital clock. "No one's there," she said wearily. "It's all right, you're only dreaming. Come back to bed, it's all right, you're safe."

"Can't you hear it? Someone's out there." He yanked the door open with such force that she was afraid he might pull it from its hinges.

"No one's there," she said more firmly. "Everything's fine." He swayed uncertainly, then stumbled toward the bed, mumbling under his breath as he collapsed next to her. She stretched out again and waited until his even breathing told her he was sleeping soundly.

Carla folded her arms, embracing her resentment. Ted not only talked in his sleep, but he also walked, alerted her to imagined dangers, debated with her, and made broad jumps across the bedroom that might have won him medals in track and field events had he been able to make them while conscious. He never remembered anything about his nocturnal activities, however much they disturbed her. He had slept quietly enough for several months with only an occasional indistinct murmur. She had believed he had overcome his somnambulism at last, but during the past week, his problem had worsened.

What annoyed her most now was her conviction that he would begin to toss and turn just as she was dozing off; she was afraid to go to sleep. She bit her lip; he tensed next to her, as though sensing her anger. She did not have to worry that he might injure himself inadvertently; somehow his usual caution protected him even in his dreams. He might fling open the front door, but never ran outside in his pajamas; he could navigate through their one-story house without bumping into the furniture. It was as though he was deliberately trying only to interfere with her sleep.

She *knew* he would start to act up again as soon as she was falling asleep; he seemed to pick up her thoughts and fears. She could almost imagine that she was, however unwillingly, controlling his actions. He would tug at the sheets, perhaps, or pick up the bedroom telephone to bark a greeting at a non-existent caller. She pulled the sheet over her head, trying to relax.

She had just found a comfortable position when Ted let out a shriek; the telephone receiver clattered against the night table. "Hello?" he shouted. "Hello?"

Carla moaned, wanting to be grateful he hadn't turned on the overhead light.

As usual, Carla had to get up early in order to rouse her apparently comatose husband. Their routine rarely varied. She prodded him when she rose, poked at him again after taking her shower, set his orange juice next to the clock before she got dressed. The juice was almost always untouched by the time the coffee was ready, and she often had to nag him into eating the breakfast she brought to him on a tray.

This morning, Ted drank the juice and coffee without protesting, but she had to pull him to his feet and aim him toward the bathroom. His grogginess was hardly surprising; Ted was more active when asleep than many people were while awake. At least he hadn't unplugged the digital clock to protect it from an imaginary power surge, as he had a few nights ago; the alarm had never gone off and they had awakened only when his car pool arrived.

She stared at her face in the bedroom mirror, noting the dark smudges under her eyes. Ted's blow-dryer hummed beyond the bathroom door. Carla assumed that he was fully conscious now, but with Ted, it was sometimes hard to tell. He was capable of hollering questions at her while still asleep, questions that almost made sense until he followed his coherent inquiries with a stream of gibberish. She swatted at her face with a makeup brush; the blusher on her cheeks only made her eyes seem redder.

She turned as he left the bathroom and began to rummage in the closet. "I can't take much more," she said. "Are you trying to drive me nuts? Why can't you sleep like a normal person?"

He closed the closet door. "How am I supposed to control myself when I'm asleep?"

"You could do something about it. It's got to be a symptom. Why don't you see a doctor and—"

"I don't have time for this. Doug'll be here any minute." He adjusted his briefs, then pulled on his slacks.

"Why don't you sleep during the day? I'll bet no one at work would notice the difference—if anything, they'd find you more lively. You ruin my sleep, and then I have to struggle out of bed early to make sure you get up on time. I can't stand it."

Ted opened his mouth to reply; a horn beeped outside. He stepped into his shoes, grabbed his jacket, and hurried from the room.

Even before they finished supper, Carla was dreading the night ahead, wondering how many times Ted would wake her. She recalled reading a piece about how totalitarian regimes treated people they wanted to break; one technique was to keep waking a prisoner, refusing to let him sleep. Ted would break her; he might do worse. She had read about a man who had strangled his wife in his sleep, then claimed to have no memory of his deed. She shuddered, afraid even to let such a thought cross her mind.

By the time she had put the dishes away, Ted was sprawled on the sofa, leafing through a technical journal while glancing at the television set. He could sit there, barely moving, for hours. Carla had learned to distrust this apparent calm, which was now only the prelude to a tumultuous night. No wonder he was so active while sleeping; it was practically the only exercise he got. Where was the Ted she had known and loved and decided to marry? He had become a man who seemed asleep while awake and awake when sleeping.

He looked up at the television screen. "Joan Collins still looks pretty good," he mumbled.

"Joan Collins probably gets her sleep."

He let the journal slide to the floor. "Was I that bad?"

"Not really. You only screamed a couple of times and you didn't interrogate me. You didn't turn on the lights or pull off all the sheets. I'm exhausted—this is the second time I've been late to work this week."

"That reminds me. I may be home late for a few days or so. Wannisky's pressuring all the engineers in my department to—"

"Good," she interrupted. "Maybe I can get in a nap before you come home. Maybe you can even get them to put a bed in your office so I can get some sleep."

"Look, it's not my fault. I've had sleep disturbances all my life. My mother had them. It's a family trait."

"They're supposed to go away," she insisted. "You're supposed to outgrow them. You're almost thirty years old. How much older do you have to get?"

"Maybe it's temporary," he said. "It wasn't that bad until recently, was it?"

"It might be a sign of some problem. Go to a doctor."

"I had a checkup just a few weeks ago."

"You weren't sleepwalking then. Now it's almost every night. I'm afraid to go to bed, and then I can barely get up. I'm afraid I'll fall asleep when I'm driving to work."

"You can't blame a guy for what he does when he's asleep."

"You could *do* something about it," she shouted. "There has to be a cause."

He was eyeing the journal, as if wanting to pick it up. He hated arguments, she knew; he went out of his way to avoid scenes. "Maybe it's your fault," he said softly.

Carla was too angry to speak for a moment, then recalled how she had felt the night before, when it had almost seemed that Ted was acting on her expectations. That idea was absurd. "My fault?" she said at last. "How can it be my fault?"

"I've been under pressure at work, and then you expect me to fix the plumbing or take you out instead of relaxing on the weekend. Or you give me that hurt look when I invite the guys over to watch a game. You don't think of me at all. I didn't have that much of a problem when we were living together."

"So now you're blaming it on our marriage."

"You take me for granted. You don't listen to me when I'm awake, so maybe I'm trying to get your attention when I'm asleep."

She bridled at the injustice of his words. "That isn't fair. I made three errors at the bank today, and if the customers hadn't caught them right away—I have to get some sleep. I'm just about ready to move into the guest bedroom."

Ted shook his head. "Oh, no. My mother always said that was the beginning of the end. First, it's twin beds, then separate bedrooms, then appointments with lawyers."

"She ought to know," Carla snapped. "No wonder she had three divorces—her husbands probably never got any sleep."

"Can't you leave my mother out of this?"

"You brought her up!"

"Why don't you go to bed early? I'll be up for a while, and you can be asleep before I come to bed." He glanced at the television screen, where Joan Collins, dressed in a silk peignoir and holding a champagne glass, was apparently preparing to retire.

Carla stood up and strode toward the bedroom.

She was unable to sleep, of course. She kept her eyes closed as Ted slipped under the sheets and wondered if he might be calmed by sex, but was too angry to make any advances.

Carla counted her breaths, commanding sleep to come, yet knowing that as soon as it did, Ted would tear the covers from her or bound toward the door. He lay still, snorting slightly at the end of each even breath. That was another thing for her to resent, his ability to nod off within moments of hitting the pillow, to calmly stack his z's before beginning to plague her.

I know what you're up to, she thought. Ted had implied

that he regretted their marriage, but would never admit it outright. He had no conscious desire to follow in his parents' footsteps to the divorce court. But his unconscious mind was craftier, would do its best to drive her away by interfering with her sleep. She would be forced to leave him just to preserve her sanity, and he could always believe that the break was not really his fault.

His unconscious mind, she was sure, was just waiting for the right moment to strike; she could almost sense it making preparations. It wouldn't stop with forcing Ted to toss and turn; he might be propelled to the light switch and then sent on a search for monsters lurking in the closet or under the bed. Ted slept on; she felt herself drifting into oblivion.

The mattress bounced under her. Ted yelled, threw off the covers, and stumbled toward the light switch. Carla moaned as the room was illuminated. "There it is!" Ted shrieked. He dropped down and crawled toward her. "See it? There it is!" He pointed under the bed.

"Nothing's there," she responded as calmly as she could. He uttered a stream of gibberish and shook his head violently.

"I can't stand it any more!" Carla screamed as she sat up. Ted sat back on his heels and stared at her. "You've got to stop it!" She was doing exactly what his mother had warned her against, trying to shock him into awareness instead of soothing him into calm. But then his mother's unconscious was probably in collusion with Ted's. Carla had always suspected that his mother had been dubious about their marriage; maybe if the woman hadn't catered to her son, Ted wouldn't have had this problem now. "If you're not going to let me sleep," she continued, "I'll be damned if I'll let you."

He blinked as he gazed back dreamily. "That isn't very rational," he replied.

"I don't care. If you insist on keeping me awake, you can at least keep me company."

"That isn't what I'd call a constructive attitude."

She rubbed at her eyes. She could not even be sure he was awake now, and kept waiting to hear the indecipherable words that would prove he was only aping consciousness.

"You've got to get treatment," she said.

"That won't help. If I repress this, I risk cutting myself off from my creative flow, the thing that makes me able to do my work. My mind has to break out somehow. My sleep disturbances are the expression of—"

"I don't care what they are! It's got to stop!"

"I have a problem I'm trying to solve, and you're only making it worse. You're disappointed in me, you think you made a mistake, and I'm picking that up." He got to his feet slowly. "You could ease me, but you don't really want to help—you're just thinking of yourself. You'd rather blame me for what's wrong with you." He turned off the light, stumbled back to bed, and lay down next to her; within moments, he was snoring softly.

She looked down at him, appalled. His unconscious had clearly spewed out that nonsense and had done so without a single cryptic word or demented shriek. His lips moved, as if he were confirming her suspicions.

Carla managed to catch up on some of her sleep that weekend during the day, while enduring Ted's restlessness at night. Feeling somewhat restored, she decided to take Ted—or his unconscious—at his word. She would solve the problem by trying to soothe him before he slept.

Their evening routine changed. Ted was often home late, but she forced herself to greet him cheerfully and prepared foods that would not give him indigestion. She offered him Ovaltine or brandy before he slept and gave him alcohol rubs before helping him on with his pajamas. She brought a cassette player and tapes designed to produce soothing sounds for insomniacs. She had sex with him even when she wasn't in the mood in the hope that this might drain some of his nocturnal energy.

Yet after a week, she saw no results. Ted cried out and sleepwalked through the house as much as before. She not only had the task of getting him up in the morning, but also the additional work of preparing him for bed, with nothing to show for her efforts except her own increasing fatigue. Her resentment blossomed, flowering fully inside her while she lay at his side, and somehow he sensed it. She would expect him to jump from the bed and he would leap to the floor; she would wait for his shrieks and incoherent babbling and then hear them. She was afraid of her own thoughts, fearful that the undercurrents in her mind were washing over him in spite of everything she did.

His unconscious, it seemed, was not going to let her off so easily. He had enslaved her, had her tied to a leash. She was exhausted by the effort of catering to him in the feeble hope of winning just a few uninterrupted hours of sleep. She had been making more mistakes at the bank and worried that she might finally lose her job. Maybe Ted secretly wanted that; if she were unemployed, she could sleep during the day and have more time to tend to him.

Her experiment ended nine nights after it began, when Ted leaped out of bed, picked up the cassette player emitting the calming sounds of a seashore, and hurled it against the wall.

This can't go on, Carla thought as she crept into the guest bedroom, feeling like a traitor. She had barely enough energy to set the alarm clock before she collapsed on top of the bedspread. She could get up and have Ted's juice ready before he awoke, and he might not notice that she had abandoned him. She no longer cared what he thought about separate bedrooms; it was time for drastic measures.

They could, of course, separate. The problem was that she didn't want to leave him. She still loved him, she supposed; she also did not care to give his mother the chance to say that she had been right about Carla all along. Her enemy wasn't Ted, but whatever was buried inside him; she had to find a way to fight it.

On the other hand, she thought sourly, maybe she was simply going crazy from lack of sleep, was beginning to believe he could pick up every angry, unspoken thought. She curled up, already missing his presence at her side.

Feet pounded down the hall; the door was abruptly flung open. "What?" Ted cried out. Carla sighed; she should have known she wouldn't escape him here. "What's going on?" He leaped toward the bed and hovered over her.

Her mouth was dry, her eyelids gritty; she could barely lift her head. You won't beat me, a voice inside her whispered; I won't let you.

Ted cocked his head, as though listening to someone.

You won't make me give up, the voice continued. If you break me, or force me to leave, Ted will deal with you. He'll get depressed, and he'll probably start drinking or taking tranquilizers just to put you in your place. You'll be sorry you ever started this, and he'll begin to hate you. And don't think you can send him after me, either—I'll hide out if I have to. See how you like sending him across town in his sleep.

She was surprised by the forcefulness of this internal voice; it hardly seemed part of her. Go to bed, she thought fiercely, if you know what's good for you.

Ted suddenly turned and left the room.

She recalled what he had said about repressing what was in him, but barely had time to consider that, or to savor her triumph, before falling asleep.

Carla started at the sound of the alarm. She stirred, realizing that she had actually slept. She shut off the alarm before creeping silently down the hall.

Ted lay on their bed with one arm around her pillow. She touched his shoulder. "Ted, wake up." She remembered how he had left her the night before, as if responding to her unspoken command, and shook her head; that had probably been a coincidence.

When she returned with his orange juice, he had actually opened his eyes; he almost seemed alert. He grabbed the juice and drank it in one gulp, then reached for her arm; his brown eyes gleamed. "We've got time," he said. "How about a quickie?"

She was too startled to protest.

Her apprehension returned that night as they were preparing for bed. Ted had been unusually pleasant that evening, had even suggested that he might give up his football game that Saturday to view fall foliage with her and to take her out to dinner. The offer made her suspicious; perhaps his other self was simply setting her up, preparing to retaliate.

But she had a plan of action now. Her suppositions about the cause of his disturbances had seemed ridiculous during the day, but darkness gave them more credibility.

Ted pounded at his pillow, then stretched out next to her. Carla waited until she was sure he was asleep before summoning her thoughts. You'll sleep soundly, she told him silently; you won't be restless, and you are not going to disturb me.

He moaned, as if trying to fight her; she seemed to feel his resistance. You're going to stay still, she thought firmly, or you know what will happen. I won't let you ruin my nights any more; you'll only hurt Ted, and then he'll do something about you. See if he finds anyone else who'll put up with this. It's time you found out who's in command, and it won't be you. Wake me up once more, and I walk.

Ted moaned again, but more softly. He was struggling against her; she felt him straining at her thoughts. Lie still, she ordered. His head jerked, as though she had pulled an invisible leash, and then he was still.

Carla opened her eyes. Ted wasn't next to her. She sat up and noticed that it was nearly time to get out of bed; as she shut off the alarm, Ted walked into the bedroom with a tray. "Good morning," he said cheerily as he set down the tray next to her. Before she could speak, he had entered the bathroom. She stared at the tray in amazement; he had not only made juice and coffee, but had provided hot cereal as well.

By the time she had finished her breakfast, Ted was getting dressed. "Good thing I got up early," he said as he buttoned his shirt. "I'll have time to make some notes before I go. Listen—instead of staying home tonight, why don't we go over to the mall and see a movie?"

She blinked. "Are you sure you're feeling all right?"

"Never felt better. Maybe we can go to Chase's after the movie—I heard the new band's pretty good." His brown eyes seemed alert—almost manic, in fact—yet his mouth hung open a little; she had seen similar expressions only when he was sleepwalking or babbling at her in the night.

He pulled on his jacket. "Got to make those notes!" He bounded toward the door in a leap that made her think of one of his nocturnal jumps. She suddenly wondered if he was awake at all.

Doubt clouded her mind for only a moment. If Ted were going to sleep peacefully, it was only natural that he would be more lively during the day. Chances were that his problem had disappeared by itself; it was silly to think that she had caused this change.

She picked up the tray and walked down the hall to the kitchen. Ted sat at the counter with a note pad and a mug of coffee. As he looked up at her, she had the feeling that someone else was peering through his eyes. She recalled that he was going to have some sort of meeting today and that he was planning to ask for a raise. It had better go well, she thought idly; we can use the money.

"I'm pretty sure I'll get that raise now," he said, "and we can use the money."

She started, then steadied herself. Something tugged at her mind; she felt herself gripping her mental leash. I've won, she thought. It didn't matter how, as long as they were both happy. She had what she wanted, didn't she?

He bolted up from the counter and grabbed her around the waist, swinging her across the floor with one arm. "Ted!" she cried.

"What?" he responded. "What?!" She heard the voice she had listened to so often during the past nights. "I think it's time to cut loose a little, don't you?"

She knew she should feel grateful for the victory, but as she thought of the energetic Ted who was likely to greet her that evening, she was already feeling exhausted.

OUTSIDE THE WINDOWS

A diner next to a gas station was the small town's only bus stop. John gazed out of his window as the driver paced near the bus. No passengers had boarded here. The driver stomped out his cigarette, then climbed back inside.

Three boys raced across the two-lane road, followed by an unleashed collie. There was little traffic here; John had seen only three cars and a panel truck moving along the street. People, he thought, should be more careful anyway. Letting dogs off their leashes was risky, and lots of children had never been taught to cross roads safely.

A white Victorian house marked the edge of the town. The bus rolled on, then passed a sign marking the way back to the interstate. John was sure the driver usually took that turn, but instead the bus continued along the narrow road. He had not taken this particular bus in over a year, but couldn't see why the company would change the route. The interstate would get the bus to its final destination in two hours; this old road would add at least one more hour to the trip.

"Don't know the way," a stocky gray-haired man sitting across the aisle muttered. His companion, an old bald man in a plaid shirt, nodded glumly. The stocky man leaned toward John. "That driver don't know the way," he continued. "Missed his turn."

"Are you sure?" John asked. "Maybe they changed the route."

"Make no sense to change the route." The man leaned back in his seat and folded his arms; the bald man next to him scowled. Apparently neither of them was going to alert the driver to his error, however annoyed they might be. This road would get them to where they were going, and they did not look like men with pressing engagements. John peered up the aisle. A big auburn-haired woman was the passenger nearest the driver, but from the way her head was lopsidedly resting against her seat, he guessed that she was asleep.

The driver probably was lost. It wouldn't surprise him; the company had been bringing in drivers from other parts of the country to take the places of those still on strike. John was fairly certain that they would soon come to another sign directing them to the interstate, and that the driver would realize his mistake then.

The sun was dropping toward the western hills; the trees were beginning to show red and orange foliage. A wooded slope suddenly blocked his view. On the interstate, the countryside had seemed spacious, the towns only distant clusters of buildings nestled in hollows. Along this winding road, the hills were barriers hiding what lay ahead.

Air travel was bad enough, John thought, but buses were much worse, and that damned strike hadn't helped. This trip was too short to justify a plane ticket, and the train had been discontinued some time back. He hadn't expected much comfort, but this rattling bus with its lousy shocks should have been retired long ago. People were forced into driving cars, with so few other ways to get to where they were going. Sometimes it seemed to him that vehicles operated the people behind their wheels, rather than the other way around, that the metallic beasts had claimed the world.

The bus suddenly swerved; its horn blared. John clutched at his armrest as the trees to his left swelled; their leafy limbs reached toward him as an invisible hand threw him back. He heard a loud, wet smack against the front of the bus before the horn sounded again.

"For crying out loud," the gray-haired man across from John shouted. The bus hurtled on for several yards, then slowed as the driver pulled over and parked along the shoulder of the narrow road. John looked down at his hands, surprised to find that they were shaking.

The driver opened the door, got up, and left the bus. The other passengers were silent. The big woman near the front of the bus was awake now, leaning across the aisle to say something to the boy in the next seat. John recalled the wet, splattering sound and closed his eyes for a moment.

"What happened?" a voice said behind him. John moved to the seat on the aisle and looked back. A young woman in a down vest and jeans was getting up from her seat; she shook back her long blonde hair. "What's going on?"

The big auburn-haired woman rose slowly to her feet. "He hit a dog," she announced in a hoarse voice as she turned toward the back of the bus. "A big black dog— looked like a Lab to me. Run right into him."

"Is he hurt?" A young black woman wearing a Cornell University sweatshirt was speaking; she was sitting next to the blonde. "Is he dead?"

"I don't know," the big woman replied. "The way we hit him—I don't know. He just run right out in front—didn't look like he even saw us coming. I'll go see."

"I wanna see, too," the boy near her shouted.

"Then come along."

The boy followed the woman off the bus. The child, who looked about nine years old, was traveling by himself; John had seen a wan brown-haired woman hug him, then press a luggage claim ticket into his hand. The big woman had been keeping an eye on him since then.

"Gross," the blonde college student murmured. John assumed that she and her sweatshirted companion were students, with their duffels, jeans, and thick economics textbooks. "Why would he want to see something like that?"

"Good thing the driver stopped," the stocky gray-haired man said. "I thought he was just going to barrel ahead." The bald man next to him nodded. "If he had, the state troopers would have radioed ahead and pulled him off at the next stop and we'd be sitting around for God knows how long. Guess he thought better of that. This way, we might lose an hour, maybe."

A young man in a leather jacket came down the aisle and left the bus. "We're going to lose more than an hour," John said, "if that driver doesn't get back to the highway."

"Could be. I meant we might lose an hour on top of whatever other time we lose."

John stood up, stretched, then decided to go outside. At this rate, he wouldn't have time to do more than call the district manager before he went to bed. John's supervisor sometimes kidded him about his eccentricity, as did the others in the home office. Luckily, he did not have to take that many business trips, and usually went by air when he did. It gave his co-workers something else to gossip about: his insistence on cabs rather than rented cars, the apartment he had moved into so that he would no longer have to drive to work.

John stepped down to the ground, then took a deep breath of the cool autumn air. The three passengers who had already left the bus were standing by the rear of the vehicle. Farther down the road, the bus driver stood near a fence talking to another man. A long driveway wound up a hill toward a large gray house; John glimpsed a woman and child on the porch.

He walked toward the other passengers. "I don't see the dog," he said.

"He got drug off the road." The big woman pointed. "That must be the owner. He came and drug the dog off the road—he was a Lab, sure enough." She pulled her long brown coat more tightly around herself. "That dog's dead."

A gray car with emblems on its doors passed the bus, then pulled up next to the two men in the distance; a uniformed man got out. "There's the cops," the boy said as he tugged at his baseball cap. "What'll they do?"

"Probably not much," the young man in the leather jacket replied. "Ask questions, maybe write out a report." His mouth hung open after he stopped talking, as if he had simply forgotten to close it.

"It weren't the driver's fault," the woman said. "I woke up just before he hit. That dog was standing by the road, and then he run right out in front like he didn't even see us coming. The driver tried to miss him, but he run right out in front. Must of killed him right away, the way we hit, but it really weren't his fault."

"He was going kind of fast." The young man brushed back a strand of his long brown hair, then thrust his hands into his pockets.

"He weren't going over the speed limit."

"He was going the wrong way, though. Why didn't he head back to the highway?"

"I would of told him to, if I'd been awake. Why didn't somebody else pipe up?"

John wandered away from the others and their pointless discussion. The policeman was writing in a notebook; the bus driver shifted from one foot to the other as he spoke to the dog's owner. The trees near the house swayed as the wind picked up; the woman and child who had been standing on the porch had gone inside. The child would be crying, his mother trying to console him.

He turned and walked back to the bus, then climbed inside. "Anything going on?" the stocky gray-haired man asked.

"A policeman's there," John said as he sat down. "The owner seems to be talking to the driver calmly enough, so we should be on our way soon." He looked back at the college students. "I couldn't see the dog. That red-headed woman said the owner dragged him off the road."

"This is all we needed," the blonde student said. "Some poor dog going about his business, then getting hit by a bus."

"Chill out, Sloane," the black student said.

John settled back in his seat. He had brought some work in his briefcase, but felt too distracted to pull it out. The incident had unnerved him. He wouldn't have been on the damned bus in the first place if those penny-pinchers in Accounting had been willing to cough up enough for a plane ticket.

The leather-jacketed man came back aboard the bus, followed by the big woman and the boy. "Don't you worry none, Ted," the woman said.

"Tad," the boy said. "My name's Tad."

"Well, don't you worry none, Tad. I'm sure your father'll wait till the bus gets there."

The boy took one of the seats in front of John, then leaned over the armrest to peer back at the other passengers. The big woman sat across from the boy. The passengers were all grouped in the middle of the bus now, as if hoping for reassurance from one another. John opened his briefcase and rummaged among his papers, hoping the others wouldn't try to drag him into conversation.

The driver soon came back. He stood in the front, rubbing at his face. "Er, we had a little accident," he said, telling them what they already knew. "I tried to avoid that dog, but if I'd gone any farther left, we'd have gone off the road and into a ditch. I just thought you ought to know. My responsibility's to my passengers." He looked around thirty years old, and had a southern accent. John wondered if he was an experienced driver or a strikebreaker the company was still training. "We'll be running about half an hour late. Sorry for the delay." He wiped his brow, then turned to sit down. John pitied him a little. Obviously shaken by the accident, he would still have to drive the bus to its destination.

The bus rolled back onto the road. The sky was growing darker; dusk shadowed the trees and made the distant hills look black. John turned on the light above him, then pulled out his newspaper.

"They shouldn't let dogs run around near roads like this," the young man in the leather jacket said in the seat just behind John's.

"Well, there isn't that much traffic." John recognized the black student's voice. "If it had been my dog, I would have assumed—"

"He might have been old, maybe going deaf," the blonde student said. "Dogs can't see very well, and maybe this one couldn't hear well, either. Poor thing."

The big woman leaned out from her seat. "Look at it this way." Her voice was loud enough to be heard above the bus's engine. "Thank the good Lord it weren't a human being." John's hands tightened on his newspaper.

He looked toward his window, unable to concentrate on reading. The unfortunate incident had apparently given his fellow travelers a sense of camaraderie; they would probably review the matter during the rest of the ride. The bus was slowing. An intersection lay ahead, and another large sign marked "I-88" with an arrow pointing east, but the driver continued along the old road.

"Missed another way back," the stocky gray-haired man

said. "Somebody better tell that young fella what to do."

"Don't look at me," the big woman replied. "I ain't about to go up there and tell that man where to go. He's probably jumpy enough already."

John stared at his paper. He could not get up and move to another seat without seeming downright hostile; the only way to avoid getting drawn into the conversation was to pretend to be reading. He was about to shift to the seat nearer the window when he saw the dog.

The animal was standing at the side of the road near a field. It was a large dog, a Labrador retriever, and before John could wonder what it was doing in that empty, overgrown stretch of land, the dog vanished.

"Whoa," somebody shouted. The boy named Tad peered around his seat at John. "Did you see that, mister? That dog—did you—"

"Lordy," the big woman cried. The dog was in the aisle. It turned and trotted toward the front of the bus, then disappeared.

John's mouth was dry. The driver, intent on his driving, had apparently not seen the dog. John glanced at the men across from him. The gray-haired man gaped; the bald man was leaning over him and staring into the aisle.

"What was that?" the young man behind John said. "What the hell—"

"A Lab." The big woman's hands tightened on her armrest. "A Lab, just like the one we hit."

"Jesus Christ."

"What's going on?" the blonde student called out. "Are we all going crazy?"

"Chill out, Sloane," her companion said.

"Holy shit, Liz, didn't you see it?"

"I saw it. Don't know what it was, but I saw it."

"It's a ghost," Tad said. "It's a ghost."

"Hush your mouth," the big woman said. "Whatever it is, won't do no good to start hollering about it." She looked back. "The driver didn't see it, and maybe we're just all kind of batty from what happened and all. We can sit here nice and quiet, or we can start acting up and get thrown off. Besides, it won't do the driver's nerves no good to have us all carrying on."

"You're talking sense, lady," the bald man said. "All we need is to get that driver even more upset."

All of the passengers had their seat lights on now. John wanted to turn his off, to slip into the illusory safety of darkness. The sun was still above the western hills, and there seemed to be nothing along this stretch of road except untilled fields and, in the distance, forested slopes. The bus had slowed; he wondered if the driver was worrying that he might hit something else. The guy can't get back to the interstate, he thought, and now we're seeing ghost dogs. Better if he had been the only one to see it; he could have explained it away as a delusion. To have everyone else see the dog was impossible. He was asleep, dreaming. That was the only explanation, but he didn't believe it.

"I am really freaked out," the student named Sloane murmured.

"It's all right, son," the big woman was saying to Tad.

A gray kitten had curled up near a shrub by the road. The bus was moving so slowly that John could see the small animal clearly, and then it was gone. No, he thought, not again.

The kitten winked into existence in the aisle; John heard a muffled moan behind him. The creature scurried past him; he followed it with his eyes. It stopped next to the leather-jacketed young man, then slowly faded away.

"Oh, my God." The young man ran a hand through his

187

long brown hair. "That cat. It's like—" He glanced from the students to John. "I hit a cat once. Killed the poor little thing right off. This girl came out of her house—she was crying like she'd never stop. I'd been drinking, so I knew it was my fault. I said I'd buy her a new kitty cat, but it didn't do any good."

"This is totally weird," Sloane said.

John did not want to look out of his window, but found his head turning in that direction. A deer was out there, standing at the edge of a field, and then it was gone.

The deer took shape in the aisle. It was a small one, not much larger than a fawn. The deer's head turned toward the stocky gray-haired man; its soft dark eyes gazed at him steadily.

"That's ours," the man said calmly, "mine and Ralph's here." He gestured at his bald companion. "We were driving along, and this deer jumps out. Now, we should have been able to miss it, but the thing is, I was driving a little fast, and jawing with Ralph, and by the time I saw . . ."

"There were signs," Ralph said. "We noticed that later, when the car was towed. Deer crossing. Signs like that all over the place, but we weren't paying much attention."

John thought of going up to the driver and asking him to stop the bus. Let me off at the next town. Hell, let me off now, even if it's in the middle of nowhere. He felt bound to his seat, unable to move. Something else would be waiting outside, and he did not want to see what it might be.

The sun was setting; deep blue clouds were growing darker against the reddish sky. Up ahead, near a billboard advertising a motel, sat a Siberian husky. As the dog vanished, John heard a cry.

"Bessie!" Tad lunged from his seat as the husky appeared near him. "Bessie!" The dog became translucent as the boy stumbled into the aisle. The big woman caught Tad as the husky disappeared. "Bessie!"

"There, there," the woman said.

"She was my dog." Tad climbed into her lap. "A truck hit her." The boy was crying now. "Mom told me to keep her on the leash, and I didn't."

"Hush, son." The woman glanced toward the driver, who apparently had noticed nothing. "Don't cry. Bessie only came to tell you it's okay, that she's in dog heaven now." Tad wiped at his face, then straightened his cap. "It's all right. Can you go back to your seat?"

Tad got off her lap. "Jesus," the student named Sloane said. "This is totally insane." Her voice rose. "Road kill spirits appearing in a bus. I can't take any more."

"Pipe down, young lady," the gray-haired man said. "You want to get us all thrown off?"

"I wouldn't mind." The blonde student crept forward, then squatted in the aisle. "We have to do something."

"Like what?" he asked.

"You're college girls, aren't you?" Ralph leaned across his companion. "You and your friend. You ought to know something. Maybe you can explain it."

"I don't know." Sloane frowned. "A mass delusion. Somehow, we're all seeing a mass delusion, but why? And why isn't the driver affected?"

"Be glad he ain't," Ralph said.

"They're outside," the young man behind John said, "and then they come in here. You can see 'em outside from this side, and then they come in here. It doesn't make sense."

"An optical illusion," Sloane said. "Maybe that's it. A trick of the light that makes something outside seem to disappear and then reflects it inside the bus."

"I don't believe it," Sloane's friend murmured. "Those

animals looked too real for that. And why would they be ones all these folks recognize?" The young black woman bit her lip. "I'm scared."

John said, "We have to get back to the highway."

Sloane turned toward him; Ralph scowled. "The highway?" The bald man lifted his brows. "Think we'll stop seeing these critters if we get back on I-88?"

"It makes as much sense as anything else."

"You gonna tell the driver?"

They were all looking at him; the big woman narrowed her eyes. Sloane rose and went back to her seat; at last John stood up. "I'll tell him."

He moved toward the front and sat down in the seat nearest the door. "Uh, excuse me."

"What's the problem?" the driver asked.

"You're going the wrong way."

"What do you mean, the wrong way?" The bus was still moving slowly, probably doing no more than thirty-five.

John said, "You're on Route 7. You should be on I-88."

"Think I don't know where I am? Look." The driver paused. "I mean, look, they've got a crew on a big long stretch of I-88. That's what the dispatcher said. If we'd gone that way, we would have been moving about as slow, maybe slower. Now, my feeling is we'll probably make better time this way, which is what the dispatcher told me, and we'll be back on 88 as soon as we pass Sidney. You won't lose much time."

"Okay. Thanks for letting me know."

"Look, I know I had an accident, but that doesn't mean I don't know my business."

"Sorry."

"And tell your friends back there that there's no alcoholic beverages allowed on this bus, and no illegal substances, and no standing around or walking unless you have to use the can."

"What?"

"From the way you're all clumped together, looks like you're having a party or something."

"We're just talking. I'll tell them." John got to his feet. He should have known the driver would try to cover up his mistakes. It was easier to make up a story than to admit the truth. No wonder the man hadn't seen the ghost of the dog he had killed. He had repressed his guilt, putting it behind him, keeping his back turned to the evidence of his deed. John understood that kind of failing.

He was nearly to his seat when the next apparition appeared, a Siamese cat this time. It leaped gracefully to the big woman's armrest and faded away.

"That's mine." The woman clutched at John's sleeve. "Only thing I ever hit—gooshed the poor thing. I was in a hurry, and my mind weren't on my driving. Going along this street with houses and little kids playing and all—I knew I should have been more careful."

John freed himself. "I spoke to the driver," he said. "He's going to get back on the highway after we reach Sidney. Apparently there's some work going on along this stretch of I-88." He straightened his tie; his hands were shaking again. "We'd better settle down. He thinks we're all up to something back here."

"He see them animals?" the big woman asked.

"I'm sure he didn't. He would have mentioned it. I don't think he'd still be driving if he had."

"I've got a theory," the student in the Cornell sweatshirt said. "I think—" She was silent for a while.

"Go on, Liz," her friend Sloane murmured.

"The driver had this accident, okay? Seems like the rest

of us folks were responsible in some way for accidents recently, and this one's reminding us of them, and because we all feel guilty, we're seeing the victims. We're blaming ourselves unconsciously—that's why we're seeing them. And the driver isn't seeing what we are because his accident really wasn't his fault."

"But why are we all seeing them?" Sloane asked. "Why aren't we just seeing the ones we hit? Why are we seeing animals someone else hit?"

"I can't explain it," Liz replied, "but it's got to stop pretty soon, because there's only three of us left that haven't seen something we remember. Unless the rest of you hit a lot of animals."

"Never hit anything," the young man said, "except that kitty cat."

"Me neither," the big woman said.

"You college girls." The stocky man turned in his seat. "You ever hit anything?"

"Yes." Liz leaned across her friend. "And I think I see it now."

A white duck was waddling down the aisle, followed by three ducklings. Liz closed her eyes as the birds disappeared. "They were trying to cross the road, and I was going way over the speed limit. Suddenly, there they were, and I was going too fast to stop. It was horrible." She settled back against her seat. "If I'd only been going more slowly, I could have avoided them."

John gritted his teeth. "What about you, dearie?" the big woman asked Sloane. "Did you—"

A cocker spaniel scurried down the aisle, panted as it looked up at Sloane, then gradually faded away. "That dog," the blonde student said in a low voice. "I was arguing with my boyfriend, and then I hit that dog—I didn't even see him. I should have pulled over until we settled it. I can't even remember what we were fighting about."

John's mouth was dry. The world outside the window was black now. He thought of another night, hands clutching a wheel, the shriek of brakes, the thud, pebbles pinging against metal as a car raced away.

"I guess that leaves the fella over there," Ralph said.

John struggled to clear his throat. "I don't drive."

"What?" the big woman said.

"Says he don't drive."

"I don't drive," John repeated, remembering how slippery the wheel had been under his sweaty palms. He had kept his secret. His neck prickled; his face was hot.

He jumped to his feet, then staggered toward the driver. "Stop the bus," he shouted. The driver hit the brakes; John braced himself against a seat as the bus rolled to a stop.

"What's wrong with you people?" The driver got up and turned toward them. "Do I have to—"

John stumbled toward the door, thinking only that he had to get off the bus. The Labrador retriever appeared in the aisle, blocking his way. The driver stared at the dog, then covered his face as the animal disappeared.

"I guess he felt guilty after all," Liz whispered.

The bus was parked along the side of the road. John saw the little girl then, on the other side of a ditch. A knife seemed to twist inside him.

He wrenched himself away from the window. She was moving toward him along the aisle; her short black hair framed her face and her hands held a doll. She stopped by his seat and gazed at him for a long time. He felt the others watching him, and thought he heard someone curse at him.

The ghostly child drew her doll to her chest, then vanished.

Eye of Flame

1

Old Khokakhchin listened as the other women gossiped. They had been going on about Jali-gulug all day, and were still murmuring to one another about the afflicted boy as they herded sheep back to camp. Jali-gulug had fled sometime during the night, unseen by the men on guard. His father Dobon had ridden out that morning and found his son wandering the steppe on foot.

The women spoke of evil spirits and possession. This was not the first time Jali-gulug had wandered off in a trance. He saw visions, fell into fits, and sometimes babbled meaningless chants. The spirits tormented him often. Khokakhchin dropped behind the other women, wondering how long it would take these people to see what the boy was.

She had sensed for some time that young Jali-gulug was destined to follow the shaman's path. Bughu should have seen that by now, and done something about it, but Bughu was not much of a shaman. He knew chants and spells and how to banish evil spirits from those who were ailing; he read the bones for Yesugei Bahadur, who was chief in this camp, as he had for Yesugei's father. But Bughu was not a shaman who could ride to Heaven or command the most powerful of the spirits. Khokakhchin suspected that Jali-gulug had much more power in him.

Koko Mongke Tengri, the Eternal Blue Sky that covered

194

all of Earth, had granted them a warm and windless day, although the late summer weather could change suddenly. The stream that had watered the sheep was a slender blue ribbon that wound in sharp loops over the endless grassland. Hoelun Ujin, Khokakhchin's young mistress, nudged a straying lamb back toward the flock with her juniper stick. With her golden-brown eyes and smooth light brown skin, Hoelun was still a beautiful woman; it was easy to see why her husband Yesugei prized her.

Khasar, Hoelun's two-year-old son, rode toward Khokakhchin on a ewe, clinging to the short shorn wool with both hands. The ewe bleated; Khasar fell from her back. His older brother Temujin quickly pushed his way through the sheep milling around the ewe, grabbed one sleeve of Khasar's short brown tunic, and dragged him to safety. The four-year-old Temujin had his father's odd pale eyes of green and gold mixed with brown, and his straight dark hair had a coppery sheen. He could sit a horse by himself and already showed skill in handling his small bow. Khokakhchin felt a pang of sorrow, remembering the son she had lost when he was no older than Temujin.

Temujin helped Khasar climb back onto the ewe, then led him toward their mother. Hoelun Ujin rested her hands on her swollen belly and smiled at her sons. The Ujin's third child would come soon. Khokakhchin would be with Hoelun during her labor, as she had been when Temujin and Khasar were born.

Knowing how to aid in bringing new life into the world had helped Khokakhchin save her own life. She thought of the first time she had seen Yesugei Bahadur, sitting on his horse with his sword in hand, yurts burning behind him as he shouted orders to his men; he had terrified her. Later, as she huddled with the other prisoners, waiting to learn if they would be put to the sword or taken away as slaves, she had heard the Bahadur speak to one of his comrades of the child his first wife would soon give him.

Khokakhchin had seen her chance and seized it. "I have some of an idughan's lore," she had called out to the man whose Mongol warriors had brought such ruin to the Tatar camp. "I know of birthing." Yesugei Bahadur had ridden toward her; she had forced herself to meet his pale greenish eyes, so unlike any eyes she had ever seen. "These Tatars attacked my people years ago," she continued, "and killed those I loved, and my life among them has been a hard one. I would more willingly serve you."

The Mongol studied her for a while without speaking. "My first wife may need your skill," Yesugei said at last. "You'll be taken to my camp. If all goes well, you'll be her servant, but if any harm comes to her or to my child, you will die, and painfully—I promise you that." He had then sent her on a hard ride back to his camp with his brother Nekun-taisi and another man.

The spirits had favored Khokakhchin. Hoelun had suffered in labor, but her son was born whole and healthy and clutching a clot of blood in his fist, a sign that he would be a great leader. Yesugei had named the boy Temujin, after the Tatar chief he had just defeated and killed.

Ahead of the women herding the sheep lay the wagons and black felt yurts of Yesugei's camping circle. Yesugei and his brothers were milking the mares tethered with their foals outside the Bahadur's tent. Khokakhchin caught up with two of the younger women, found that they were still talking about Jali-gulug, and fell behind them once more. She did not want to hear talk of Jali-gulug and spirits and magic. She had dealt in magic once, long ago, and had sworn never to do so again.

★ ★ ★ ★ ★

"Dobon's son has the makings of a shaman," Hoelun said to Sochigil, Yesugei's second wife. Khokakhchin fed more fuel to the fire burning in the metal hearth. She had come to respect Hoelun's wisdom during her years as the young woman's servant, and was pleased the Ujin finally understood what Jali-gulug was.

"Do you think so?" Sochigil set a platter of dried curds and strips of cooked lamb on the low table in the back of the tent. "I saw Bughu riding to Dobon's yurt from the tent of Orbey Khatun. I thought she might have sent him there to drive the evil spirits from Jali-gulug."

"Bughu ought to be teaching the boy some of the shaman's arts," Hoelun said as she took her place next to her husband.

"Perhaps he will," Yesugei Bahadur muttered. "Let us hope Jali-gulug has the shaman's calling. He's not good for much else."

Yesugei was sitting on a felt cushion at the north of the tent, with his four sons on his right and his two wives at his left. He was a handsome, broad-shouldered man with sharp cheekbones, long mustaches, and black braids coiled behind the ears of his shaven head. Belgutei, Sochigil's three-year-old son, jostled against Khasar at the low table. Khokakhchin settled on her cushion and shot a warning glance at Bekter, Sochigil's older son, who got into fights with his half-brother Temujin far too often. Hoelun handed her husband a cup of kumiss. Yesugei dipped his fingers into the mare's milk and scattered the drops while whispering a blessing.

The Bahadur seemed contented tonight. The herds of sheep, cattle, and horses had found good grazing this summer. There had been no raids on his camp during this season, and none of the sudden fierce and deadly storms that even summer could bring, while his scouts had reported that Yesugei's Tatar enemies were now camped farther to the east and south, away from these lands. This autumn, Yesugei and his men would make a foray against the Merkits, who camped in the northern lands. They would be richly rewarded for that effort by Toghril, the wealthy Khan of the Kereits, who hated the Merkit tribes as much as Yesugei did. Even Jali-gulug's afflictions and wanderings could be seen as a good omen; Yesugei might eventually have a powerful shaman in his service.

Such contentment, Khokakhchin knew, might endure for an evening, a moon, a season, but rarely for longer than that. Yesugei needed accord among his people if they were to stand against their enemies, but the unity he had brought about could easily fracture, as it had before among the Mongol clans. Sooner or later, the Bahadur would again be arguing with his younger brother Daritai over such matters as when and where to move camp and which men were to herd the horses to their new grazing lands. Orbey Khatun still believed that her grandson Targhutai should be chief in this camp instead of Yesugei, even if she no longer said so openly. Orbey, the widow of Ambaghai Khan, was consumed by two ambitions: wreaking vengeance on the Tatars who had sent her husband to his death, and having a leader in this camp whom she could control.

Khokakhchin listened to Yesugei and his wives as they talked of Orbey and Bughu and Jali-gulug, but said nothing. She was used to keeping her thoughts to herself, knowing that the safest course for a servant or slave was to be useful, trusted, and silent. She would follow the ways of the marmot, burrowing into her hole, keeping her ear to the ground, surviving.

★ ★ ★ ★ ★

The dream came to her again. The spirits always sent the same dream to her after she had come to believe herself free of it forever.

She was running for the horses, hearing her husband's voice calling to her above the curses and screams of the others. The steppe was a plain of fire, the flames a wall moving closer to the camp. People were fleeing the flames on horseback, in wagons, on foot. She cried her husband's name and saw him in the doorway of a burning yurt, the tent collapsing around him. In the distance, she heard the war drums and the shouts of the enemies who had sent the flames against them.

Khokakhchin woke with a start. The dream did not tell all of the truth, only a part of it. A fire had consumed her camp long ago, when she was still a young woman. Her husband Bujur had died in the flames. Tatar warriors riding against her people had used the fire as their shield in attacking the camp; Khokakhchin and others who had survived the attack had been taken into captivity. But the Tatars had not sent the flames against them.

The only sound inside the yurt was the deep, steady breathing of sleepers. Temujin and Khasar lay on beds of felt cushions on the western side of the tent; Hoelun was asleep in the bed in the back. Yesugei had gone to Sochigil's tent for the night. It was good for him to divide his attentions as equally as possible between his wives, and Hoelun was too heavy with child now to take much pleasure from her husband, but Khokakhchin knew that the Bahadur preferred Hoelun's bed to Sochigil's.

Khokakhchin lay under her hide, wondering why her old dream had come to her that night, then got up, covered her head with a scarf, and crept from her bed toward the hearth. The argal burning in the six-legged metal hearth under the cauldron glowed dimly. Fire was sacred; without it, people could not have cooked their food, could not have been purified by passing between two fires before entering a camp, could not have found warmth when the winter winds swept across the steppe, could not have lighted their way through moonless and cloudy nights. She could not imagine the world without fire. But fire was also something to be feared.

Khokakhchin knelt by the fire and stretched her gnarled hands toward the heat. Her thoughts often wandered to the past, especially at night. Sometimes what she recalled was so clear that she almost felt that her spirit had been carried back to her old life, to live through it again. Now she thought of the man who had shown her the eye of fire so long ago.

He had come to her camp with a caravan not long after her marriage to Bujur. The traders in the caravan had gone to the northern forests to trade with the Uriangkhai, the Reindeer People, for sable pelts. Most of the caravan's goods had been traded, but there were still a few bolts of silk, some sharp knives, carved goblets, and polished mirrors to trade for sheep, wool, and hides before the strangers returned to their own Ongghut lands in the south.

One man, who had small brown eyes, a round cheerful face, and a wisp of beard on his chin, had shown Khokakhchin a mirror. She had never seen her face clearly before, having caught only an occasional glimpse of herself in a still pool of water or a polished piece of metal. She stared at her image, making faces at herself, until the women around her were laughing and demanding time to look at themselves. Bujur called her his beauty, but the mirror had shown Khokakhchin a broad face with reddish-brown cheeks and eyes that were a bit too long and narrow.

Another woman was making faces at the mirror as those near her giggled. The men, after riding out to greet the traders, rummaging through their packs of goods, leading the visitors between the fires outside the camping circles, and getting five horses in exchange for two camels the traders needed for their journey south across the desert, had left it to the women to trade for other goods. The women passed the mirror around, then got down to the serious business of trading wool for silk.

The traders laid out their goods on the ground in the center of the chief's circle of wagons and tents. Khokakhchin's yurt was in the chief's camping circle, since Bujur was his younger brother, so she had brought out her soft beaten wool and secured a trade for a bolt of blue silk by the time others were returning with their hides, rolls of wool, and pieces of felt.

"And what for the mirror?" the trader asked her.

She was tempted by the mirror, but could see well enough in a small piece of metal to braid her hair and secure the braids under her bocca, the square headdress of birch bark that sat on her head. "I need no mirror," she replied, unwilling to trade good wool for something that would only make her more vain.

The man shrugged and was about to put the mirror back into his pack when his coat fell open. Around his neck, on a thin gold chain, hung a clear disk that looked like a piece of ice encased in a round golden band.

"What is that ornament?" Khokakhchin had asked, gesturing at the disk.

"It is what the people of Khitai call a lens." The trader slipped it from his neck and held it out to her. "But the old sage who traded it to me called it a firemaker. He claimed that he could do magic with it, that by holding it in a certain way when the sun was shining, he could bring fire."

Khokakhchin shook her head. "I don't believe it."

"I saw him do it. He had other such pieces, and gave me this one for much silver. I was happy to have it at that price."

"Too much to give for such a bauble," Khokakhchin said.

More women had collected near them. The man glanced up at the cloudless blue summer sky, then said, "This is no bauble, Lady."

He asked for something that would burn easily. Two of the women sent their children for some bits of wood and dry grass. The trader directed them to stand back, then held the disk over the tinder; a point of sunlight appeared on the fuel.

The women watched for a long time in silence. Just as Khokakhchin was about to ask when magic would be made, the tinder flared up and she saw a tiny flame.

The women gasped, threw their hands over their eyes, and made signs against evil. The tiny fire quickly burned out. Khokakhchin gazed at the blackened tinder, thinking of what could happen if such a disk were left lying in a patch of dry grass away from the camp. The steppe might go up in flame. She had heard about such fires, of animals and people fleeing from them, of people moving to new grazing grounds only to find them burned away.

Lightning could bring such fires, and everyone knew that only evil deeds and grave violations of custom brought lightning to strike at the Earth. When lightning flashed across Heaven, people threw themselves to the ground in terror; to be caught out on the steppe away from camp and hear thunder was especially frightening. Lightning could strike anywhere. It came to Khokakhchin that the trader's disk had summoned a kind of lightning; she thought that she had seen a tiny bolt as thin as a thread under the disk before the tinder burned.

"Put it away," she said, waving her hands at him. "You . . . you . . ." She shook her head. "Your eye of fire will put us all under a curse."

The other women were too frightened to trade with him after that. The traders were fed that evening, given places to sleep inside the yurts in the chief's camping circle, then left the next morning, and no one spoke again of the eye of flame that could make fire and summon lightning.

Why had she thought of that trader's ornament now? Another memory came to her, of how she had fleetingly longed for the disk and its power before pushing that longing from herself. It was wrong to want such power. She would never have been able to make such a disk work its magic.

Once, she had felt the call to become a shamaness. She had heard the spirits as a child and had wandered from her camp one night to meet spirits that had torn her body apart, sent her wandering among the dead, and restored her to life once more. She had gone to Kadagen, the old shamaness who lived among her father's people, to learn of herbs and spells and chants and how to beat on a small drum to summon spirits.

The training was not wasted. Khokakhchin learned ways to banish some of the evil spirits that brought illness and how to ease women in childbirth. But after a year, Kadagen had told her that she would teach her no more. "You are not an idughan, Khokakhchin." She could still recall the old woman's words. "I don't know what it is that you are. There is power in you, and to have you nearby seems to aid my spells, but I sense that you are not a true shamaness. You cannot use whatever lies inside you."

A dream had come to Kadagen, telling her that Khokakhchin should not follow the shaman's path. The spirits had told her that Khokakhchin had much power, but that to use it would only bring evil. For her to learn any more from Kadagen would only tempt her to use powers that she could not control, powers that should have been given to only the most powerful of shamans. Hers might be a power that others could draw upon for good, yet if she summoned it herself, she risked losing it and bringing ruin to those she loved.

Kadagen did not know why the spirits would give a girl a great gift that she could not make use of herself, but it was not for her to know their purpose. The gift of great beauty could sometimes make a girl no more than a prize to be fought over by men, a captive with a succession of masters. The prize of great strength could be wasted by men in violent, drunken, pointless displays that ended in injury, death, and blood feuds. Gifts were not always the blessings they seemed to be.

Kadagen had been right. Khokakhchin's gift had brought only suffering and death. She supposed that was why she had so easily accepted her captivity among the Tatars; it had been no more than she deserved.

A dog barked outside once, then was silent. Khokakhchin listened, then got up and moved to the doorway. Hoelun had left the flap partly rolled up. Yesugei's tugh, the pole adorned with nine horse tails that was his standard, stood in the ground just outside the entrance. The

Bahadur's big black dog was stretched out under the tugh, head on his front paws, whimpering softly at Jali-gulug.

Khokakhchin tensed, surprised. The dog would snarl and bark at anyone approaching Yesugei's dwellings, howling until his master hushed him. Temujin, brave child that he was, went out of his way to avoid the animal. No one else could do anything with the creature, yet he was cringing before Dobon's son.

Jali-gulug motioned to Khokakhchin. She slipped outside, seeming to feel the pull of invisible cords. When she was closer to the boy, he said, "Something in you called to me."

In the moonlight, she could make out his features. His hollow-cheeked face was calm, his dark eyes focused on her. She thought of all the times she had seen him prattling gibberish and the other times when he had rolled on the ground outside his father's tent, his body shaking and twitching.

He beckoned to her again. She followed him to one of the wagons at the edge of the circle. He sank to the ground and motioned to her to sit.

Khokakhchin knelt, then sat back on her heels. The night was almost too quiet. The sheep resting near the yurts were still, the dogs chained near other yurts as silent as Yesugei's.

"What do you want from me?" she asked.

"Why are you not a shamaness?" Jali-gulug said.

"Once, I thought the spirits had called to me," Khokakhchin replied, "but I was wrong. The spirits decreed that I turn away from the idughan's path."

"There's more power in you than in Bughu." His voice usually shook, breaking when he pitched it too high, and often his tongue tripped over his words, but now Jali-gulug

205

sounded like a man. "Bughu is a poor shaman. I might have learned more from you."

"I know only a little of a shamaness's lore. Whatever you may think of Bughu, he has more such learning than I do—he'll teach you much of what you need to know. After that, you may have the power to learn more by yourself."

"Your dream called to me," Jali-gulug whispered. "I saw a wall of fire. I heard the cries of people."

Did he have the power to touch thoughts and enter dreams? She thrust out her hand and made a sign. "If you can sense that much," she said, "then you must know why I can't use whatever power I have."

"I know only that you somehow summoned the fire I saw in your dream."

Khokakhchin bowed her head and pulled her scarf closer around her face. "I thought that I could help my people. Instead, I brought them terror and death."

"Tell me of what you did."

Jali-gulug seemed to be drawing the words from her. "I've always had sharp ears," Khokakhchin murmured. "Those in my camp used to say that they couldn't keep their secrets from me even if they whispered them." She rested her hands against her knees. "It was late summer, a night much like this one. We had made camp to the west of Lake Kolen and the lands the Onggirats wander, hoping to find better grazing, because there had been so little rain that summer that even the watering holes were drying up. I woke while it was still dark. The air was too still, as if a storm was coming, and I thought I heard distant thunder, but the patch of sky above my smokehole was clear and black and filled with stars." She found herself unable to speak for a moment.

"Go on," Jali-gulug murmured.

"My children were asleep, my husband Bujur resting at my side. I left my bed without waking him, without even troubling to put on my boots, and went outside. I still sensed thunder, but the sound seemed to be coming from below instead of above me. I dropped to my knees and put my ear to the ground. Then I knew the sound for what it was, the sound of horses galloping in our direction."

She paused to take a breath, remembering how fear had welled up inside her. "The Tatars were riding against us. It couldn't be anyone else. The Merkits camped to the north of our pastures were on the move toward Lake Baikal, and the Onggirats and our people were at peace." Her voice shook; she swallowed. "There had to be hundreds of them. The sound I heard was that of an army. We couldn't fight them—our only chance was to get away."

As she spoke, she saw herself back in her camp, outside her yurt on that last night. She had cried out to Bujur; in moments, everyone was awake. By then the wind was rising, blowing from the northwest to the southeast, toward the enemy. She ran into her yurt, pulled on her pants under her shift, and told her two daughters and young son to bring only their weapons and what food they could carry. She was running for the horses when she saw a spark leap from the watchfire just outside the camp to the grass.

"That flame died quickly," Khokakhchin went on. "The men on guard by the fire put it out and mounted their horses. We still couldn't see any Tatars, but others had put their ears to the ground and heard the enemy approaching." She was silent for a bit. "The sight of that flame leaping into the dry grass had made me long desperately for another way to defend ourselves. The Kerulen River lay to the south of us. A few of the men could cross and set fire to the grass. The wind was blowing toward the Tatars—it would carry the fire toward them. We would have time to get safely away while the fire held them back."

Jali-gulug recoiled.

"It was madness," she continued, "the wish of a moment, the words of a malign spirit whispering inside me. To misuse fire is one of the gravest of sins." She made a sign to ward off evil. "But my wish had roused the spirits. They granted my wish. Almost at once, lightning flashed from the sky and struck the ground to the south."

Convinced that she had summoned the lightning, she fell to the ground and covered her face, terrified and yet fascinated by the power now flaring inside her. Flames danced where the lightning had struck. Her skin prickled. She looked up as another bolt hit the ground and knew that she had called it to Earth.

"People were flinging themselves to the ground, trying to hide from the lightning," Khokakhchin said. "Thunder came, and more lightning flashed across Heaven, but no rain fell. The wind grew stronger, and the flames spread over the grass until a wall of fire was moving south."

She had forced herself to her feet, crying out to the others. A few people stood up, then ran toward the pen where some of their horses were kept. Lightning was no longer flashing overhead, and the wind was dying. The fire spreading across the steppe on the other side of the river would hold off their enemies until they could escape.

Then the wind rose once more and shifted, shrieking past Khokakhchin as it blew north. She watched in horror as sparks flew across the narrow stream of the Kerulen and flared up in the grass along the river's northern bank. She ran for her yurt, screaming for her children. Her son scurried through the doorway, clutching his child's bow; she swept him up in her arms. The fire was upon the camp by the time Khokakhchin reached the horses; by then, she was praying, calling upon the spirits to forgive her for calling down the lightning.

She looked back. Her daughters were running toward her, their masses of long black braids whipping in the wind. She saw Bujur dart back inside their yurt for a moment, perhaps to get his bow or his sword. The wagon next to the yurt was beginning to burn; the wind quickly carried the flames to the tent's felt panels, and then a curtain of fire hid the dwelling from view.

"A few people got away," Khokakhchin murmured. "Others died in the flames. Tengri showed the land some mercy then by sending rain to douse the fire. By then, the Tatars were in sight. They killed most of the men they captured and raped the women and girls. I think no more than forty of us survived—our camp was small, much smaller than the Bahadur's here. My daughters were taken away by one band of warriors, and I never saw them again. My son was put to the sword. He was only a child, no more than four, but the Tatars had sworn to kill all the men and boys of our chief's family, and my husband was brother to our chief."

"I weep with you, old woman," Jali-gulug said. "I pity you."

"One of the men who raped me took me under his tent as a wife, but he fell in battle before I could give him a son. His first wife made a slave of me." Khokakhchin sighed. "I brought our fate upon us by wishing down the lightning, by treating fire so carelessly. I earned my suffering." She covered her eyes for a moment. She could weep for all of them, her dead son and her husband and her lost daughters, even after all these years. "And that is more than I have said to anyone about this ever since that evil night."

"I will not tell this tale to others."

"I'm grateful for that."

"You have suffered enough, Old Woman Khokakhchin. You don't have to suffer more by hearing your story retold. It would also do no good to have others here know of your powers."

She had heard the coldness in his voice even while he was speaking kindly to her. His concern was not for her, but for whatever abilities she might still possess. The shamaness Kadagen had told her that others might draw upon them for good. Perhaps a powerful shaman, the kind of shaman this boy might become, could use them to protect Yesugei's people.

No, she told herself. She would not allow a moment's arrogance to bring more ruin upon others.

Jali-gulug said, "The spirits will use us as they wish. What we want doesn't matter."

Khokakhchin got to her feet. "You have much power, young one. I saw that sooner than anyone here. Take care that you don't make my mistake."

2

Hoelun Ujin gave birth to her third son, Khachigun, in early autumn, just after Yesugei and his men rode off to raid their Merkit enemies. The birth went more quickly and easily than had those of Temujin and Khasar. Khokakhchin stayed with her mistress during her labor, summoned Bughu to bless the child, and nursed Hoelun during the days when the Ujin was confined to her tent with the infant.

Yesugei returned with little loot and tales of having to pursue Merkits into pine-covered hills and losing their trail there; someone had warned the enemy and given the Merkits time to escape. Hearing of his new son soon cheered him, and there was still the prospect of Toghril Khan's reward for the foray against the Merkits. The Bahadur's followers broke camp and moved south, to the Senggur River valley. From there, Yesugei, his two brothers, and his close comrade Charakha rode west to meet with Toghril and his Kereits and claim their payment.

The Bahadur came back from the Kereit Khan's court with only a couple of gold goblets, a few trinkets, some goats, and three breeding mares past their prime. Toghril might be Yesugei's sworn brother, bound to him by an anda oath, but he was apparently unwilling to give away any more of his great wealth until the Mongols had killed more Merkits.

By then, it was time for Yesugei to meet with the leaders of clans and tribes that often joined him for the annual great hunt. Jarchiudai, an Uriangkhai chief and comrade of Yesugei's, arrived with his men and announced that he would join the Bahadur for the hunt before returning to his lands north of the Kentei Mountains. A Jajirat chief rode there soon afterward, and Seche Beki brought men of his Jurkin clan, but Khokakhchin saw that fewer men would be hunting with Yesugei this year. Men unwilling to hunt with him this season might later refuse to fight under his command.

The men gathered to make a sacrifice for luck during the hunt and began arguing almost immediately. Orbey Khatun's grandson Targhutai openly demanded command over more men of his Taychiut clan, and Daritai took Targhutai's side. Yesugei and Daritai nearly came to blows before Nekun-taisi interceded, begging his two brothers not to fight. Bughu then read the bones of a sacrificed sheep and predicted a hard winter.

The men left the camp to fan out in two wings and gradually encircle their prey; the women took down the tents again and followed with the children in their carts. By the time they had caught up with the men and had finished skinning the carcasses of the deer that littered the ground, a snowstorm struck. The women dried as much of the meat as they could, cutting it into strips and hanging it up to dry before the howling winds and the sharp lashing of the snow forced them to stay inside their yurts and huddle by their hearth fires.

They made their winter camp near the southern slopes of the Gurelgu Mountains, not far from the Senggur River. The mountain cliffs offered protection from the fiercest winds, but Khokakhchin knew that this winter would be harder than many; the rivers had hardened into ice early. Bughu, whatever his failings in other respects, had read the bones correctly.

More snow came, a thick blanket that covered the ground. The women and children had to uncover the snow with brooms and sticks so that the sheep and cattle could graze, while the smaller lambs had to be fed by hand. Soon, even Orbey Khatun, who usually left the harder work to her servants, was leaving her tent with Sokhatai Khatun, Ambaghai Khan's other widow, to help with the sheep and goats.

In spite of these efforts, too many animals died. The women butchered the carcasses and dressed the hides with salted milk, fearing that not enough lambs would be born that spring and summer to make up for the losses. Yesugei and his brothers, who were often away from the camp either to hunt or to guard the horses grazing near the mountains, returned with stories of wolf packs attacking stray horses and of tiger tracks in the snow.

A tiger soon struck near the camp, killing a stray lamb. Three nights later, the tiger came near Daritai's yurt, killed a dog, and dragged off another lamb. Esugei, Daritai's wife, had heard the bleating of frightened sheep, the howls of other dogs, and the snarling of the tiger, but had not dared to go outside.

Yesugei returned to the camp with Daritai, then sent for Bughu. The shaman arrived with his apprentice Jali-gulug. Khokakhchin poured broth for the visitors while Hoelun set out jugs of kumiss, then sat down next to her husband, Khachigun's cradle at her side. Temujin and Khasar sprawled by the hearth, playing knucklebone dice; Khokakhchin sat with them, close enough to hear what would be said in the back of the tent.

"Is that tiger only a tiger," Yesugei was saying, "or is it a spirit in the guise of a cat?"

"It isn't a ghost," Bughu replied in his high soft voice. "I'm sure of that. If we set out a poisoned carcass, we'll rid ourselves of the beast. I'll prepare the poison tonight."

Jali-gulug said, "This tiger won't take the poison."

Khokakhchin lifted her head. Hoelun was staring at the young man, eyes wide with surprise; Yesugei frowned. Bughu's dark eyes had narrowed into slits.

"Can you be so certain?" Yesugei said. "Bughu served my father as a shaman. You've only begun to learn what he knows."

"That is so." Jali-gulug's voice was firm. "But I think setting out a carcass filled with poison will only waste good meat. This tiger killed one of Daritai's dogs and carried off a lamb without the other dogs attacking it. I don't think it will be foolish enough to eat poison."

Bughu was struggling to restrain himself. His mustache twitched; Khokakhchin saw his left hand tremble. She was suddenly relieved that Sochigil was in her own tent with her sons. Had Yesugei's second wife witnessed this, talk of the apprentice's challenge to his master would have flown around the camp, shaming Bughu. Yesugei and Hoelun would at least have the wit to keep silent, knowing that even a weak shaman could be a dangerous enemy.

"And how do you mean to rid us of the tiger?" Bughu pointed his chin at Jali-gulug. "By hunting it? I've never seen you bring down anything larger than a hare."

Khokakhchin tensed. Young Temujin glanced up from his dice, clearly aware of the shaman's anger.

Yesugei held up a hand. "Enough. Bughu has served me well for some time. We'll do as he advises, and set out the carcass." He turned to Jali-gulug. "If the tiger doesn't take the bait, you'll get your chance at it. Until then, you'll follow Bughu's instructions."

Khokakhchin did not look at Bughu and Jali-gulug as they left. Jali-gulug should have known better than to disagree with the shaman in front of their chief; better to have taken Bughu aside later and spoken to him alone. But Jali-gulug was barely more than a boy, still learning. Bughu, old enough to have learned some forbearance, had only made matters worse by insulting him in Yesugei's presence. She wondered if the shaman was still blind to Jali-gulug's growing abilities.

The shaman set out the poisoned carcass of a lamb. Sochigil claimed to have heard that Bughu had mixed the poison alone, refusing to show Jali-gulug how to prepare it.

For four nights, the carcass lay just outside the camp, untouched. On the fifth night, the tiger killed a ewe outside Charakha's tent. Charakha's son Munglik had awakened to the sound of howling dogs, and left his tent to find a large white cat feeding on the dead animal. He had never seen such a tiger before, white and without stripes. He had not dared to move, afraid the tiger might leap at his throat, and had waited until the beast slipped away over the snow.

Charakha rode with his son to Yesugei's camping circle. The Bahadur listened to Munglik's tale, then sent Charakha and Munglik to fetch Bughu and his apprentice. Jali-gulug arrived alone, but Bughu was accompanied by Targhutai. Khokakhchin saw the Bahadur scowl as Bughu explained that Targhutai had come here to volunteer to hunt the tiger. She did not believe it. Targhutai was here so that he could later tell his grandmother Orbey Khatun what had been said.

Khokakhchin served jugs of kumiss, then seated herself with Hoelun and the children on Yesugei's left. "Munglik," Yesugei said, "have you told the shaman your story?"

Munglik nodded. "Never have I been so frightened." He was a good-looking, sturdily built lad of thirteen, not the sort to admit easily to being afraid. "Even our dogs were cowering." Munglik drew his brows together. "The more I think about that tiger, the more I wonder if it was a tiger at all."

"Maybe it was a shape-changer," Charakha muttered, making a sign against evil.

"If it's a tiger, it can be brought down," Targhutai said. "I'm willing to lead the hunt. If it isn't a tiger, but something else, then it means a curse may lie upon us here. Perhaps the spirits don't want us grazing these lands."

Khokakhchin studied Targhutai's chubby, petulant face. How obvious the young Taychiut man was. If by some miracle he captured the tiger, more of the men would view him as a possible new chief, and Yesugei's position would be weakened. If the tiger escaped him, but continued to prey on their flocks and herds, more would come to believe that this land was under a curse. Yesugei would be blamed for that, since he had chosen the site. Some of his men might even desert him for another chief.

215

"There will be no tiger hunt," Yesugei said. "I won't put men at such risk until we've tried everything else. You know how dangerous and treacherous a tiger can be."

Jali-gulug leaned forward. "Bahadur," he said softly, "I ask for my chance at this tiger."

Bughu shot him a glance. Yesugei stroked his long mustaches, looking thoughtful. "I'll need Bughu's help," Jali-gulug continued. "He will have to cast a spell to protect the camp from evil spirits and ghosts. I will go outside the camp and wait for the tiger there." Bughu looked relieved that his apprentice had acknowledged needing his aid.

Targhutai snorted. "Wait for the tiger? Do you think it'll just walk up to you so you'll have an easy shot?"

"That is my plan. I can say no more about it."

"Very well," Yesugei said. "Bughu will cast his spell, and you'll wait for the tiger. If you have no luck, Targhutai can lead his hunt."

Targhutai's cheeks grew even rounder as he grinned. The men talked for a while, finished their kumiss, then made their farewells. Khokakhchin went to the entrance to roll up the flap for the men. Charakha and Munglik were to ride out and relieve some of the men guarding the horses, and Targhutai would probably ride directly to his grandmother's yurt.

"I will cast a powerful spell," Bughu said as he got to his feet. "Perhaps my spell alone will be enough to rid us of that tiger."

Jali-gulug stood up slowly. "I have one more request, Bahadur."

"And what is that?" Yesugei asked.

"Someone else must wait for the tiger with me. A dream has told me this. The one called Old Woman Khokakhchin must come with me."

Startled, Khokakhchin let go of the rope, letting the flap at the entrance fall. Bughu, in the middle of pulling on his long sable coat, turned toward his apprentice. "That old woman? Of what use can she be?"

"A dream came to me," Jali-gulug replied, "and you know well that the spirits speak through dreams. A dream told me that Khokakhchin must wait with me if I am to succeed."

"I have something to say about this," Hoelun said. "Khokakhchin is my servant, a good woman who has helped me in childbirth, done her work without complaint, looked out for my sons, and earned my trust. We would all grieve if any harm came to her." Khokakhchin warmed at her mistress's words, pleased and surprised that Hoelun thought so much of her.

"I can't promise that she won't be harmed," Jali-gulug said. "I can only swear to do what I can to protect her. She must come with me—my dream said it."

"This is madness," Bughu muttered. "Yesugei, are you going to listen to—"

"Silence!" Yesugei raised a hand; his pale eyes glittered, as they always did when he was about to lose his temper. "You had your chance. I promised the boy he would have his." He rested his hands on his knees. "You'll cast your spell, Bughu. Jali-gulug will take Khokakhchin and go where he must to await the tiger." Hoelun seemed about to protest, but one angry look from her husband kept her silent.

"I will come here tomorrow for the old woman," Jali-gulug said. "I'll need two horses, a boiled lamb, a small tent for shelter, and a cart. The rest I can provide for myself."

"If this works," Yesugei said, "you'll both be richly re-warded, you for your efforts and Bughu for his spell."

Bughu looked mollified as he left. If Jali-gulug failed, the shaman could not be blamed; if the young man succeeded,

Bughu was likely to claim part of the credit. Khokakhchin lowered the flap after Jali-gulug, went outside, tied it shut, then moved toward the hearth. "If this works," Hoelun said to Yesugei, "Khokakhchin will deserve a reward as well. I insist upon that."

Someone tugged at Khokakhchin's sleeve. She looked down into Temujin's small face. "You'll be brave," the boy said. "I know you will."

She knelt to embrace the child, fearing for herself.

Jali-gulug came for her just after dawn, as she was sipping her morning broth. Hoelun helped her load the felt panels and willow framework of a small yurt into the two-wheeled cart, then handed her two oxhide jugs of kumiss. "Take care," Hoelun whispered through the woolen scarf that covered most of her face. "I'll pray for you, old woman."

Jali-gulug mounted his horse and began to trot north. Another of Yesugei's horses had been hitched to the cart. Khokakhchin climbed up to the seat and picked up the reins.

The air was cold, dry, and still; the wind that had been howling through their camp for days had died. Khokakhchin followed Jali-gulug across the icy white plain toward the cliffs looming in the distance. To the west, the horses grazing away from the camp were small dark specks against the whiteness.

They rode until they came to a finger of rock that pointed out from the nearest cliff, then halted. Khokakhchin raised the yurt, tying the felt panels to the frame, while Jali-gulug unsaddled the horses and set out some of the boiled lamb. It was cold inside the small yurt; in winter, at least three layers of felt were needed against the cold, and this tent had only one. Khokakhchin longed for a fire, but the flames would keep the tiger away.

It was growing dark when Jali-gulug came inside the tent and sat down at her right to face the entrance. "How long will we have to wait here?" she asked.

"As long as we must."

He was so calm. Did he lack the wit to be as frightened as he should be?

"I am afraid," he said then, as if hearing her thoughts, "but it will do no good to give in to my fear." He handed her a piece of lamb.

"I thought," she said, "that this food was for the tiger."

"It's for us as well. That tiger would come even without the meat I set out. It isn't a tiger, you see."

"What is it?"

"A ghost. Bughu should have seen that for himself from the start, when Daritai's dogs wouldn't fight it."

Khokakhchin made a sign. "Why did you bring me here? What good can I do you? I swore that I would never meddle in magic again after what I brought upon my people."

"You have power I can use, Old Woman Khokakhchin. But that isn't the only reason you're here. My dream told me that the tiger is seeking you."

She forced herself to eat the piece of lamb, nearly choking on the food. "You aren't a shaman yet," she said. "You're still learning how to be one. How do you know—"

"Be quiet, old woman. The tiger is not far away."

She listened, but heard nothing. Jali-gulug was staring at the entrance. He had not even brought a small drum to beat upon, to aid him in calling upon the spirits. She wondered how many chants he had mastered, how many spells he had learned to cast.

The smokeholes of Tengri glittered in the night sky. The

219

plain outside glowed blue; there were no clouds to hide the full moon. Jali-gulug set his weapons at his side; he had brought along his bow, a quiver of arrows, and a sword, for all the good they would do him. No man would willingly hunt a tiger. Everyone knew how dangerous the creatures were. This boy was setting her out to lure the cat just as he had done with the meat.

Jali-gulug tensed. A pale blue creature was slinking across the snow toward them. Khokakhchin squinted, thinking the light might be playing tricks on her, and then the form became that of a tiger.

"The ghost knows you're here," Jali-gulug said softly. "We must go outside to meet it."

She was an old woman. She had lived her life and there had been times when she had longed for death. If this tiger was to carry death to her, she would meet it bravely and hope that the creature tore out her throat quickly without making her suffer too long. Khokakhchin got to her feet and felt her knees tremble; her breath came in short, sharp gasps.

Jali-gulug ducked through the entrance; she crouched down and followed him outside. The horses, still tied to the cart, had their ears flat against their heads and their nostrils distended in fear, but made no sound. The meat had been set out several paces from the cart. The tiger crept toward the food, lowered its head, and began to feed.

"Aaaah," Jali-gulug cried. His arms were suddenly flailing about him like whips; he threw himself to the ground, writhing and twisting.

Why did the boy have to fall into one of his fits now? Khokakhchin watched his thrashings helplessly, afraid to move, expecting the tiger to leap upon him at any moment. The tiger lifted its head from the meat and stared directly at her. She wondered if she would have enough time to go for the weapons inside the yurt.

Jali-gulug let out a wail, then stiffened. At that moment, the tiger howled, then fell to the ground as if dead. Khokakhchin stepped back, terrified, as Jali-gulug sat up slowly, his face twisted into a grimace.

"Khokakhchin," he said in a voice much deeper than his own, a voice she had never thought to hear again in this life. "Khokakhchin, am I to have no rest? Am I to roam in this world, hearing the blood of our son cry out for vengeance?"

"Bujur," she whispered, making a sign, "my dear lost husband. I still ache for you and our children. I've never forgiven myself for what I did. Are you here to punish me for daring to call down the lightning?"

"You have suffered enough for that already," her husband said from Jali-gulug's mouth. "You endured the loss of all those you loved and suffered a hard life among our murderers. The spirits must have ended your captivity and brought you to live among these people for a reason. I cannot see their intentions clearly, but it may be that the power you possess will be used for good. It may be that I and all the ghosts of your people will have the revenge we seek."

"My power is useless." Khokakhchin covered her eyes briefly, afraid she would weep and that the tears would freeze on her face. "I swore never to call upon it again."

"Listen to me. I have wandered the steppe in the body of a wolf, searching for you. I came down from the mountains as a tiger, waiting for you to see me and know what I was. You swore not to use your power, but that does not mean refusing to let others draw upon it."

"Are you telling me that Jali-gulug—"

The boy let out a shriek. His body was writhing again, and then he leaped to his feet. The tiger was watching him.

221

She sensed that the ghost of her husband had fled, that the cat housed only a tiger's spirit now. She wondered which of them the cat would go for first.

"Khokakhchin." Jali-gulug was now speaking in his own voice, but so softly that she could barely hear him. "Fetch my bow and one arrow. Move very slowly, and keep facing the tiger as you move. It's under my spell now, but I don't know how much longer I can hold it."

She backed toward the tent as slowly as she could. The weapons should be just inside the entrance. She bent low and backed inside, still keeping her eyes on the cat. The tiger snarled and got to its feet. She knelt and moved her hand over the ground; her fingers brushed against the sword, then touched the quiver. She drew out an arrow and found the bow.

Holding the bow and arrow close at her side, she crept outside. One arrow, she thought. Would he shoot that accurately, even at close range? It did not matter. He would not get a second chance.

The tiger snarled again, showing its sharp teeth, then went into a crouch. She thrust the bow and arrow into Jali-gulug's hands. He fitted the shaft, drew the bow, and slowly took aim.

The tiger leaped toward them. Khokakhchin stumbled back, throwing up her arms. Jali-gulug's arrow flew from his bow, but the great cat struck the young man, knocking him onto his back. Khokakhchin reached under her coat, found her knife, and pulled it from her belt, even while knowing that her weapon would be useless against this creature.

The tiger was very still. Then the beast moved, but she saw that Jali-gulug was pushing the cat from himself. He sat up, his hand still around his bow.

"It's dead," she murmured.

"Help me up." She pulled him to his feet, then peered at the carcass. The arrow had pierced the roof of the tiger's mouth. A lucky shot, she thought; not many men could have made it. Perhaps the spirits had guided his aim. Jali-gulug stared at the animal that had carried Bujur's ghost to them, then knelt and cut its throat, spilling blood over the silvery snow.

Khokakhchin took down the yurt, hitched her horse to the cart, and rode with Jali-gulug back to the camp. The dead cat lay in the back of her cart. Jali-gulug's horse had been too skittish to carry it, whinnying and pawing at the ground as if still fearing that the cat harbored a ghost.

The sky was still dark, but growing gray in the east, as they approached the camp. Three men were on guard near the two fires to the north of Yesugei's circle of yurts and wagons. Jali-gulug dismounted and walked between the fires, followed by Khokakhchin. One of the sentries spotted the tiger; the others moved toward the cart to stare at the body of the white cat.

Jali-gulug did not speak. She saw how the men looked at him, eyes wide with awe and a little fear.

"Is that the tiger that was killing our sheep?" one man said at last.

"It is," Khokakhchin replied.

The guard gaped at her, then turned to order one of the others to ride to Yesugei's tent with the news.

3

In a day, the story of Jali-gulug and the white tiger had flown to the farthest circles of Yesugei's camp. The young man had spoken to a ghost, driven it from the tiger, and

223

killed the beast with one arrow. The ghost, it was said, had been someone known to Hoelun Ujin's servant Old Woman Khokakhchin, but that spirit was at peace now and would trouble them no more.

Yesugei gave Jali-gulug a man's bow made by old Baghaji, the best bowmaker in the camp, and also one of his prized white mares. He was careful to reward Bughu for his spell with three soft-wooled black-headed sheep and a jade goblet. Khokakhchin was given a long tunic of green silk, despite her protests that such a garment was much too fine for her.

Jali-gulug spoke of his deed only once, when reporting it to Yesugei. Khokakhchin told the story to Hoelun and Sochigil, then to other women in the camp. By the end of winter, the tale had grown in the telling until many believed that Jali-gulug had vanquished the ghost and killed the great cat only after several nights of battling evil spirits. Khokakhchin soon disappeared from the story, and by spring people had nearly forgotten that Jali-gulug had taken her with him to meet the tiger.

This was just as well with her. The white tiger pelt Jali-gulug wore over his coat was a constant reminder of his deed; she had occasionally glimpsed the envy and hatred in Bughu's eyes when he glanced at his apprentice. Bughu would be thinking of the rewards he might lose to Jali-gulug, of the influence he might no longer have. Khokakhchin was content not to have any of his hatred and resentment directed at her.

In spring, they moved north, toward the Onon River, and made camp within sight of the Kentei massif and the mountain of Burkhan Khaldun. The mountain harbored a powerful spirit, and Yesugei was soon riding there with his shaman and his close comrades to make an offering and to pray.

They returned to the camp without Jali-gulug. Some said that the spirit of the mountain had kept him there, even that the young man had been given the power to ride to Heaven from Burkhan Khaldun. Others, noting Bughu's easier mood during the absence of his apprentice, whispered that Bughu had told Jali-gulug to remain there in the hope that the spirits, or the rigors of spending days alone on the tree-covered slopes, would send the lad to dwell among the dead for good.

Hoelun heard the whispers, and repeated her suspicions to Khokakhchin while preparing to join the other women for the spring sacrifice to the ancestors. "Bughu thinks only of himself," Hoelun murmured as she adjusted a square birch headdress adorned with feathers on her head, then pushed her thick black braids under its cap. "He knows that Jali-gulug might someday be a great shaman, perhaps even one who could strike fear into my husband's enemies. He should have stayed with the lad on the mountain to guide him."

"Bughu had to return to set the time for the sacrifice," Khokakhchin reminded her mistress.

"He could have done that before he left." Hoelun stamped her booted feet and smoothed her long pleated tunic down over her trousers. "Instead of training Jali-gulug, he avoids him whenever he can. Instead of using his magic to help us, he curries favor with Orbey Khatun in case her grandson ever decides to challenge my husband."

Her mistress, Khokakhchin realized, was irritated not only by the shaman, but also by the prospect of spending the day with the old Khatun. Orbey and Sokhatai, as the widows of Ambaghai Khan and the oldest women in

Yesugei's camp, always presided over the spring sacrifice. They would be picking at Hoelun as they dined on their sacrificed sheep, trying to affront her while being careful not to openly insult her, resenting her because she was Yesugei's wife.

"When Jali-gulug knows more magic," Hoelun went on, "I'll advise Yesugei to consult him more often. Maybe by then—" She fell silent. Sochigil was calling to her from outside. Hoelun tightened the sash around her waist, secured her knife, slipped on a coat, then left the tent.

Khachigun crawled to her over the carpet. Khokakhchin picked up Hoelun's youngest son and went outside. Blue and white flowers dotted the land; women were riding toward the yurt Orbey had raised beyond the camp. The wives of Yesugei's brothers and his close comrades would honor the ancestors today, and Hoelun would no doubt be hoping that the two old Taychiut Khatuns would soon join those forebears.

Temujin and Bekter were watching the sheep. The scowls on their faces as they glanced at each other told Khokakhchin that the two half-brothers were working themselves up to a fight. Khasar and Belgutei stood to one side, their eyes on the two older boys.

"Bekter!" Khokakhchin shouted as she approached. "You and Belgutei will go to your mother's tent, fetch baskets, and gather argal for the hearth. Make sure you bring only the driest of the dung back. Temujin, you and I will look out for the sheep. Khasar, you'll watch Khachigun."

Bekter glared at her with eyes as black as kara stones. "Why do I have to—"

"Silence!" Khokakhchin raised a hand. "Temujin and Khasar will gather fuel later, while you watch the sheep. Any more from you, and I'll tell your father you've been disobedient and deserve a good beating."

Bekter hurried off with his brother. Khokakhchin moved toward the sheep. Yesugei's camping circle was near the Onon, and a few sheep had wandered toward the river to drink. One black-headed ewe would drop her lamb soon, perhaps today. They would need many lambs to replace the ones lost over the winter.

"Khokakhchin," Temujin called out. He was gazing northwest, toward Burkhan Khaldun. She turned and saw the tiny form of a man on horseback riding over the snow-strewn land below the massif. Jali-gulug was returning from the mountain. Her eyes were still sharp; even at this distance, she saw that he was slumped over his horse, barely staying in his saddle. She was suddenly afraid.

"What's wrong with him?" Temujin asked. "Even I can ride better than that."

"Watch the sheep," she said.

Bekter and Belgutei had returned with dry dung, and Temujin had gone to gather more fuel with Khasar, by the time Jali-gulug neared the camp. By then, the men near the horse pen and the men churning kumiss behind Daritai's tent had paused in their work to stare at him. Temujin, usually quick about doing his chores, had stopped picking up dung and was watching with the men. Jali-gulug's face was thinner, his cheeks hollow, and his dark eyes had the entranced look of one who had communed with spirits.

He rode toward Yesugei's circle, stopped by the horse pen, said something to the men there, then continued toward her. Temujin ran after him, Khasar at his heels. Jali-gulug's bay horse was moving at a walk; by the time he reached Khokakhchin, the boys had caught up with him. Khachigun whimpered and pulled at the hem of her coat; she handed him a small skin of kumiss to keep him quiet.

227

Bekter, standing near one of the dogs, made a sign against evil.

Jali-gulug reined in his horse. His braids had come undone; his matted hair hung down from under his wide-brimmed fur hat. "Old woman," he muttered, "one can see much from a mountain." His voice was so low that she could hardly hear him. "The spirits have spoken to me. They warned me . . . they . . ." He toppled from the horse; his body writhed against the ground, then stiffened.

She ran to his side and knelt. His body was as rigid as a board; his eyes were half-open, with only the whites showing. Two of the pouches hanging from his belt had spilled their contents. Khokakhchin carefully picked up the small bones used in casting spells and the large round jada stones that were used to make rain and slipped them back inside the pouches.

Khasar reached for Khachigun, holding his younger brother's hand tightly. "I'll fetch Bughu," Temujin said, and ran off before Khokakhchin could stop him.

She managed to drag Jali-gulug into Hoelun's tent and stretch him out on a felt carpet. His body was cold; she covered him with a blanket and moved him closer to the hearth. Too late, she thought of how the yurt and everything in it would have to be purified if he died here. If she was at his side when his spirit left him, she would be forced to stay outside the camp and under a ban for months.

Bughu soon arrived, and spent several moments prodding and poking the inert young man. "He won't die," the shaman said at last as he stood up.

She wondered if she could believe him. Bughu knew something of healing, even if he lacked the gifts of a great shaman. But he also resented his apprentice. He might be thinking of how to use his knowledge to rid himself of Jali-gulug.

The young man moaned. Khokakhchin sat back on her heels, determined not to leave him alone with the shaman. The sky above the smokehole was growing dark; she heard the voices of men outside the tent. Yesugei suddenly came through the entrance, drawing himself up as he caught sight of Jali-gulug lying by the hearth.

"Bahadur," Jali-gulug gasped.

"A spirit is inside him," Bughu said. "It must have seized him on the mountain. Pitch a tent for him outside the camp and I'll do what I can to drive the spirit from him."

Jali-gulug was trying to sit up. Khokakhchin slipped a pillow under his shoulders. "No spirit is in me now," he whispered. "I need no help. Bahadur, listen to me. On the mountainside, I dreamed, and in my dream I flew east until I saw black birds hovering over your camp. Your tent was below me, Bahadur, its frame broken and its household spirits desecrated. I saw no people in your camp, only a great bull standing by your tent with a yoke around its neck." Jali-gulug closed his eyes for a moment. His sallow face had grown even paler; Khokakhchin saw how weak he was. "This was the only dream that was sent to me on Burkhan Khaldun. It was a warning—you must not go east when we break camp."

Bughu snorted. "I read the bones on the mountain. I saw no such omen in the cracks."

"I tell you—"

Bughu stood up and faced Yesugei. "I served your father," he said in his soft high voice. "I've read the bones for you ever since you were chosen as chief. I have told you what the stars decree for your sons. Does this boy know more than I do?"

Yesugei's mouth worked. "He rid us of the ghost-tiger." He gestured at the furry white pelt that covered Jali-gulug's shoulders.

"And my spell protected your camp while he was going to meet that tiger." There was a coldness in the shaman's eyes, an empty look as he gazed at Yesugei, the kind of look a man might have after his spirit had flown from him.

"If we're not to go east," Yesugei said, "exactly where would you have us go?"

"I'm not certain." Jali-gulug sounded hoarse.

"He doesn't think we should go there," Bughu said, "yet he can't tell us where else to go."

"West," Jali-gulug murmured. "We could camp near the Tula River."

"Those lands are Kereit pastures," Bughu said. "Toghril Khan would surely let us graze our herds there, but you would have to offer him some tribute in return. I don't know how much we have to give him after the winter just past."

Khokakhchin knew what Yesugei would decide; he had little choice. He would heed Bughu because he could not afford to slight him. If he did, the shaman would turn to Orbey Khatun, who would grasp at any reason to cast doubt on the Bahadur's ability to lead. The men would also wonder how much Yesugei's oath of brotherhood with the Kereit Khan meant if they had to lose even more of their depleted flocks and herds in exchange for grazing on Toghril's land. Jali-gulug might have met and overcome a ghost and a tiger, but he was still young, still learning; he could be wrong. They would go east, whatever Jali-gulug's dream had told him.

"Are you well enough to move?" Yesugei said to Jali-gulug. The young man nodded, sat up, and slowly got to his feet. "Good. Old woman, give him some kumiss and send him on his way." The Bahadur motioned to Bughu. "Come with me while I finish milking my mares. The women will soon return from their spring sacrifice. I'll want to know what the bones told Orbey Khatun."

The two men left the tent. Khokakhchin rose and went to the eastern side of the tent, where jars of kumiss hung from goat's horns set in the yurt's wicker frame. She took down a jar and brought it to Jali-gulug.

"Here," she said as she sat down. He knelt and whispered a blessing as he poured out a few drops. "I must be rude and beg you to drink it quickly, so that I can fetch the Bahadur's sons, settle the sheep, and prepare supper."

"You must tell Yesugei Bahadur not to go east."

"Oh, yes." She shifted her weight on her felt cushion. "I, a servant and an old woman without sons, will tell a chief, a man with Khans among his ancestors, what to do."

"You could tell his chief wife. He listens to her."

"I'll tell no one. Hoelun Ujin would say only that it's not something for me to meddle in."

"It's something you don't want to meddle in. You think your life ended for you on the night you called down the lightning. You've lived in your body like a ghost ever since. Hoelun Ujin cares for you, her children seem to have affection for you, and Yesugei Bahadur probably holds some fondness for you, even if he won't admit it. But you'll do nothing to try to shield them from harm."

"Stop it," she said, knowing he had struck close to the truth.

"I didn't think you were a coward. I thought you were more than that. After we faced the tiger together, after you spoke to the spirit of your husband, I thought you'd see how your power might be used for good, how you might make up for the suffering you brought to your people. I

231

could draw on the force inside you, Khokakhchin. Tell the Bahadur and Hoelun Ujin what they must do, and I'll draw on your power to cast my spell. They'll listen—"

"They will not listen!" She looked into his eyes and saw only the glazed stare of a madman. "Leave me alone. I want nothing to do with your magic. Bughu hates you already, and I don't want him seeing me as another enemy. He's more dangerous than you know."

"I know what Bughu is." Jali-gulug set down the jug. "He has no true power, and no great gift, because he doesn't believe in the spirits. No voices sing to him in the wind, and no spirits speak to him in his dreams. He wouldn't know them even if they did, for he doesn't think they exist."

Khokakhchin was too shocked to speak.

"His spells are meaningless," the young man went on, "his chants empty gestures. I've seen it for some time, while he was teaching me, I heard it in the way he spoke. The world to him is a soulless place. That's what makes him so dangerous, Khokakhchin. He has knowledge, but will not use it to serve the spirits, to honor Etugen, the Earth, or to bow to the will of Heaven, but only for his own ends."

She had glimpsed the emptiness inside Bughu without knowing what it was. The horror of what lay inside him nearly made her choke. That had to be why he had been so blind to Jali-gulug in the beginning, and refused to see his talents even now.

"He has some skill," Jali-gulug continued. "He can cast a few spells. It wouldn't be hard for him to make the Bahadur see you as merely a useless old woman and me as no more than an afflicted boy."

"That's why we must keep out of his way," Khokakhchin murmured.

"It is also what gives us a chance to stand against him, because that is all he sees." He leaned toward her. "Say only that you'll lend me your power if I need it."

"I promise nothing." She stood up. "I am going to get the Bahadur's children. Please be gone from this tent before I return." She moved toward the doorway, whispering a prayer.

The bones were saying different things. Bughu had seen no evil omens in the bones he had read on Burkhan Khaldun, but Orbey Khatun, at the spring sacrifice, had burned a clavicle that refused to crack at all. Yesugei demanded another sacrifice, with an exact question to be put to the spirits: should they appeal to the Kereit Khan for the use of his lands, or go east?

Bughu killed three sheep and burned their bones. All three of the clavicles split down the middle. The omen was clear.

Yesugei's followers took down their tents and moved east. Yesugei rode in front of the procession with most of the younger men and the horses, the women followed in their ox-drawn carts with the sheep and cattle, while the boys and older men brought up the rear. They went at a slow pace, so that their animals would not lose fat.

Yesugei had sent scouts ahead of his main force with orders to treat with the Onggirats for the use of the lands bordering their pastures. His scouts returned to him with disturbing news, while the Bahadur's people were still far from Lake Kolen, in land bordering a mountain ridge and foothills. The Onggirats were camped along the Urchun River and near Lake Buyur, farther south than they usually were in late spring. A large encampment of Tatars led by Ghunan Bahadur were traveling north of the Yellow Steppe and the Kerulen River to the lands the Mongols had hoped to graze.

Yesugei cursed when his scouts brought him this report, but Khokakhchin noticed the half-smile on his face after the men had left his tent. The Tatars would pay for encroaching on lands that bordered Mongol pastures. War would come now, and Yesugei welcomed the prospect of fighting the Tatar chief Ghunan. This was too good an opportunity to be missed. The Tatars might be prepared for one of Yesugei's raids, but not for a larger Mongol force.

Yesugei sent out messengers, summoning his allies to a kuriltai. Other chiefs were soon riding to his camp for the war council. Seche Beki and his brother Taichu came with a few of their Jurkin retainers, Yesugei's cousin Altan swore to lead his men into battle under the Bahadur's command, and the Arulat chieftain Nakhu Bayan was willing to fight at his side. The horses tethered outside Yesugei's yurt grew so numerous that one might have thought a Khan dwelled in this camp.

The men practiced their archery, raced their horses, honed weapons, dined in Yesugei's tent, went hunting with their falcons, got drunk and recited stories, and spent the rest of their time talking of war and planning their tactics. They would strike at Ghunan in summer, when he would not expect an attack, and exterminate his people.

Khokakhchin thought of Jali-gulug's prediction as she moved among the men, helping her mistress and the other women serve boiled lamb and airagh, the stronger fermented mare's milk offered on special occasions. Yesugei had ignored Jali-gulug's advice, and now more Mongols would join him in punishing the Tatars. At the agreed time, each force would advance east before converging on Ghunan's camp. With a victory, they would destroy one of the most powerful Tatar chiefs and strike terror into the other Tatar leaders. More people were saying that the Mongols, who had lacked a Khan since the death of Yesugei's uncle Khutula, might soon have a Khan again, that the chiefs would elect Yesugei. Even Orbey Khatun would soften toward Yesugei if he took Ghunan's head.

Khokakhchin listened to the loud drunken voices of the Mongol chiefs as they sang their songs and told herself that she was wrong to worry. Temujin, who was learning about his ancestors, recited the tale of Bortei Chino and Maral Khohai, the Blue-Gray Wolf and the Tawny Doe who were the forebears of all Mongols, and won high praise from the men for both his performance and his memory. The warriors complimented Yesugei on the beauty and the cooking of his wives, the strength and swiftness of his horses, the soundness of his strategy. The omens were favorable, the early summer weather was warm, wildflowers were blooming on the steppe, and there was every reason to think that the war against Ghunan's Tatars would go well.

Yet Khokakhchin could not keep her darker thoughts at bay. Bughu had told Jali-gulug that he would no longer instruct him, that he had shown himself unworthy to be a shaman. When she glimpsed Jali-gulug taking his turn at archery practice with the younger men, or riding in one of the races across the steppe, she saw how poor his aim was and how awkwardly he held himself in the saddle. The young man belonged in the rear guard, casting his spells and protecting his comrades from harm with his magic, not in the midst of battle. If one of his fits came upon him during the fighting, he would not survive.

The kuriltai was over. Khokakhchin circled Hoelun's tent, seeing that the sheep at the back of the yurt were set-

tled for the night. The other Mongol chiefs had left
Yesugei's camp. They would ride against the Tatars after
the twenty-first day of the summer's first moon; Bughu had
chosen the time.

The camp seemed more quiet than usual, after the past
nights of hearing men singing and shouting tales of past
battles. She remembered how Yesugei had danced the night
before, when everyone had gathered outside for a last feast
to celebrate the end of the kuriltai. His booted feet had
pounded the ground with such force that he had made ruts
in the grass. His shaven head had gleamed with sweat, the
braids looped behind his ears had come undone and
slapped against his back like whips. He had looked like a
Khan.

Two men rode past her, on their way to join the night
guard just outside this camping circle. Daritai's wife Esugei
left her yurt to throw a few bones to her dogs, then went
back inside. To the northwest, above the sparsely wooded
foothills bordering the steppe, a high black mountain ridge
thrust toward the stars, reaching for Tengri. Khokakhchin
was near the entrance to Hoelun's tent when she saw another man ride out from a circle of tents and wagons to the
south.

He was riding in her direction, slouched in his saddle;
she recognized Jali-gulug. He had tied a band of cloth
around his head and wore his tattered dark wool tunic
under his pale tiger skin. People were quickly forgetting the
courage he had shown in meeting the ghost-tiger. Even she
could think of that night and wonder if only luck had
guided his arrow, if an evil spirit rather than her husband
had spoken to her through Jali-gulug. She watched him ride
toward her, pitying him.

Fifty paces beyond Yesugei's circle, he reined in his

horse, then beckoned to her. Khokakhchin refused to move until he motioned to her more vehemently. Cursing under her breath, she went to meet him.

"What is it?" she muttered.

He dismounted. A bowcase and quiver hung from his belt, next to his sword, but no man could have seemed less of a warrior. He still wore the pouches that contained his small bones, amulets, jada stones, and other tools of magic, even though he would never become a shaman. A faint mustache had begun to sprout on his upper lip, but his face was still that of a sickly, hollow-cheeked boy.

"I came to tell you—" His voice stumbled over the words; his stammer had grown worse. "I've been sent to join the men grazing the horses."

Khokakhchin sighed. "You made me walk all the way out here to tell me that?" She spoke softly; even a feeble voice could carry far on a nearly windless summer night.

"M-my father—my father s-said—" He shook his head and wiped his mouth with one hand. "He ordered me to look after his spare horses when we ride against the enemy," he said in steadier tones. "He wants me in the rear, you see."

"Your father's wise," she said, relieved. "That's the best place for someone who hasn't done much fighting to be."

"Young men my age, even many of the older boys, know more of fighting than I ever shall." She heard the despair in his voice. "I'm not going to guard the horses, Old Woman Khokakhchin, or ride with my father to war. I came to say farewell, to tell you that I'm leaving this camp."

She drew in her breath sharply. "I can't believe it. There's nothing lower than a coward, nothing worse than a man who would desert his comrades. Are you the same man who faced a ghost and killed a tiger?"

"The spirits are tearing at me again." He looked up at the sky. "They're driving me from this camp. I'm useless here, I can do nothing."

"You can fight with your chief against his enemies. You can—"

"The same dream still troubles me. The enemy will trample on the threshold of Yesugei's tent. The great bull will wear a yoke."

He was mad, she told herself. Bughu's shaming of him and his own fear of battle had driven him mad. "I ought to do my duty," she whispered, "by going to the Bahadur now and telling him that you're deserting us. Bughu would be happy to see you punished for your cowardice and your head lying on the ground."

"I must go, old woman. The spirits tear at me. Perhaps they'll show me what to do, how to—" His chest heaved. He turned away and mounted his horse. "Farewell."

"The Bahadur will send men after you, you cursed boy." She shook her fist. "Or you'll die out there all alone, without shelter, without—" But he was already riding away.

The men grazing the horses would not miss him for a while. Two or three days might pass before Dobon found out that his son had not ridden there. His trail could be followed, but by then everyone would be preparing for war, and Yesugei would not change his plans to search for Jaligulug.

She had once sensed power in him. Maybe his madness had touched her, making her see what was not there. She tucked her hands into her sleeves and walked back to Hoelun's tent.

The men sharpened and oiled their curved lances and knives, polished their lacquered leather breastplates, fletched arrows, and selected the horses they would use in the campaign. On the day before they were to ride out, another sheep was sacrificed, and Bughu predicted victory. Yesugei took off his belt, hung it around his shoulders, and poured out some kumiss as an offering to his sulde, the protective spirit that lived in his nine-tailed standard.

No one spoke of Jali-gulug's desertion. Yesugei had gone into a rage when Daritai suggested going after the coward. Even Dobon seemed content to regard his son as dead. They would have their war, and then Jali-gulug, if he still lived, would be punished.

The men rode out on a day when the blue sky was so clear that it hurt Khokakhchin's eyes to look toward Heaven. The nine horse tails of Yesugei's tugh, carried by Nekuntaisi, danced in the wind. Women and boys on horseback galloped after the men, shouting their farewells. Hoelun was astride one white horse, calling out to her husband.

Khokakhchin gazed after the men, her fingers around Khachigun's small hand, thinking of the times she had sent her husband Bujur off to war. If Yesugei had his victory, they would have the better grazing land they needed for their herds. There would be loot in Ghunan's camp, riches given to his people by the rulers of Khitai so that the Tatars would not attack the villages outside Khitai's Great Wall. Yesugei would win the respect of other chiefs and clan leaders and a measure of vengeance for all the Mongols who had died fighting the Tatars; he might even be raised on the felt and proclaimed Khan.

But eventually the Tatars would find a way to strike back at him. The fighting would go on, Khokakhchin thought; there would never be an end to it. She tried to shake off the darker spirits that had entered her thoughts. She had suffered among the Tatars; Yesugei would be avenging her.

239

Temujin was riding back to her, his brother Khasar on the saddle in front of him. Temujin sat his horse well for one so young. "Khokakhchin," he shouted, "I want to go to war. When will I ride with Father?"

"When you're older," she said.

"Father told me he'd bring me a Tatar sword." His horse danced under him. "I wish I could ride into battle now."

"Don't be so impatient." She let go of Khachigun; he sat down and stretched his arms toward his brothers. "You'll have your chance. There will always be wars, Temujin."

Khokakhchin sat with Hoelun near a cart, making rope from horsehair and wool. She had been beating wool with Hoelun for most of the morning, while Sochigil and the children looked after their sheep. Hoelun was making a shirt from a hide for Khasar. Esugei was working near them, separating the softer wool from the coarser fleece in the cart. Most of the sheep had been sheared, and they had less of the coarser wool they needed for making felt this summer than last.

The oldest men and the boys under fourteen were still in the camp; all of the others, except the few left to guard the grazing horses, had gone to fight the Tatars. By now, Khokakhchin thought, the Mongols would have met the enemy in battle. Maybe Yesugei was already celebrating a victory.

"Hoelun." Esugei was looking east; she let the wool drop from her hands and stood up slowly. "Someone's riding here." She narrowed her eyes. "It's my husband."

Khokakhchin set down her rope and looked up, shading her eyes. The tiny black form was so small against the horizon that it was a few more moments before she recognized

Daritai. His mount was raising dust, pounding the dirt into clouds that hid his horse's legs. He would not have been riding like that, without a spare horse and risking death to his mount, to tell them of victory.

Hoelun got to her feet, still holding her hide. As Daritai came closer, Khokakhchin saw more riders appear behind him.

By the time Daritai was clearly visible, Hoelun had sounded the warning. The women and boys with the sheep quickly herded them back to the camp; others were saddling the horses in the pen near Yesugei's circle. Daritai's chest heaved as he galloped toward them; his face was caked with dirt and dust. His horse gleamed with sweat; specks of foam flew from the animal's mouth. Khokakhchin wondered that he had not ridden the horse to death already.

"Yesugei sent me," Daritai shouted. "Take what you can carry! Leave everything else behind! Head for the foothills and make a stand there—the enemy's after us!"

More of the men retreating with Daritai soon reached the camp. By the time the sun was setting, people were fleeing in carts, wagons, and on horseback toward the foothills and the wooded mountain ridge in the northwest. They took food, weapons, skins for water and jugs of kumiss, and little else. The sheep and cattle were driven off, to fend for themselves until they could be rounded up once more. Most of the yurts were left behind, along with much of the new wool, the newly dressed skins, and most of the household goods.

Khokakhchin rode in an ox-drawn cart with Belgutei, Khasar, and Khachigun sitting behind her. Hoelun and Sochigil had ridden ahead on two horses, carrying Temujin and Bekter in the saddles with them; there had not been enough horses for them all. Khokakhchin lashed at the ox, willing it to move at a quicker pace.

Night was upon them, and the Golden Stake, the star at the center of Heaven, was high in the sky when they reached the foothills. They rode on until they came to the lower slopes of the mountain ridge, then unhitched the horses and oxen. The wagons and carts would become barricades; they might have a chance against the Tatars on higher ground.

Hoelun was rallying the women, riding from one group to another on her horse. She would be telling them to be brave, to hold together, to fight with their husbands and sons. Khokakhchin sat with Sochigil and the children by their cart, listening as one of the men who had retreated with Daritai told Nekun-taisi's wife what had happened.

As Yesugei's forces had converged, the Tatars had flanked them. Near Ghunan's camp, another force, led by the Tatar chief Gogun, had struck from the south. Yesugei had not known that Gogun and Ghunan had joined forces, but the Tatar chiefs were prepared for the Mongol attack. They had begun to close around them in a pincer movement. Yesugei had ordered a retreat, telling the chiefs with him to scatter and draw off the enemy. Instead, the main force of the Tatars was pursuing Yesugei while letting the other Mongol commanders escape.

"They mean to put an end to Yesugei," Khokakhchin heard the man say. "He's the one they want. All we can do is hold out here and hope the other chiefs come to our defense."

"They won't," another man said. "They'll get ready to defend their own. Yesugei would tell them to lie low for now and fight the enemy another day. And some of them may already be blaming the Bahadur for this rout. They'll wait before they fight again."

"It's almost as if the enemy knew our plans," the first man

said. "Someone might have told them. That son of Dobon's, the false shaman—maybe that's why he disappeared. He wouldn't have lasted long in battle, and Bughu wanted nothing more to do with him. What did he have to lose? Maybe he rode to the Tatars thinking he'd get a reward."

Khokakhchin did not believe it, but others would. The story would spread; people would be ready to believe that an outcast and coward who had often seemed mad was also a traitor. It was an easy way to explain defeat.

The children slept soundly, curled up under the cart, their heads on packs. Sochigil tossed restlessly at Khokakhchin's side. Khokakhchin could not sleep. The sky was growing gray in the east when Hoelun rode back to them. Munglik, Charakha's son, was with her.

"Our people are united," the Ujin said in a weary voice as she dismounted. One of her braids had come loose, trailing down from under her scarf; Hoelun fingered the thick plait absently. "Even Orbey Khatun is offering me support instead of complaints." She took a breath, then knelt by Khokakhchin. "I must ask something of you, old woman. I want you to take the children to higher ground and find a place for them to hide."

Khokakhchin nodded; she had expected such a request. "Munglik will go with you." Hoelun motioned at the boy, who was still seated on his horse. "He'll help you look out for the boys."

"No," a child's voice said. Temujin crawled out from under the cart. "I won't go. I'll fight with you, Mother."

"You'll go with your brothers," Hoelun said.

"Why?"

"Because you and your brothers are Yesugei's sons. You're the first ones they'll kill if we're captured." Hoelun put her hands on Temujin's shoulders and drew the boy to her. "You are your father's heir, Temujin. You may have to avenge him if—"

"He'll win," Temujin said.

Hoelun turned to Khokakhchin. "Take a little food with you. If—" Hoelun fell silent, clearly not wanting to say aloud that her husband might fall in battle. "If what I most fear happens, make your way to the camp of Charakha's uncle, where the Kerulen River meets the Senggur. His Khongkhotats will give you refuge. From there, send a message to Toghril Khan, begging him to take the sons of his anda and sworn brother into his household."

"I'm honored," Khokakhchin said, "that you would trust me with your sons, Ujin."

"Go, before it's light." Hoelun crawled under the cart to wake the other children.

They went up the slope on foot. The underbrush grew thicker as they climbed, and the tangled roots of the pines that covered the ridge's southeastern face would have made passage on horseback difficult.

Hoelun had strapped Khachigun to a board and tied him to Khokakhchin's back. Barely a year old, he was the least likely of the children to survive. She would do what she could to save him, but not at the risk of losing the others. She refused to think of how slight the chances of survival were for all of them.

A creek, barely more than a trickle, ran down one patch of the slope before disappearing under rocks. Khokakhchin told Temujin and Bekter to fill the empty skins Hoelun had given to them. They had some dried meat, dried curds, and their weapons—knives, bows, and arrows. She hoped that they would not have to use them; the smaller bows of the boys would not offer much of a defense against those of men.

It was dark under the trees. They came to stonier ground where the trees grew more sparsely and Khokakhchin saw that it was growing light. She continued to climb, ignoring the weight of Khachigun on her back. A great rock blocked their path, and they were forced to go around it.

They went on until Khokakhchin looked up to see a small rocky ledge jutting out from the slope. The mountain-side had grown steeper. They had to move away from the ledge, making their way slowly up the slope, then double back to reach it.

Khokakhchin untied the straps binding Khachigun to her, then sat down under the trees bordering the ledge. The children settled around her, panting for breath. From here, she could see the plain and the barricades lining the bottom of the ridge.

"Listen to me," she said to the boys. "Stay under these trees, not out on the ledge where you might be seen from below. Temujin and Bekter, you'll look out for your younger brothers. Munglik, you'll help me make a shelter. If all goes well, we'll be able to come out of hiding before too long." She wondered if the Tatars hated Yesugei enough to search the ridge for his sons.

Khokakhchin and Munglik made a makeshift shelter of branches and dead tree limbs, then sat down to rest. The younger three children were soon asleep under the shelter on a bed of pine needles. Temujin and Bekter were silent as they gazed out at the land below.

The sun was high when Khokakhchin saw three dust clouds on the horizon to the southeast. Soon she could make out the forms of the men and horses amid the dust. The army in the center was Yesugei's; his tugh was in the middle of a forest of curved lances. On either side of his force, two wings of the Tatar light cavalry were firing on his men, the archers turning in their saddles to shoot at the Mongols. Gorge rose in Khokakhchin's throat as arrows arched through the air and fell toward Yesugei's men. The Tatars were driving the Mongols toward the mountain, the two wings closing around them as if they were game.

Khokakhchin trembled with fear. Temujin said, "I see Father."

Khokakhchin narrowed her eyes and spotted the Bahadur's leather helmet with its metal ornaments and white horsetail. Yesugei's men were massed around him. The Tatar forces were allowing them a retreat, but in the distance, another dust cloud had appeared against the sky. That would be the enemy's heavy cavalry. When Yesugei's men reached the foothills and the people barricaded there, they would have to turn and fight.

"We're outnumbered," Munglik muttered.

"Father's worth ten of their men," Temujin said.

More arrows flew toward Yesugei's men. The Mongols fired back. An enemy archer rode closer to the Mongols; Dobon's curved lance swept out and unhorsed him.

"If the Bahadur can hold them off until dark," Munglik said, "he and his commanders might be able to escape. Maybe we should try to get away then. I could sneak down to steal us some horses, and—"

Temujin glared at the older boy. "Father won't leave his men, and I won't run away until I have to."

"We're staying here for now," Khokakhchin said. "The Bahadur isn't beaten yet." She tried to sound confident. "Pray for him, young ones. Perhaps the spirits will listen."

Yesugei's forces reached the foothills before dusk. Arrows flew toward the enemy from the wagons lining the ridge. The Tatar forces fell back, out of range of the people behind the barricades, but were soon massing in the distance. Khokakhchin had been watching the fighting all day. Yesugei had held off the enemy for now, but the Tatars would attack again in the morning.

Khasar crawled out from under the shelter. "I'm hungry," he said.

"Munglik will be back with food soon," Khokakhchin replied, wondering why the boy was taking so long. She had sent him to gather ripening berries from some bushes she had spied farther up the slope. The little food they had might have to last for some time.

On the plain, the Tatars were lighting their fires, getting ready for the night. She shivered, longing for a fire; the air was turning sharply colder and the wind moving the trees overhead was now blowing from the north.

She heard footsteps behind her and turned to see Munglik descending the slope. He had found enough berries to fill his fur hat. He knelt by the shelter and divided them among the boys, then gave Khokakhchin a small handful.

"You eat them," she said. "I can do without food for one night."

"Take them. I ate some off the bushes." He got up and tugged at her arm. "There's something I must tell you." He drew her aside. "By the bushes, I found broken branches and trampled underbrush and the droppings of a horse," he said softly. "I followed the trail and it led me to a small spring. A horse was there, still with its saddle and reins, drinking from the spring. It looked almost as thin as a horse in spring, as if it hadn't grazed well in some time." He lowered his voice still more. "It was Jali-gulug's horse."

Khokakhchin caught her breath. "Are you certain?"

He nodded. "It was his saddle, and I've seen him on that bay gelding of his father's many times."

"Then he must be on this mountain, too." Jali-gulug had spoken of spirits tearing at him on the night he left Yesugei's camp; perhaps they had driven him to this ridge. That he was here proved he was no traitor, that he had not gone to the Tatars with Yesugei's battle plan.

"Yesugei will kill him," Munglik said.

"The Bahadur would first have to admit that Jali-gulug's prophecy was truer than Bughu's," Khokakhchin said angrily. "You'll say nothing of this to the boys. In the morning, you will take me to where you found the horse. If Jali-gulug still lives—"

"What are you going to do?"

"Ask no more questions, Munglik. You're not to speak of this—do you understand?"

He nodded. They walked back to the shelter. Jali-gulug had asked her to lend him her power if he ever needed it. She hoped that she had not waited too long to offer it to him.

The plain below was as dotted with tiny fires as the night sky overhead. From the number of fires, she guessed that the Tatars outnumbered the Mongol forces four times over. Khokakhchin kept watch for a while, then woke Munglik to take his turn on guard.

She dreamed as she lay under the shelter, and fire burned in her dream. She was holding a small transparent disk, an eye of flame like the one a trader had shown her so long ago. As she lifted it to the sky, a bolt of lightning flashed toward her, passed through the disk, and struck near her. Flames leaped from the ground; she had called down the lightning, yet felt no fear.

She woke, knowing what she would have to do. Temujin stirred next to her; she gently nudged him awake. They crawled out from under the twigs and branches toward Munglik and the ledge.

The sky was gray. A strong wind was blowing across the plain from the north, making waves in the grass and whipping at the yak tails of the Tatar standards. "Munglik," Khokakhchin said, "you and I will gather more berries. Temujin, you keep watch."

Munglik went ahead of her, leading her up the slope. When they came to the berry bushes, he pointed out the flattened underbrush of the trail he had found.

"Gather some berries and go back," Khokakhchin said. "I'll follow this trail."

"By yourself? But—"

"I remind you that Jali-gulug took me with him when he hunted the ghost-tiger," she said. "I'm not afraid to meet him now."

Munglik shook back his long black hair. "He may be dead, after so many days alone."

"Then I will say a prayer for him." She made a sign. "Keep the Bahadur's children safe. Don't let them wander from the shelter. I'll return as soon as I can."

She left him and followed the trail to the clearing. Jali-gulug's horse, the same one he had been riding when she had last seen him, was drinking from the spring. The gelding's bay coat was dull and marked by scratches; it lifted its head and whinnied as she approached. She circled the clearing and soon found more underbrush with broken branches; Jali-gulug had not troubled to hide his tracks.

The trail led her higher, to another clearing. Above her, Jali-gulug sat on an outcropping, eyes closed, back against the fallen trunk of a tree. She climbed up to him, clinging to the bushes and branches as she ascended the steep hillside.

Jali-gulug's face had the tight dry skin of a corpse; the hands resting on his folded legs were claws. His shaven head was uncovered, his braids hanging over his chest. At first she was sure that he was dead, and then he opened his eyes.

"Khokakhchin."

She sat down next to him on the rocky outcropping. Over the tops of the pines below them, she saw the battle-field. The Tatars had put out their fires; the men of their heavy cavalry were mounting their horses. Near the man bearing Ghunan's tugh, the Tatar war drummer was astride his horse, his drums hanging at his mount's sides. The warriors looked so small from here, waiting for Yesugei to ride across the empty expanse to meet them. This had to be how Tengri saw men, as tiny creatures that could be swept away in an instant.

"Do you have water?" he asked.

"Yes." She slipped her waterskin from her belt and lifted it to his lips. He drank only a few drops, then feebly pushed the skin from himself.

"You found me," he said. "The spirits sent you to me."

"My mistress sent me up the mountain with her children. Your trail led me here." But he had spoken the truth. Her dream that night had sent her to his side.

"I know now why the spirits led me here," he said. "I can save our people, but I must draw on what's inside you to do it."

"What are you going to do?" she asked.

"You must help me, Khokakhchin. I need a basin, a cup, anything that can hold water."

"I didn't bring such things with me."

"Then give me your waterskin."

She handed it to him. He leaned forward; seeing how weak he was, she slipped an arm around him to support him. He poured some water into a small cavity in the rocky ground, then fumbled at his waist.

He drew out one of his pouches and opened it, his fingers fumbling at the leather ties, and shook several large round white stones as smooth as jade into his hand. Khokakhchin tensed, realizing what he intended to do.

"Your jada stones," she whispered. "You mean to call down rain."

"I mean to call down a storm."

"You mustn't," she cried, drawing away from him. "A storm might turn on us."

"Khokakhchin." His voice had changed. "You still deny me my vengeance against the Tatars. You deny rest to the ghosts of your people." Her husband was speaking through Jali-gulug once more. "You must consent to this," the young man continued in his own voice, "or I cannot call down the storm."

"Do what you must," she said, bowing her head, knowing she was now no more than an eye of fire in Jali-gulug's hand.

He put his jada stones in the small cavity of water, then poured more water over them as he chanted. She did not know the words he spoke, and wondered where he had learned the spell. Bughu might have taught him the words, or perhaps a spirit had whispered the spell to him.

The wind rose. She heard the wind shriek above them, crying out as it swept toward the plain. She felt it rise inside herself and knew that Jali-gulug was drawing on her strength. Khokakhchin screamed; the wind howled back at her, wailing through the trees.

Jali-gulug kept chanting. The wind was coming over the

mountain ridge, gusting to the southeast. If the wind did not change, Yesugei's people, behind their barricades at the bottom of the ridge, would escape the brunt of the storm. The wind would not shift; she would aim it at the enemy. She screamed again, feeling her soul feed the storm.

Thunder rolled over the ridge, bringing thick clouds as black as felt. The dark clouds billowed over the sky above the plain; lightning slashed through the darkness. The Tatars milled around on the plain, their battle plan forgotten in their terror of storms and lightning. Horses reared, throwing their riders. Men threw themselves to the ground as a bolt of lightning flashed from Heaven and struck the Earth.

The trees below bowed in the wind. Khokakhchin's skin prickled; her face flamed as more lightning forked and struck the plain. Lightning severed a mass of dark clouds. A gust tore Ghunan's standard from the hand of the Tatar warrior holding it. A bolt shot down from the sky, stabbing into the midst of a knot of Tatar warriors on horseback. Some of the enemy rear forces were already in retreat, streaming east.

The rain came in sheets, hiding the battlefield from Khokakhchin. She called out to the spirits and another bolt pierced the plain. Thunder beat against her ears with the sound of a war drum. Jali-gulug was taking all her power. The air grew sharply colder, and soon the rain had turned to ice.

Sleet lashed her face; ice glittered on Jali-gulug's coat. Shielded as they were on this side of the ridge, they could not escape the storm altogether. Khokakhchin huddled against the tree trunk and covered her face with her arms, feeling her power ebb from her. There was a hollowness inside her; the strength given to her by the spirits had been spent. She would die here, she supposed. It did not matter. Yesugei's people would survive, and her mistress's children would be safe. Her husband's spirit would be at peace; she would join him at last.

The wind was dying. Khokakhchin lay still, waiting until the spirits among the trees were speaking only in sighs. She sat up slowly, marveling that she still lived.

Tatar bodies littered the plain. Panic had probably killed as many of the enemy as the storm. The enemy was retreating. Two wings of Yesugei's force were already in pursuit, fanning out as they galloped after the Tatars. They would pick off more of the enemy, then close around them like talons. Both the Tatars and Yesugei's allies would tell stories of how Heaven had come to the Bahadur's aid.

"Jali-gulug," Khokakhchin said, "you are the greatest of shamans. Even Bughu would admit that now."

He did not reply.

"He will of course claim that his prophecy of victory turned out to be true after all."

Jali-gulug was silent. She turned to him. He lay against the tree trunk, his legs folded, his bony hands resting against his thighs. His lips were drawn back from his teeth; his dark eyes stared sightlessly at Heaven. His chest did not move, he made no sound, and she saw that his spirit had left him.

Yesugei's people would never know of his greatness. They would not believe an old woman who was the only witness to his power, and who had lost what power she had in aiding him. She bowed her head and let her tears fall, mourning Jali-gulug and the honor he should have been granted but would never have, then wiped her face.

Some of the Mongol men and boys were moving among the enemy dead, stripping the bodies. She reached for Jali-gulug's jada stones, put them into his pouch, then slipped the pouch under his shirt. She would make a shelter of tree limbs to house his body before she left him.

She stood up and began searching the ground near the outcropping for dead branches. Munglik would be waiting with Yesugei's children, perhaps fearing that she had been lost, and Hoelun Ujin would be worrying about her sons. She could tell Munglik truthfully that she had found Jaligulug and that he had died on the mountainside. She would have to pay her respects to the young shaman quickly. She would pray for him later, when Yesugei and his people celebrated their victory.

ABOUT THE AUTHOR

PAMELA SARGENT has won the Nebula Award, the Locus Award, and has been a finalist for the Hugo Award. She is the author of several highly praised novels, among them *Cloned Lives*, *The Sudden Star*, *The Golden Space*, *The Alien Upstairs*, and *Alien Child*. Gregory Benford described her novel *Venus of Dreams* as "one of the peaks of recent science fiction." *Venus of Shadows*, the sequel, was called "a masterly piece of world-building" by James Morrow. *The Shore of Women*, one of Sargent's best-known books, was praised as "a compelling and emotionally involving novel" by *Publishers Weekly*.

Sargent is also the author of *Ruler of the Sky*, an epic historical novel about Genghis Khan. Her *Climb the Wind: A Novel of Another America* was a finalist for the Sidewise Award for Alternate History. *Child of Venus*, the third novel in Sargent's Venus trilogy, called "masterful" by *Publishers Weekly*, came out in 2001. Two collections, *Behind the Eyes of Dreamers and Other Short Novels* (Five Star Publishing) and *The Mountain Cage and Other Stories* (Meisha Merlin), were published in the spring of 2002.

Pamela Sargent makes her home in Albany, New York.

Additional copyright information: